ONE OF AMAZON'S TOP 100 BOOKS OF THE YEAR

Praise for *Security*

"True ingenuity in a novel is hard to find, and Gina Wohlsdorf's debut has it in spades. Much like its resort setting, *Security* is a cutting-edge novel that showcases its creator's impeccable design and eye for detail. Wohlsdorf writes a razor-sharp thriller with a clinical approach to gore, guaranteed to unsettle even the most seasoned crime reader . . . *Security* introduces a fresh, inventive talent to the crime fiction scene. The influence of horror 'greats' like Stephen King and Edgar Allan Poe can be felt heavily throughout this novel, but Wohlsdorf infuses the story with a madness all her own. I will be recommending this book for years to come." —*Crime by the Book*

"This thriller plays around with experimental form, and delivers an exciting and unusual reading experience . . . If you love thrillers and are looking for something a little bit out of the ordinary, this is the perfect book to stay up all night reading." —Bookish.com

"Staff at the luxurious new resort Manderley (think *Rebecca*) are killed off before the place can open in this vivid thriller." —*St. Louis Post-Dispatch*

"Debut author Wohlsdorf delivers a shocking thriller, a narrative puzzle, and a multifaceted love story in this novel set at a California coast hotel." —*The Wichita Eagle*

"*Security* isn't your run-of-the mill thriller. Not by a long shot. Original and imaginative, the story is told in so clever a manner that it could almost obscure the story itself . . . were it not for Wohlsdorf's gasp-inducing plot and fully engaging characters whom she develops without any sacrifice to the gripping suspense, the sheer terror, or the wrenching love story. When reading the last half of the book, I didn't take a breath." —Sandra Brown, author of *Friction*

"Be surprised, be very surprised: Gina Wohlsdorf brings more than just plot twists and a terrifically tender love story to this thriller about a disastrous opening for a luxury beachfront hotel. It's her playful homage to Hitchcock and du Maurier that had me reading, howling, and just plain loving this novel. I can't wait to read her next!" —Sara Gruen, author of *At the Water's Edge*

"Film and literature have been each other's trampolines for a long time, each providing a platform to launch the other, with each genre's inherent benefits and limitations. So this is the novel that wouldn't exist without film: an elaborated screenplay of a movie that exists only in our minds, with every advantage the written word has over the visual. This literary text shows its architecture and is written in vivid and beautiful, nuanced language. It's also shocking and filled with Tarantino-ish dark humor, along with the writer's attentiveness toward constructed worlds and constructed identities, their limits and inevitabilities (the first Manderley—du Maurier's—also went up in flames). Structurally reminiscent of the amazing Jennifer Egan, Gina's book is certainly a hybrid, like nothing else. Get ready."
—Ann Beattie, author of *The State We're In*

"The thrill of this novel goes beyond its wickedly clever, split-screen, high-tech wizardry—a kind of video gamer's literary retake of Hitch-cock's *Rear Window*—and emanates from its strange, disembodied narrator: a consciousness not just godlike in its ability to see every room on every floor, nor just helplessly voyeuristic, but a conscious-ness also moved by the bloody cat-and-mouse playing out before it to contemplate such mysteries as human vulnerability, desire, sex, security and—finally—love. The effect is terrifying, sexy, dizzying, and impossible to look away from."

—Tim Johnston, author of *Descent*

"*Grand Hotel* meets *Psycho* in the age of surveillance: Gina Wohls-dorf's *Security* is cinematically vivid, crisply written, and sharp enough to cut. As the body count rises, the question becomes: Just who is telling this story? Lee Child fans, in particular, will be able to appreciate how brilliantly Wohlsdorf subverts our expectations of the action genre in this smart, shocking, poignant thriller."

—Emily Croy Barker, author of
The Thinking Woman's Guide to Real Magic

SECURITY

□ □ □

SECURITY

A NOVEL

Gina Wohlsdorf

ALGONQUIN BOOKS OF CHAPEL HILL 2017

Published by
Algonquin Books of Chapel Hill
Post Office Box 2225
Chapel Hill, North Carolina 27515-2225

a division of
Workman Publishing
225 Varick Street
New York, New York 10014

First paperback edition, Algonquin Books of Chapel Hill, May 2017. Originally
published in hardcover by Algonquin Books of Chapel Hill in June 2016.
Printed in the United States of America.
Published simultaneously in Canada by Thomas Allen & Son Limited.
Design by Steve Godwin.

This is a work of fiction. While, as in all fiction, the literary perceptions and
insights are based on experience, all names, characters, places, and incidents
either are products of the author's imagination or are used fictitiously.

LIBRARY OF CONGRESS CATALOGING-IN-PUBLICATION DATA
Names: Wohlsdorf, Gina.
Title: Security : a novel / by Gina Wohlsdorf.
Description: First edition. | Chapel Hill : Algonquin Books of Chapel Hill, 2016.
Identifiers: LCCN 2015034365 | ISBN 9781616205621 (HC)
Subjects: LCSH: Hotels—Fiction. | Murder—Investigation—Fiction. | GSAFD:
   Mystery fiction | Suspense fiction
Classification: LCC PS3623.O46 S43 2016 | DDC 813/.6—dc23
LC record available at http://lccn.loc.gov/2015034365

ISBN 978-1-61620-693-2 (PB)

10 9 8 7 6 5 4 3 2 1
First Paperback Edition

For Sara, Jen, and Dani

You know.

"That feast was laid before us always,
and yet we ate so little."

—Daphne du Maurier

CAMERA 1

□ □ □ □ □ □ □ □ □

The maze is twenty-five hundred yards square. Destin Management Group planted hedges before they even began construction on the hotel, since plants can't be paid to hurry like contractors can. The hedges are twelve feet tall, lush, rounded smooth as sanded wood, and currently a dark black green. This is because the hotel is straight and monolithic, a stark white block on a flat stretch of Santa Barbara beach, the kind of building that inspires arguments about whether its simplistic appearance is a great leap forward in design, or whether a child with a crayon and a napkin could have drawn it while waiting for a five-dollar grilled cheese. It's visible from the Pacific Coast Highway but only just. The driveway is quite long so as to accommodate the hedge maze, which is the size of half a football field, and it is darkening, now, in the hotel's shadow.

In the maze's center, the dark red roses are immaculate, thanks to four hours of grooming and possibly because Sid, a freckled and obese landscape technician, is singing "O Danny Boy" in his surprisingly gentle tenor. He told the landscape architect that romantic serenades are the secret to growing flawless red roses; fragile flowers need to know they're loved. He also told the landscape architect he hated the hotel and would take the contract on the condition he never had to go inside. "It looks like a goddamn tooth. Like a tooth somebody yanked out and stuck on the beach." He pointed at the hotel and spat in its direction, unaware anyone was listening. "Like it'd bite you when you weren't watching close."

Manderley Resort does look somewhat like a tooth. Kinder metaphors like "jewel" and "main sail" are more prominent in the marketing materials. Ads in every medium have ensured that Manderley is the talk of its demographic. Every third billboard in Los Angeles splashes a quote from *Travel* magazine about how tasteful, how opulent, and how special Manderley will be once it opens in August. It is now mid-July. More tasteful and more opulent invitations arrived at the households of L.A.'s elite yesterday. It's going to be the Party of the Year. It says so on the invitation. Charles Destin—owner of Destin Management Group, owner of Manderley Resort—does not know how to throw a party that is anything but the Party of the Year.

Destin's father was a diplomat who died in a hotel in Sierra Leone because a waiter agreed to take a contraband tray to Lamont Destin's room. The waiter agreed to do this for seventeen American dollars. The tray had a bomb glued underneath it—a cheap bomb, composed of household products. Charles Destin was notified of his father's death after a lacrosse match. He was ten years old. He won the lacrosse match, and he always includes this detail when the subject of his father's death meanders into conversation. He also always mentions that the bomb was cheap, and the spray-tanned skin around his capped teeth tightens when he says this, as though to be incinerated by an expensive bomb is somehow less offensive.

In the maze, Sid's wrist beeps, signaling the end of his workday. He croons his final verse to the dry, rose-heavy air—"For you will *bend*"—snipping deep into a hedge so that a perfect bloom's absence isn't blight on the foliage. He slides his large clippers through a fat loop in his tool belt and takes a smaller pair from a thin loop, trimming the thorns from the rose's twelve-inch stem. Sid goes to the fountain at the center of the maze. Immense, made of stone, themed on fruit and hummingbirds, it sits dank and murky, its wide rim holding the detritus of Sid's labor: excised leaf clots and thorny branches overflowing a black bucket, and plastic sandwich bags bunched in a rusted silver lunch pail. Sid tweezes the rose between thumb and forefinger, setting it on the fountain's rim with exaggerated care. Using a schmaltzy pianissimo for the final strains of his ballad, he picks up the bucket, shuts his lunch pail and locks it, and departs from the maze's center, taking the first right turn in his favored route, which is effective but not remotely efficient.

On the nineteenth floor, Tessa is boarding the elevator. Its soft ding carries to the ballroom's ceiling, thirty feet above her, and bounces off the mural there: a sunset sky in muted pinks and oranges, playing host to a dozen subtle, and subtly modern, cherubim. Their fleshy faces all stare down instead of up. The ballroom's enormous west-facing windows trap the earliest phases of an actual sunset. Bars of light and shadow crosshatch tables set with china finer than bone. White napkins are folded in the shapes of swans, magnolias, seashells. Only a few are folded in the shape of napkins. A clutch of red roses serves as each table's centerpiece, and if a guest asks, staff is to confirm that the roses are from Manderley's garden, though they're not. Tessa placed a standing order with a florist last week to deliver fifty dozen every Monday.

She holds the elevator's glass doors open with her left boot and takes a final look at the southeast corner of the ballroom, where Jules is holding the base of a twenty-foot ladder. Jules's husband and catering partner, Justin, is finishing the pyramid of a thousand champagne flutes they began at seven this morning. At the Party of the Year, Charles Destin intends to climb this ladder and pour a bottle of champagne, the fizz of which will overflow the glass at the apex, to the four glasses under it, and so on, into a thousand glasses. A thin plastic hose worms up through the pyramid. The hose runs to a storage room, where four large tanks of champagne will finish the work that Destin's pouring will start. Destin compared the illusion of the single bottle of Cristal filling a thousand glasses to the miracle of Jesus and his disciples feeding the five thousand with five loaves and two fish. When Destin made this comparison, Tessa rolled her eyes so hard, one of her contact lenses fell out.

In the elevator, she presses the button for the eleventh floor. The glass doors slide shut, the nineteenth floor rises in front of her, and Tessa's posture slackens, an exhale showing in her shoulders. She's pretty, but not an obvious pretty. She tried modeling in college ("Because I'm a twig," she said once), and the photographers told her she only looked right in three-quarter profile, due to a face that's a little long, a chin that's weak, and cheekbones that don't protuberate. Tessa's the kind of person who latches onto criticism thankfully and treats compliments like insults. It's infuriating.

She makes a check mark on her clipboard as the eighteenth floor passes, and another as the seventeenth floor appears underneath her.

The elevator is excruciatingly slow. This is because it is diamond shaped and made of glass. Every day at five o'clock, Tessa descends from the ballroom to the foyer, scrutinizing each floor for problems, and the process takes an hour. She usually walks the halls, but she doesn't have time for that today. Her view from the elevator consists of the long hallway that links the north and south wings of guest rooms—the middle stem of a letter "I"—and this doubtlessly grates on her, to check off the premises as passing inspection without inspecting them thoroughly. The front sheet of her clipboard shows a diagram of Manderley's layout with floors numbered one through twenty. The twentieth floor is shaded.

Tessa makes a check mark on her diagram for the sixteenth floor. She taps her boot impatiently. Before the fifteenth floor appears, she makes a check mark in its space. She pinches the bridge of her nose, her eyes falling shut and staying that way, which means when the fifteenth floor does appear, and Vivica in the bright white hallway spies Tessa in the elevator and waves, Tessa doesn't see her. Vivica is carrying a purple bottle of carpet cleaner and a white cloth, which she flaps ineffectually until Tessa sinks out of sight. Vivica's mouth draws down in disappointment. She walks toward the north end of the hall, turns left, and sinks to her knees in the entryway of Room 1516. She sprays the carpet cleaner on a round, red stain the size of a quarter and curses it in a flurry of Spanish. She thinks an electrician cut himself. This is not what happened.

The Killer is on the seventh floor. He's washing his hands in Room 717, scrubbing vivid red from his nail beds and knuckles into the bathroom sink. He picks a fine, light hair from his shirt cuff, studies it with brief interest, and flicks it behind him. It lands on the white bath mat. The water in the sink is paling from a strange, swirled red orange to a shade that matches the gold leaf of the taps. A knife the length of an average man's forearm is drying on a white towel beside the basket of assorted guest soaps.

Tessa opens her eyes at the fourteenth floor, nods, and makes a firm check mark.

She waits, and makes another for the twelfth floor.

There is no thirteenth floor; Charles Destin is extremely superstitious.

As the eleventh floor grows beneath her, Tessa winds a section of her thick, black hair into a twist at the nape of her neck. She does this many times throughout the day. She says her hair is too heavy to tie it all up, but her neck gets too hot if she leaves it all down. The elevator dings, the tone soothing, but when the doors slide open, she cringes at the scream of a drill. She follows the sound to the south end of the hallway and turns right, where the thickset lead electrician lets off his drill's bulky trigger. He smiles, showing bad dental work.

"Dirtbag leave?" he says.

Tessa cocks an eyebrow. She would look disapproving, except her lips curl upward on one side.

The lead electrician laughs. "All right, sorry. Did Charles Xavier Destin the Third leave yet?"

"Imagine going through life with that name," says Tessa, glancing around Room 1109 to make sure it's pristine. "I think you're doing fine, Pat." She glances at a few flecks of drywall by his feet. "Not great, but fine."

The lead electrician stoops. His meaty fingers look incongruous picking drywall out of carpet. "I thought Chucky wanted us to stay on till we finished. Actually, I think his words were, 'You fucks can stick around until your old ladies seal the fuck up from waiting—'"

Tessa holds up a hand. "Yeah, I know. But we're only using luxury suites for the party. That's fourteen through seventeen, and they're done. Right?"

"Yes. Yes, ma'am, floors fourteen through seventeen are good to go."

"Then there's no need for you guys to pull overtime, unless you want to." She backs up a step, says, "Let me know," and heads for the elevator.

"That's an easy one," the lead electrician says, following her. He unclips a walkie-talkie from the waistband of his jeans. "I'll tell the guys we'll knock off now, but only if you're sure Chucky Destin won't come yelling at you tomorrow."

"Let me tell them," Tessa says. "And Charles doesn't yell at me. He knows better."

Tessa smirks as she leaves the lead electrician laughing, satisfied she has undone the damage Destin inflicted when he threatened to fire the lead electrician and ruin his reputation by telling everyone who mattered anywhere that his company was a pathetic operation fucking incapable of following a fucking timetable and that he would have to relocate from California in order to ever work again. Destin made the same threat to every employee in the hotel. He does this whenever he visits. He is now very probably lounging in his limousine en route back to the city, on his cell phone to a business associate—Destin thinks he has friends, but he doesn't—chatting about how scared employees are productive employees. There are apprentice electricians in Room 921, Room 525, Room 511, and Room 301, and Destin yelled at all of them. So Tessa visits all of them, one by one, and deploys her professional yet conspiratorial smile. She calls them each by their first names. She implies insults to Charles Destin without precisely insulting him. She is not above bending a shapely knee when the apprentice in Room 301 sulks that on top of everything, he lost his walkie-talkie today. Tessa relates a story about losing one shoe at a concert festival in college and hopping across the park like an idiot to buy flip-flops at Walgreens. She leaves him laughing, boards the elevator, and checks her watch when the third floor rises away.

The Killer is in Room 717, sitting on the edge of the king-sized bed. A walkie-talkie crackles by his hip and says, "Okay, guys, you heard the lady. Pack it in and make sure you're not leaving crap in the carpet. We're outta here in twenty." The Killer looks at the clock radio on the cherrywood night table. It's difficult to tell where he's looking, as he's wearing a mask. It's the same mask from the Halloween movies, the ones with Jamie Lee Curtis. He's also wearing navy blue coveralls. He is an amazingly large man, and, one could tell even without firsthand experience, incredibly strong.

Tessa does not exit the elevator on the second floor. When the doors slide open, familiar sniffs and squeaks reach her from the direction of the housekeeping storage area. There, among shelves of supplies, Delores, the head of housekeeping, is counting toilet paper and crying. Tessa stands in the yawning elevator, her right foot arrested in a step forward, her expression torn, then pitying, then decisive. She reverses and presses the button for the foyer. Tessa likes Delores, but Delores cries at pet food commercials, spilled all-purpose cleaner, surprise homemade birthday cupcakes—the list is endless. Delores is inconsolable for at least ninety minutes after a profanity-laden tirade from Charles Destin.

Tessa never cries. She hardly ever lets herself look exhausted—at least, not in front of people. She frequently looks exhausted when she is alone—or, when she thinks she is alone.

She leans against the elevator's back wall and lets her neck go slack. Her head bonks against the glass, once. Twice, three times, while the first floor swells around her. In the morning, sunlight makes the glass elevator into a prism as it arrives in the foyer, but not now. Tessa shakes her head at the chandelier, a piece of modern art with white sconces in the shape of a pinecone. It cost seven million dollars. Even if it were lit, it would not prevent the foyer—which boasts east-facing windows every bit as long and impressive as the ballroom's facing west—from looking like a gargantuan, vaulted tomb in the late afternoon, with its white counters, white sofas, and white marble floors. Tessa's apartment is a one-bedroom in Anaheim—the good part of Anaheim, but still. Her apartment has indoor-outdoor carpet and a stove on which only three out of four burners work, and her savings account surpassed six figures long ago.

As the main elevator slows still further to settle at its terminus, Tessa's chin lifts. The elevator dings, and the doors slide open. Shoulders back, she walks to the manager's office, where the lone person on the first floor sits behind a desk, holding his head in his hands. Destin really let Franklin have it. Franklin leaves his head in his hands, though he must hear Tessa's boots clacking on the foyer's Italian marble. She arrives at his office, leans in the doorway—clipboard held parallel to the crease in her black skirt—and waits.

"Don't tell me he didn't mean it, Tessie," Franklin says.

Tessa doesn't like being called "Tessie"—or anything other than "Tessa"—but she's never told Franklin that.

"I won't," Tessa says. "But I will tell you he barked at everybody in the hotel. Everybody. Including apprentice electricians he'd never met before."

Franklin raises his head, but keeps a hand over his face. He does this to look silly. It is effective, but not in an endearing way. "He told me I'm not fit to manage a McDonald's."

"Aw, Frank," says Tessa. Her mouth twitches. "Of course you're not."

Franklin reclines in his ergonomic office chair. He is short, muscular, hairy, and gay. "Shit on that." Now he's grinning. "I could manage the shit out of a McDonald's."

Tessa said once that the trick to managing Franklin is to feign amusement at his moods and support his own bouts of insecurity so that his narcissism comes to the fore to galvanize his tenuous sense of self. She didn't use these exact words. She said, "Tell an asshole he's an asshole nicely and he'll fight you." But she also feels sorry for Franklin. She once said, "He has all the backbone of a jellyfish on a clothesline." Her expression softens as he reaches to the bottom drawer of his desk and extracts a bottle of scotch and two cut crystal glasses.

"Frank," she says with a tone.

He pours an inch of scotch. Tessa takes the glass he hands her, but she dumps the liquor in a potted banana tree by the door. Franklin knocks his back.

Tessa says, "Charles thinks he understands people, but he doesn't. Makes him dangerous." She sets her glass on Franklin's desk blotter.

"Dangerous." Franklin laughs, lightened by Tessa's confession. "It surprises me you would use the word 'dangerous.'"

Tessa makes a mark on her clipboard. "It's the right word."

"How are we doing? For real?"

"We're in great shape. We're two days ahead on the ballroom setup, and housekeeping can't do anything but stock counts until electric's done on three through twelve—"

"That's not my fault."

Tessa's posture stiffens, so slightly that only a knowing eye would see it. "It's no one's fault. Charles didn't allow for overtime, Pat didn't notify him the timeline got wonky because of it, nobody told me any of *that*, so how could I tell you?" She tucks a hair into the twist at the nape of her neck and doesn't wait for Franklin's answer. "I have to catch Sid before he leaves. I doubt Charles trekked all the way into the maze, but he might've."

Franklin calls a thank-you. Tessa waves without looking around. Passing the information desk and the check-in counter, she walks to the front entrance and out. She turns around in the reception driveway, looks directly into Camera 3, and says, "You know how Charles is. Don't take it personally."

I almost laugh. Tessa holds the camera's gaze for several seconds, her face firm. She's imagining my team members on the twentieth floor. She thinks they're nodding at the monitor and scoffing over hot cups of coffee. Her imaginings are vague, because Tessa's never been to the twentieth floor.

She turns, jogs three steps, and then walks again when she sees that two vans still squat at the maze's entrance. One is dirty and green with "Donaldson Landscaping" stenciled on the side panel. The other is clean and dented, black and blank; it belongs to the electricians. Tessa rounds the vans just as Sid materializes in the maze's narrow opening. His girth, his bucket of greenery, and his jolly smile at seeing her make Sid look like an oversized garden gnome. Their body language is casual, and their conversation lasts less than four minutes. Toward the end, Sid shakes his head. He points toward the maze and mimes a rich-man walk by sticking his nose in the air. Tessa laughs, smug she was correct that Destin wouldn't dirty his suit simply to hurl curse words at the man who tends the hedges. She smiles fondly at Sid: here is one fewer person for her to placate. She tells him with fake sternness that she's off to check his work, and Sid wipes his brow with fake worry. Tessa waves good-bye. She disappears.

She reappears, via Camera 2. She's checking her watch. It is five fifty-eight p.m. Her body wilts, her feet slow, but her route is much more efficient than Sid's. Her neck sags to one side, then the other. Tessa unties the twist of her hair and shakes the full weight of it back, unaware how lovely and calm the gesture makes her look, certainly unaware that as she arrives in the maze's center, Camera 1 motion-activates and shows her trudging toward the fountain, exhausted.

Sid tosses his equipment in the back of the van. He slams the rear doors and gets in the front seat, emerging a second later to pick a brochure out of his windshield wiper. He frowns at it. Destin placed it there before diving into his limousine and racing back to Los Angeles.

"Safety. Luxury. Manderley."

It's a slogan that means whatever the prospective guest wants it to mean. The brochure is illustrated with the cliché ocean vistas and eerily clean interiors of any coastal hotel, but it hints at a level of privacy unattainable anywhere else. It promises a movie star sojourn from a bad breakup. It tells the hedge fund manager discretion will be afforded his mistress. It informs the dignitary who has committed terrible atrocities that his transgressions are of no interest here. This is a business that understands business. The background checks for employees are extensive, the hiring process complex. There will be no waiters spiriting bombs upstairs for seventeen American dollars— and especially not cheap bombs—because the hotel pays its employees extremely well.

But Sid is a subcontractor. He makes twelve-fifty an hour, and he has moderate to serious class rage.

Destin knows this. He laughed about it with his driver. His driver is Somali and speaks no English.

Sid throws the brochure over his shoulder. He's good-humored but not stupid, and he'll proudly tell someone on first meeting about his quick Irish temper. He slams the van door behind him. The starter grinds. The brochure puffs from the gravel as he blows by it, soaring much higher than one would expect, and flutters down like a serene bird to land on a hedge's smooth, squared top. The van's tires squeal down the driveway.

Tessa blinks at the noise. Her brow furrows, but then it relaxes. She's busy perusing the roses that spit from the hedges like a million arterial bleeds. Cursory inspections here are fine. Sid does excellent work. She's only ever had to reprimand him once, for defecating into a shrub to save himself a trip inside the hotel.

She sits on the fountain's wide rim. Her clipboard crushes the flower Sid left her. She's unzipping her left boot. There's the click of the zipper down the teeth, to the heel. She winces pulling it off. Then she does her right. She pivots around on her behind to face the fruit and hummingbirds carved in gray granite. She looks at her feet submerging. A *plub* sound. The black water is warm, oily from a long July day, and she moves her feet in overlapping circles, smiling tiredly at the Venn diagram they create. Or smiling at their motion, as if they existed separately from her. Or at the water, its ridges and scales, the *shush* they whisper rippling outward from her soft knees. One can be forgiven for wondering—especially one who sees her do this every day at six p.m.—where her mind goes when she watches her feet draw circles underwater, what window to what world lies at the bottom of that dark fountain. She never looks so sad as when she looks almost happy. And it's very nearly possible, seeing her at peace for the last time, to delude myself that she will remain there, static, safe.

To ignore the Killer in Room 717, rising from the bed.

Or the motorcycle zooming up Manderley's long driveway, which wraps around either side of the maze like a noose.

CAMERA 2/3, 4, 4/12, 3

□ □ □ □ □ □ □ □ □

The electricians have arrived in the foyer. They took the stairs. Their voices were indecipherable in the stairwell, but here, in the spacious foyer's excellent acoustics, each is distinct. They're making fun of the apprentice who lost his walkie-talkie. "Vin, buddy, you gonna lose your dick next—"; "Nah, Vin's girl got it in a jar on the—"; "Yeah! Ha! Woo! She's—"; "Important. Expensive, too," says the lead electrician, who has a hand on Vin's slouching back. "I know every kid had a walkie-talkie, but they were cheap kids' toys, and these are part of the trade, Vin. Okay?"

Tessa's head snaps up from the fountain. She looks terrified. Her breath stops; it's Pavlovian. She grabs her clipboard and tries to calm herself—some internal conversation, counterargument to a nightmare. The motorcycle engine gives a final grunt and is silent. Tessa's chest collapses in. Rises-collapses. The sound of her panicked respiration is enough to make an invested observer panic, too, but she grabs her left hand with her right and digs her thumbnail into her palm. Pain pulls her eyes wide open, and her breathing normalizes. She laughs, not happily, dismissing her fear of a revving motorcycle like a judge would a case with no evidence. She's brutal about putting her boots back on and yanking the front pieces of her hair into a low knot.

A young man in a motorcycle jacket eases down his kickstand with bizarre physical grace. He levers himself off the bike the same way. His clothing and transportation bespeak an idolization of Steve McQueen, but he's tall, slight. He looks up at Manderley, and he pales. The hotel can have that effect at twilight. Its flat white façade with several hundred panes of clear glass is intimidating—the tired simile of empty windows as eyes. He touches his motorcycle's handlebars, as if for comfort. He stuffs his hands in his pockets and begins to pace. Occasionally he puts a rough hand through his short, dark hair.

The young man in the motorcycle jacket becomes the central point for two approaching parties: Tessa, from the hedge maze, her boot heels punching divots in the soil and the electricians, from the foyer, whose cacophony is dying down at Vin's lack of reaction to their mockery. The electricians' exit from the foyer doors and Tessa's exit from the maze are nearly simultaneous. Nearly, but not quite. The electricians are first.

Vin says, "Whoa!" He's staring at the motorcycle parked by their van.

"Dude!" says another apprentice.

The young man turns to them. Tessa sees him in profile, and she drops her clipboard. It clatters against a low marble plaque recommending that any guests who fear tight spaces should forgo the hedge maze. Attached to the plaque is a cube of Plexiglas; it is designed to hold maps of the maze, which Tessa hopes will obviate guest complaints that the path is too difficult. The young man turns back to Tessa. He's looking at her like she's a mirage.

"Domini?" says Pat, who's looking at the young man like he's a mirage.

Seconds later, the young man in the motorcycle jacket has vanished, surrounded by the five electricians. Their gruff handshakes and slaps to the young man's back give Tessa, who remains standing stiff as an ax handle, a chance to pick up her clipboard and compose her features, which briefly slide into an arrangement completely foreign to her face: skin crimped and pinking, mouth pressed thin, eyes wet. She swallows, her throat convulsing several times, like whatever she's feeling is something she must digest. It appears to work. She walks toward the huddle of men with the hard façade she wears on mornings when she has important meetings on her schedule.

The electricians are behaving like girls at a dance who want to be looked at, listened to: "Damn, that jump at Saratoga—"; "Watched it the night my kid was born. Wife kept telling me to turn off the—"; "Haven't seen you. Heard you're mostly promoting—"

"Brian?" Tessa says. She makes a check mark on her clipboard. This action is an excuse to study the hedge maze, and not the young man in the motorcycle jacket, whose name, one supposes, must be Brian.

"Listen," says Pat to Brian, fumbling in the pockets of his drywall-specked jeans, "I know you must get this all the time, but—" He shoves a pen and perhaps a receipt into Brian's hand. "For my son. He's a fan. I mean, I am, too, but he'd flip shit if I came home with—"

"Sure," Brian says, and more pens and odd scraps of paper appear by his hands. "What's your son's name?" He grins at Tessa. It's not a creepy or smarmy grin. It's boyish. Kind.

Tessa doesn't smile back. As Brian scrawls personal messages for each of the electricians and signs in swooping cursive underneath, Tessa is fighting a civil war behind her eyes. They want to weep, but they want to scream—but they want to weep for other reasons. Tessa is a difficult woman to love. She likes sex, but she also likes boxing. She looks at her opponent, at least, when she's boxing. And when sex does weaken her a little, usually right at the end, she looks exactly like this.

Except, not exactly like this. This is exponential. She's building her resistance to emotion up so high, it's crumbling under its own unbelievable weight, as if she's begging this kid—this *Brian*—to go away before her powers of resistance expire.

He's finishing his last autograph, the bastard. "It's nice you guys remember. Thanks. Really, thanks." He hands a scrap to Vin, who holds it as though terrified to fold it.

"Man," Vin says, "when Mitch wiped out—"

"Shut up, shithead!" hisses Pat.

Brian's smile dims.

"Sorry," says Vin. "Sorry, Domini, man. I didn't mean nothing, I just—I remember that." Vin looks at the autograph. He points at where the paper's still blank, like something's missing. "It was like my brother died, too."

"You even have a brother?" Tessa says, her voice hard as nail heads.

Vin looks at her, surprised. So do the other workmen. They forgot her, if they made note of her at all. "Yeah, I do."

Tessa moves closer. The men make a space for her, and she occupies it. "Is he your twin brother?"

"No," Vin says. He hangs his head. "No, he's not."

Brian puts out his hand. He doesn't touch Tessa. He puts his hand in the middle of the circle of men that Tessa's invaded, and they all look at it. It seems to ask for peace. His short fingernails have rings of black underneath them. He says again, "Thanks, guys. Really, I mean it." Before they can thank him in return, Brian asks, "Tess, could I talk to you a second?"

The men disperse with halfhearted waves and mumbled thank-yous. Pat waits until all his apprentices are in the van and then shakes a finger at Vin. It is doubtful this scolding involves walkie-talkies.

Tessa watches the van.

Brian watches Tessa, catches himself, and watches the van.

It reverses, pebbles popping in its tire treads, and makes a U-turn in the north parking lot, which contains ten vehicles among spaces for two hundred. It passes Brian and Tessa, dividing them at an angle from the

front door, where Franklin pokes his head out, furtively, before the van's bulk rolls away. He's holding a large pair of scissors. maze. The van's shadow almost obscures Brian's arm as it reaches on instinct for Tessa, in case the van gets too close.

Brian puts his hands in his pockets as if he doesn't trust them. "You're wondering what the hell I'm doing here."

Tessa crosses her arms and bends one knee.

"And there's a great reason." Brian's mouth and eyes squinch. He's trying to effect charm but achieves only constipation.

She twists at the waist and peers at Brian haughtily. Usually, this stance of Tessa's unnerves men. But Brian first smiles, amused at her pose, and then hides a laugh in his fist. Tessa glares at him. Brian pretends to cough, his teeth flashing despite the hotel's towering shadow. He says, trying not to laugh, "I was in the neighborhood."

Tessa stomps her foot, her mouth puckered angrily, her entire body suddenly open, yet defiant. Brian shakes his head, laughing loudly now, and reaches as if to hug her. But Tessa is in that same instant stalking toward the hotel. She looks gray in its long silhouette.

The Killer has left Room 717. He is approaching the seventh-floor cleaning closet at the south end of the hallway. If one were stepping out of the glass elevator, one would turn right and walk forty feet, and there would be no mistaking the slatted door that bends outward in three sections (in the style of laundry facilities or other functional household areas) for a guest room. There would be no reason for any guest to open it. The Killer opens the cleaning closet: plastic bottles full of primary colors, white towels of various sizes, vacuum attachments, furniture polish, and carpet cleaner. There would be no reason to suspect the sturdy shelves or their contents. The Killer holds a controller—it resembles a garage door opener—in his left hand. He double-checks that the hallways are empty, presses the controller's single button, and the cleaning closet's shelves slide sideways. The Killer boards the secret elevator. He pulls the cleaning closet's door closed—flattening its three folds—before pressing the controller's button again. The cleaning closet shelves reposition. The secret elevator is not beautiful, like the glass elevator. Fluorescent-lit and blond-wood-paneled, it's the kind of elevator that belongs in a bureaucratic institution. But it is much faster than the main elevator. The Killer presses the button marked "8."

Brian says, "Wait. Wait, Tess, wait. Wait." He doesn't touch her. He cuts off her path to the front doors instead.

She tries to get around him. "Bri? Move."

"I need to talk to—"

Tessa's quite quick, particularly at ducking. Anyone who's boxed with her would know that. She rushes past Brian, and inside, and is most of the way across the foyer—watching him over her shoulder— before his voice rings toward the gaudy chandelier, shouting, "Tess, for God's sake, don't be—"

The blade slices her cleanly.

"Mon Dieu!" Henri cries, and drops a large knife. A thin stream of red splashes from its tip.

Tessa grabs her left palm. She squeezes her eyes shut as her mouth falls open.

Brian is also, it becomes obvious, quite quick. He shakes Henri by the lapels of his white chef's coat—"What the damn hell!"—and shoves hard enough that Henri's considerable girth tumbles back- ward over a reception sofa. Brian, in seemingly the same movement, bends low to Tessa and tries to coax her hands apart. His forehead is touching her forehead. One can imagine how their exhales must be mingling. He is saying something, whispering it, and this—his whispering—appears to cause Tessa much more pain than the cut across the palm of her hand, which she eventually shows him. Blood fills it in a shallow pool.

"It's nothing," she says.

"It's not nothing." Brian shucks his jacket and tears the sleeve off his black T-shirt.

Tessa laughs a little. "So macho, Bri."

"Thanks," he says, tying the cloth like a crude bandage. "I'll take you to the hospital."

"If you think for one bald second I'm getting on that motorcycle—"

"We'll take your car."

"No," she says, "we won't. I'm not leaving, I have tons of work to do."

"Mon Dieu," Henri says again, his legs akimbo on the reception sofa, his snowman's torso struggling for the torque to right itself on the plush rug. "This is why chefs die of the heart failure! This is absurde! I come to you with problem, as you tell me to do, and I become victim of assault."

"Hey." Brian points at the knife on the floor. "Who assaulted who? Why're you running around with Ginsu knives? Riddle me that, Pepe, okay?"

Henri, finally managing to sit up, says to Tessa, "Pepe? Who is Pepe?"

Tessa massages her closed eyes. She might be battling a grin. "What problem, Henri?"

"The dishwasher. She is broken!" He shakes a fist in the air. Fat and on the floor, he looks like a spoiled toddler. "I bring the knife to show you."

"So it's a dirty knife," Brian says. "Great. Good, that's great."

Tessa picks the knife up, turns it. Her blood glistens on the edge. It's beautiful. "You couldn't have shown me a spoon."

Henri farts thunderously as he stands. "You claim to me this is not a problem? Four days until the soirée and no dishwasher? This night is for the testing of the coulis. How do I make many coulis without dishwasher? I *pile* dishes until tomorrow, when man for repairs can come? This is what I do? This is what you ask of me? This is why the chefs die young. Mon Dieu, c'est tragique!"

During Henri's tirade, Brian tried to take Tessa's arm. She wouldn't let him. So he gestured to a reception armchair with one shoulder high in aggravation and the other low like a supplicant's. Tessa is now sitting down. Brian again examines her cut as if he might have missed something the first time.

The Killer has been wandering the eighth, ninth, and tenth floors. It's methodical wandering. He's traced each floor's layout, a predictable square on either side of the elevator's long hallway. Door after numbered door, slowly, taking his time, passing every guest room. He is now passing Room 1016.

Vivica, in the entryway of Room 1516, is making progress with the stain on the carpet.

"No hospital," Tessa says to Brian. He throws his hands up and goes to the lobby's modern fireplace (white marble, deep—children could have a tea party in it), where he hits his head against the mantel for show, only it hurts worse than he planned. He hides a wince from Tessa as she tells Henri, "I can call a repairman out tonight."

"Repairman will not come! Repairman will say tomorrow, and I will waste a day in the dishes. They are not to use when dirty." Henri reaches for the dirty Ginsu knife, which Tessa placed on an end table.

Brian points at him. "You touch that knife again, I'll kick your ass." The threat wouldn't work on a man who knows threats. The effortful tone is all wrong.

But Henri whimpers, "Mon Dieu."

"We'll figure it out," Tessa says. She presses her bandage, and her fingers come away sopped red.

"How about this," Brian says. "If I fix the dishwasher, will you go to the hospital?"

Tessa looks out the long windows at his motorcycle. "Not on that."

"I said already we'd take your car."

Henri stares at Brian like he might be Jesus. "He can fix her?"

Tessa gets up and goes to the main elevator. "Yeah," she says, "he can fix anything."

Tessa's a difficult person to get to know. Conversations about family or childhood get brushed aside as unimportant, irrelevant, dumb. The past is over, she'll say. Haven't you read any self-help? You're supposed to live in the present. She sidesteps and counters with questions of her own that focus conversation back on the questioner.

But there are files. Some of them are juvie files, but then there are bribes.

Tessa was found in a Dumpster when she was two days old.

Tessa's holding the main elevator open. As he gets in, Henri is describing the dishwasher in detail to Brian, who looks at Tessa like he wishes she'd look at him. When the elevator

disappears with Brian and Henri and Tessa inside it, Franklin darts from the stairwell and scurries across the foyer like a tweed rat. He shuts himself in his office, placing the large pair of scissors in his desk.

passes the second floor, Tessa sees Delores wiping her eyes en route to the housekeeping office. Tessa moves to make a note and says, "Damn it. My clipboard." Brian hides a snicker in a fake sneeze.

The Dumpster was in Spokane. Tessa went into foster care. She had twelve homes in eight years, all in northern Washington State. When she was eight years old, she went to live with Troy and Lorraine Domini. Troy and Lorraine had two other foster sons, twin boys, Mitch and Brian, ten years old. Tessa lived at Troy and Lorraine's until she turned eighteen, and then she went to UCLA. Yet she is not *over* being abandoned in a heap of trash, wrapped haphazardly in a white blanket patterned with blue and yellow duck-lings, her hair light then, and wispy, her mouth a round, wailing hole in the police photographs—no one gets *over* that. Tessa needs to be liberated from those memories. She should confide them. And if she won't confide them, there are files.

But information from files can be as irritating as it is illuminat-ing. Files don't mention, for instance, that even in an elevator with an annoyingly verbose chef describing every conceivable challenge in-volved in creating the perfect cherry coulis, Brian is jocular. His eyes laugh. Tessa bites her lower lip to keep from laughing with his eyes. Their bodies, even with a considerably wider body between them, possess a kind of visible static. Tessa's hips seem overactive. They tick outward or rest on the elevator's railing, in turns. The blood on her hand has pooled past the bandage. Brian picked up his jacket before getting in the elevator, mostly—it seems—so he'd have pockets to shove his hands into. His hands are so far in his jacket pockets that they make conspicuous forward bulges. He is fit, but not so fit as to seem vain.

It doesn't seem fair that men preoccupied with being fit are natu-rally assumed to be vain.

The Killer is boarding the secret elevator on the twelfth floor. Vivica, on the fifteenth floor, is telling the stain in Spanish that it is no match for her, and she is right.

There is no thirteenth floor.

Tessa sees something from the glass elevator that makes her forehead furrow. Henri doesn't notice, because he's ranting to Brian about the unstable flavor of cherries. Brian notices Tessa noticing something and says, "What's wrong?"

"I thought—the closet at the end of the hall—" She huffs and blows a strand of hair out of her eyes. "Forget it. I'm sleep deprived."

"The profile, I tell you," says Henri, "it has a volatility that the common mouth does not comprehend. To add cinnamon is to make them too sweet, liquor and it is overspicy. I try vinegar. I get desperate, monsieur—I try vinegar! And this fucker Destin says he ruin me, says I am mad. Who made me mad, this I ask you!"

The glass elevator passes the fourteenth floor. At the south end of the hall on the fourteenth floor, in the secret elevator, the Killer presses his controller's single button, and the cleaning closet's shelves shift sideways. He looks through the slats in the cleaning closet door to make sure the glass elevator has passed. He must have seen Tessa glimpse him. He's holding a knife much sharper than the one with which Henri accidentally sliced Tessa's hand. It's a knife the length of two of the sets of scissors Franklin used to disable the dishwasher. The Killer walks the fourteenth floor, methodically checking the door of each luxury room. They are all locked. Downstairs,

Franklin picks up the phone in his office. He looks at the receiver in bewilderment and joggles it a few times to confirm the landlines are not working. He laughs an unpleasant laugh that reminds the ear of a weasel. He takes a cell phone from his top desk drawer. Cell phones are against hotel protocol. Charles Destin himself made it clear he believes cell phones compromise employee productivity and, by extension, guest satisfaction. He dictated that all employee cell phones and other devices be deposited in the

Delores hears the intercom in the housekeeping office. The office is next door to the housekeeping storage area, where Delores is discarding a bulk bottle of expired shampoo. She crabs down a ladder and hurries toward the tinny voice. She wouldn't hurry toward the voice if it weren't Tessa's. Delores hates men. Delores has a right to hate men, but that doesn't make it any less frustrating for a man to whom she is supposed to listen. Delores's office has the only security feed anywhere in the hotel besides the break room lockers on the second floor. Franklin presses his phone's screen to blue it, taps, and puts the phone to his ear. "Tell the boss I messed with the dishwasher . . . Yeah, little things adding up to big things, like he said . . . And—uh—the phones. I got the landlines down, too." Franklin is lying. The Killer disabled the landlines. "Yeah, later . . . No, I'll wait till it's dark . . . Right, nobody gets hurt—hey, we've got flashlights . . . Yeah." It's easy to infer that Franklin is on the phone with Cameron Donofrio, or, more likely, an associate of Cameron Donofrio. Donofrio Properties is the principal rival of Destin Management Group. Charles Destin has long suspected Cameron Donofrio was infiltrating and sabotaging his properties. To a sane mind, Destin's paranoia seemed like so much rich-boy bullshit. The revelation of Franklin's call makes one wonder about Destin's reasons for building a hotel with the most sophisticated surveillance capacities ever attempted in the private sector. How much they had to do with catching the mole, Franklin, in a conversation like this one. "All right . . . Yeah, I'll report later tonight."

twentieth floor. It's a tiny television that streams motion-activated activity from everywhere in Manderley. Delores is supposed to have this television on at all times. The television is on, but Delores has taped her to-do list over the screen, in order to stick it to the head of security, who told her she was very important, his number two, the last line of defense. Delores is the only person in the hotel—besides security—who knows about the secret elevator. If her to-do list weren't taped over the screen, Delores would see the Killer boarding the secret elevator on the fourteenth floor. She would see *her* number two, Vivica, still warring with the blood-stain on the fifteenth floor. Delores hates men because her husband beat her for ten years. She tried to leave him four times, and he found her four times. The fourth time, she shot him. She didn't kill him. This is all in her police file. Her lawyer got her off. She limps slightly because her husband broke her tibia with a baseball bat when she was twenty-two. She was pregnant at the time. She limps into the housekeeping office. "Hi, Tessa. Sorry for the wait. I'm here."

Tessa kicks the glass elevator's door frame, probably cursing its slowness, and speaks into the emergency phone, which can access the intercom system if one has the proper pass code. "Del, how're you doing?"

Delores says she's fine.

"I saw you crying, hon. I'm on the elevator," Tessa says. The elevator sings its soft note for the nineteenth floor. Its doors slide open. Tessa signals Henri and Brian to go ahead. Henri rushes for a quartet of sous-chefs; they're sitting at a table playing Go Fish. "Don't let Charles get to you," Tessa tells Delores. "You know how he can be." Brian leans against the elevator doors to keep them open. Tessa signals again that he should go ahead. Brian shakes his head and smiles—at her, then at his feet.

"I'm fine now," Delores says. She wipes her tears, determined to make the statement true since it's Tessa who's asking. "Really, I'm okay. Why're you calling on the intercom?"

"The landline isn't working. Electricians probably nicked it." She asks Brian, as if it is a long-dead habit to always ask Brian, "Is that possible?"

Brian says, "It's possible. I doubt it, though. Electric and phone are kept separate for just that reason." He adds, for false modesty's sake, "But I'm no expert."

Tessa says, "Del, would you do me a favor?"

Delores sounds relieved, agreeing. She's a large, fifty-two-year-old hausfrau, but her emotional maturity arrested at fifteen, when she got married. The psychologist who evaluated her for her competency trial noted she was most tranquil in the domestic sphere, and that domestic duties aroused her maternal side, which had been frustrated by the miscarriage she suffered after her husband broke her tibia with a baseball bat. It is obvious that Tessa also arouses Delores's maternal side.

As when Tessa says, "I accidentally—look, don't freak out—but I cut my hand down in the foyer—"

"Oh my God! Are you—"

"But I'm completely fine. There's some blood on the marble. I'd really appreciate your cleaning it. Will it stain?"

Tessa knows the answer. She's asking so Delores can tell her, with confidence, "No. No, Tessa, it'll wipe right off with a little ammonia. The seal on the floor's still nice and fresh, and marble only stains easy if it's porous."

Tessa smiles. She likes hearing Delores be confident. "Awesome. Thanks. Wear gloves. The whole blood-and-puke protocol—keep OSHA happy."

Delores laughs. It's an old joke between them how much Henri hates OSHA and how much Delores loves it. "Will do, kid," Delores says. "You get that cut fixed."

"Bye." Tessa hangs up.

Brian gestures to indicate Tessa may pass him exiting the elevator, so she does. The ballroom rises around them. It feels like emerging from a mountain's long, narrow crevasse into the vastness of an enormous cave, only it's bright, and warm, and the finished pyramid of a thousand champagne flutes glistens like a waterfall on their far left. Long, athletic legs take two minutes to cross from one end of the ballroom to the other. Tessa's legs are athletic, but not long, and Brian keeps pace to stay beside her. The chandelier up here is simple so as not to distract from the cherubim mural. Tessa picked this chandelier. Destin picked the seven-million-dollar pinecone in the foyer.

"This place is something," Brian says. "I read about it. Supposed to be the safest hotel in the world, right?"

"Something like that." Tessa pauses halfway through the tables to move a salad fork to a surprising position. She makes a sour face and moves it back. "Yeah, that's the idea. Starlets can come here to recover from plastic surgery, that kind of thing." She walks, and the clicks of her boot heels sound like cracking bones. Brian nods to show he's listening, to show he knows she's not done talking. "Charles really wants the government bigwigs—political figures, diplomats. That's where the money is."

They're on the wooden dance floor now. Their steps are louder.

Brian says, "We should get your hand taped up. Before I deal with the dishwasher."

"It's done bleeding, I think."

"If you duck out of the hospital—" He reaches for the small of her back when she makes a sharp turn around the grand piano. The grand piano's not on the bandstand yet. Tessa doesn't see Brian reach, or feel it, because she executes the turn perfectly, and Brian's hand goes back in his jacket pocket. He doesn't look embarrassed about having reached. He doesn't look like he even noticed doing it. "I might go all big brother on you."

"Oh no," Tessa says. "Not that."

"Don't smile or anything, Tess."

"I won't." She is.

"Don't smile. You're annoyed with me, so don't smile."

"I'm not. Not at you. I'm thinking of a joke."

"Yeah?" Brian's smiling, too. "Tell it to me."

"Why'd the rabbit cross the road?"

Brian doubles over, laughing so loudly it startles Henri at the other end of the ballroom, where he is ranting at his underlings in French. It startles Justin and Jules in the kitchen, where they are staring at the dishwasher in utter confusion.

Brian's laugh at half a joke makes it easy to identify with utter confusion.

Tessa pushes into the kitchen, which is huge and industrial. Its sheer size and its Tetris game of tables, cabinets, tools, and appliances ensure that neither Henri nor the sous-chefs saw Franklin tampering with the dishwasher.

The kitchen's size also means that Brian's laughter echoes through it as he and Tessa come inside. Tessa's mashing her lips together so she doesn't laugh, her effort not to laugh worse than a laugh, because it means if she did laugh, it would be genuine. Not professional or proper or polite or cautious. It would honk like a Canada goose, obnoxiously endearing. She treats her past like a secret. She becomes very, very, very upset if someone mentions her upbringing in the foster system. She says, You're trying to *use* this. Don't you dare try to *use* it. Quit trying to *crack* me like I'm a vault in a bank! She throws things.

Such behavior breeds suspicion that emotional trauma resides in those memories, and therefore, leaving them alone is the proper approach if one wishes Tessa to relax her defenses and allow one to love her. But her efforts now to stifle laughter, combined with Brian's helpless laughter, added to Justin's and Jules's looking up from the dishwasher and performing the same addition as I am, arriving at the same sum as I have and sharing a glance of excitement at Tessa's odd mixture of perfect ease and paralytic unease with this young man—these phenomena put together suggest that Tessa's upbringing in the foster system included periods of great happiness. Her refusal to discuss them could be indicative of a desire to keep those memories closed off and sacred—a place she can go where no one can follow her.

In the entryway to Room 1516, Vivica gives a final daub with her rag. She pumps her fist in the air and gives the conquered stain a smug middle finger. Behind her and around the corner and down the hall, the cleaning closet door folds open. The Killer steps out of the secret elevator, onto the fifteenth floor.

CAMERA 33

□ □ □ □ □ □ □ □ □

Vivica reaches deep into her apron and pulls out a miniature hair dryer. She stuffs the bloodstained rag into her apron pocket, does likewise with the carpet cleaner—the bottle's handle overhangs the pocket like a baby kangaroo innocently surveying its surroundings—and tips onto all fours to plug the hair dryer into the nearest outlet. She aims the nozzle and turns it on "High." Only when the carpet is dry can a stain-fighter tell if any discoloration remains, if her enemy has been truly vanquished. This is the final step of Vivica's stain-fighting procedure. Tessa once told Vivica she should patent the process and teach classes. Tessa wasn't kidding. Vivica is petite and thin, her dark hair always in a tight bun. The errant gray strands in her hair emphasize how lineless and youthful her face is.

The Killer is passing the main elevator. He turns left. His feet are fluid, silent. The hair dryer is loud.

Tessa introduces Brian to Jules and Justin. Handshakes. A discussion takes place. Pointing and gesturing at Tessa's hand. Justin and Brian agreeing on something. Jules pointing to herself and offering an alternative. Tessa agreeing with Jules. Brian rolls his eyes and throws up his hands, but good-naturedly. Justin and Jules laugh. Tessa succeeds at not laughing, again, barely. Jules grabs the first aid kit from its special cabinet on the wall. She studied nursing but found she disliked the hours. She and Tessa leave the kitchen. Brian watches Tessa leave, his expression that of a stupid, forlorn puppy. He asks Justin a question and squats to the dishwasher's controls. Justin produces a toolbox from a stainless steel cabinet beside the walk-in refrigerator. Brian's head is no longer visible. High-capacity dishwashers are mounted on stainless steel countertops, to make loading more ergonomic. Brian's head is underneath the countertop. It would be unfortunate if the dishwasher crushed Brian's pretty-boy smile. Justin rifles through the toolbox and passes a flashlight to Brian's protruding hand.

The Killer stands behind Vivica. He points his knife at the back of her neck. He moves it to the space behind her heart. He watches his knife like a man under hypnosis. Vivica's from El Salvador. She survived the upheaval there and came to America. She stares at the drying carpet like the mere possibility of remaining discoloration is the military faction that cracked her country in two. She shuts off the hair dryer and mutters in Spanish with an El Salvadoran accent, cursing the electrician she thinks cut himself there. But that is not what happened. What happened is: a member of my team, Twombley, escaped the twentieth floor. The Killer chased him onto the fifteenth floor and caught him at the entryway to Room 1516, where Twombley was fumbling with a card key. The card key worked, but too late. The Killer grabbed Twombley, dragged him to the bathroom of Room 1516, wrestled him into the tub, and stabbed him. I don't know how many times. I lost count in the thirties; I was distracted. As the Killer left Room 1516, his pant cuff dripped onto the carpet. Thus the blood. Now—

Vivica unplugs the hair dryer and strokes the carpet as if it were a cranky toddler's hot head: There, see, isn't it easier if you behave? She probably feels lucky she found the blood when it was fresh, at five fifteen. It is now ten minutes to seven. She winds the cord around the hair dryer. She's turning around as she does it—she is fifty-seven years old, married thirty-six years, four children, seven grandchildren; one has MS, and Vivica runs a half marathon every spring, fund-raising for a cure—but the Killer is not there. She walks toward the cleaning closet to throw away the rubber gloves she used, in compliance with OSHA protocol. Delores forwarded the joke about OSHA and Henri to the entire housekeeping crew. It made the housekeeping crew like and feel loyal toward Tessa, and also motivated them to comply with the protocol. Tessa's a genius.

Vivica opens the cleaning closet. The Killer is not there. The shelves are in place. The hallway is empt— The Killer comes down the hallway behind Vivica as she peels off her gloves and bags them in plastic. He was sitting on the bed in Room 1512. He has a card key that unlocks every guest room in the hotel, except Room 1802, the deluxe penthouse. The Killer doesn't know his card key won't unlock Room 1802. The Killer stole his card key from Twombley, whose blood Vivica just finished cleaning out of the carpet. There are only two people with card keys that access Room 1802.

Vivica is humming a pop song. The Killer is directly behind her. She's throwing her bagged gloves down the trash chute. She sets the carpet cleaner in its place on the shelf, drops the rag into a dirty linens hamper, straightens a bottle of furniture polish, and turns around. She jumps, screams. Then she laughs. "You scare me, Mr. Franklin." Franklin likes to play pranks. "Mr. Franklin, you a bad man." Vivica pokes him. It occurs to her, abruptly, that this man is a foot and a half taller than Franklin. The Killer has pressed the controller's single button. The shelves behind Vivica move. "Mr. Franklin?" The Killer pushes Vivica into the secret elevator. He shoves her so hard, she bounces off the secret elevator's far wall. She cradles her elbow and sinks against the dull wood paneling. The Killer follows her inside.

"Knife, looks like," says Brian, who has reappeared from under the dishwasher, "or scissors."

"Seriously?" Justin says.

Brian gets up and sorts through the tool kit. "It's a good thing whoever did it cut the wires, because he cut the hoses and piping, too. There'd have been water all over this floor if he'd left the power connected."

Justin watches Brian's hands. They're grimed black. They push bolts and screwdrivers and pliers through the toolbox's pristine tiers, rejecting them in pursuit of something else.

Justin says, "So you're the foster brother."

"I could patch it if I had duct tape. MacGyver it for now." He keeps searching the toolbox, though he's done so already, and effectively. "You'll still need a repairman out here tomorrow. It'll be a temporary fix, hold for a day or two, max."

Justin goes to a cabinet beside the industrial stove, where ingredients for cherry coulis are flung and dribbled everywhere, as if there's been a food fight. "Heads up," Justin says, and Brian catches a roll of duct tape still wrapped in cellophane.

"Nice." His face lights. He stabs a box cutter through the plastic. His phony offhandedness is revolting as he asks, "Tess talked about me?"

"To Jules," Justin says, "not to me. Tessa isn't exactly an open book."

Brian laughs through his nose. He cuts lengths of tape. His swipes with the blade are expert, practiced. "Depends who's reading."

Justin waits. He has a master's in psychology from UC Davis. That's where he and Jules met. Jules was doing a double master's in psychology and business management, after quitting nursing school and earning a BA in art history. They both like to cook. Justin is a better cook than Jules. Jules does a kind of cooking there's a special word for; it means she makes everything with a side of foam. The foam is supposed to improve or contrast or enhance the flavor of whatever it's served beside, but the main thing one thinks when being served steak with a side of mushroom foam is: Weird. Justin and Jules opened a catering business straight out of grad school. It was foundering when they met Tessa at a catering conference three years ago. Tessa folded them into Destin Management Group, but they still do side projects on their own. Weddings, mainly. Justin now owns a hang glider, and Jules teaches Pilates. They like to rib Tessa by saying she saved them. This wouldn't count as ribbing, except Tessa hates it, because it's a compliment.

"I was ten," Brian says. "She was eight." He's still cutting duct tape. Flaps of it hang like silver tongues off the counter. "Me and Mitch—that's my twin brother. Did she tell you I had—?"

Justin nods.

"Me and Mitch—I mean, it's, 'Boys, say hi to your new little sister.' You're a foster, you're laughing at that. It's funny, because she'll be gone. You'll never see her again. Six months, nine months. Maybe a year. Maybe." He points at the fifteen or so strips of duct tape. "Hand me one every time I say, okay? You got a bigger flashlight? Something that can stand on its own?"

Brian could hold the small flashlight in his mouth. But Justin unclips a large one from the wall, by the fire extinguisher. Brian disappears under the counter again, only his legs and groin visible, but his voice continues, bolder. "First day of school? Tessa's first day—it's the middle of the year, February, I think. She's a second grader, got all the body fat of wheat chaff, just tiny. Tape."

Justin sticks a strip to Brian's outstretched finger.

"And we're taking the bus, because Lorraine's lazy as shit. Me and Mitch sit in the back. We're cocks of the walk on that bus. You know, made it clear early that if you messed with one of us, you messed with both of us. We weren't big guys, not ever, but there's a mystique with identical twins, and we played it way up. Tape."

Justin sticks a strip.

"Now, Tess hasn't said a word. Not to me, Mitch, Lorraine, nobody. And me and Mitch, we're fine with that. Whatever, right? She'll be history pretty soon. Tape. But there's this bully. His name's Lance. Swear to God, a bully named Lance. I mean, polo shirts, gel in his hair. Kid's eleven, and he gels his hair. Tape. Tess is wearing this hat. Blue with green polka dots. Got a little pom-pom on top, blue and green yarn. It's a funky shape, looks handmade. I'd bet anything a foster made it for her. And Lance starts in on her, calling her names, making fun of her secondhand clothes, and—tape—and Tess doesn't say anything. Won't even look at him. So Lance takes her hat and throws it out the window. I start getting up, but Mitch pulls me back in my seat, looks at me like I'm nuts. I still should've—tape—I mean, she didn't cry. She didn't do anything. She just sat there, her hair sticking up, static-y. Her hair—even then, you couldn't look at Tess and not kind of—even then, she was—her hair was really nice, but that's . . . So we get to school, and the bus's door opens, and Lance is at the door first because he's a d-bag like that. Tape. And Tess just—wham! Out of nowhere. Shoves him with everything she's got. He goes *flying* off the top step—"

Justin laughs, because Brian is laughing.

"Face-first into a snowbank. Breaks his nose. Except Tess isn't done. Tess runs down to him, starts stuffing snow in his mouth, down his coat. I'm sure as hell out of my seat now, got Mitch right behind me, and we pull her off him. It's like pulling a pit bull off a ham bone. Tape. Lance tried to tell on her, but me and Mitch both said he tripped. The bus driver was this deadhead who didn't care one way or the other, so Tess never got so much as a hard look about it."

Brian scoots out from under the dishwasher. Justin gives him a hand up.

"There a load in here?" Brian says, knocking on the dishwasher's shut door.

"Yeah."

Brian presses the power switch. Sound of spraying water. He peels the remaining strips of tape off the sink and makes a silver ball. "After that, if you messed with one of us, you messed with all three of us."

"And that's when Tessa started talking?"

"Call a repairman anyway. This'll hold three days, absolute maximum." Brian starts scrubbing his hands in the sink.

Justin realizes that's his answer. "I'll go get Henri so he can kiss your feet."

"It's no big deal, honestly," says Brian. "Some tape in the right places."

Justin leaves the kitchen and crosses the ballroom, widthwise, to where Henri is still berating his sous-chefs, who have banded their playing cards so as not to incense their boss further. Justin winks across the ballroom, lengthwise, to where Jules is cleaning Tessa's hand with hydrogen peroxide. Tessa must have insisted they sit as far from the dining tables as possible, so as to avoid getting blood on the linens. She must have insisted they not use the kitchen sink, so as to comply with OSHA protocol. She didn't want to get on the elevator again and use the break room or housekeeping storage area, in case she bled on more marble, which Delores would then have to clean.

Delores is cleaning Tessa's blood off the foyer floor. She wrapped Henri's knife in a hand towel from her apron pocket. Delores has everything imaginable in her apron pocket, now including the knife. She turns on the chandelier, because the lobby, facing east, is now dark.

Franklin, at his desk, is drinking more scotch. When the chandelier brightens his dark office, he squints, annoyed.

The Killer finally delivers a fatal wound to Vivica's heaving chest. Blood spurts outward in a foul, black splash. It would create a horrible red stain, but the entirety of the secret elevator is horribly stained already. It looks like a slaughtering pen.

"So," Jules says, "that's him."

A pile of cheap paper napkins, as opposed to expensive cloth napkins, catches the blood from Tessa's hand. She and Jules are sitting on cheap folding chairs equidistant between the dining tables and a long table against the east wall. The long table is there to hold upscale items for a silent auction, proceeds of which are earmarked to benefit foster children in the state of California. Destin does not know or care where the proceeds of the silent auction go. It's likely that Tessa's insistence on cheap napkins and cheap folding chairs meant more time required to set up this makeshift triage station, and that Tessa's insistence on cheapness vis-à-vis treating her injury made Jules impatient, which—even though Tessa hasn't answered right away whether that's "him"—is why Jules's voice has an uncharacteristic edge when she says, "The foster brother? Brian?"

"You're a sleuth, Jules." Tessa hears Henri's overjoyed "Grâce à Dieu!" and tries, *again*, not to smile. "He fixed it."

Jules exchanges a cotton pad for a cotton swab. She's exacting. This is probably why she cooks with foam. "You didn't mention he was hot."

"It's the motorcycle jacket."

"That helps. He looks about twenty years old. He's our age?"

"Older. Thirty-two. Ow, Jules—okay. Okay, it's clean."

"It's clean when I say it's clean, kid." But Jules changes back to the cotton pad. "And there were two of that hotness? Mmm, double trouble. You were a lucky little girl."

Henri doesn't kiss Brian's feet, but he does kiss each of Brian's cheeks, twice, though Brian still has his hands under the kitchen tap, trying and failing to get the grease out of his knuckles and nails. Water from Brian's hands splashes his motorcycle jacket as he tries and fails —also—to angle his face so that Henri's kisses land far away from his mouth. Justin and the sous-chefs watch all this with extreme amusement, because Henri hates everyone, except Tessa.

Tessa says, "One of that hotness is dead." Now her voice has an edge. "Remember?"

"Yeah, I remember. That's all you'd tell me, though."

Tessa is a wretched storyteller—unless the story is about lost shoes and music fests and Walgreens. If it's Jules asking, Tessa usually tells, but obfuscation is such a habit with her that she leaves things out and doesn't know she's doing it. "Troy was a—"

"Troy? Was that the other twin?"

"No, the other twin was Mitch." Tessa doesn't mind Jules interrupting; she finds the interruptions a welcome relief. "Troy was our foster father. Lorraine was his wife. Troy was a professional motocross racer."

"Motocross?" Jules says, scissoring bandages and gauze. "Like motorcycles?"

"Right. He was on the road something like three hundred twenty days a year." Tessa's body shifts around in the folding chair, as though the story's a cocoon she wants to be free of. "But when he was home, it was like a different house."

"Different how?"

"Lorraine was a bitch, that's how. No, not like that. She didn't hit, she yelled. A lot. A *lot* a lot. But when Troy was home, she was a saint. It was so bizarre."

"Why would a bitch take in foster kids?"

Tessa laughs bitterly. "Functional adults don't take in fosters. No, that's not true. Very few functional adults take in fosters. Jules, I didn't sever my jugular here—I think you've cut enough gauze."

"Let the nurse work, control freak. So, what? She yelled Mitch to death?"

"No. Troy taught Mitch and Brian motorcycles whenever he was home. Riding, repairing, racing. It was crazy. They were ten years old, racing hunks of junk in the fields behind the house." Tessa pauses, maybe so Jules can ask a question.

Jules doesn't.

"They built a ramp," Tessa says. "I helped. They started doing tricks."

Jules tapes the bandages. She's slow about it. She watches her work and not Tessa's face. Tessa doesn't like being watched.

Brian is attacking the grease on his hands with a kitchen towel. The towel has red stains on it, most likely cherry coulis. One cannot rule out the possibility that the stains are not cherry coulis. He goes to the swinging door and peeks out at Tessa and Jules across the ballroom. He lets the door swing shut and watches Henri direct the sous-chefs through desperate slicing and spicing of volatile fruit. Justin pulls a rack of dishes from the dishwasher, and Brian, tossing the towel aside, goes to the sink. He starts rinsing red-soiled plates and bowls.

"You don't have to do that," Justin says. "You can go find Tessa if you want."

"They're girl-talking. I don't mind." He arranges rinsed dishes in an empty tray.

"So," Jules says, after a long silence, "he died doing a trick in the backyard?"

Tessa shakes her head. "They dropped out of school when they were sixteen and joined the circuit. The Domini Twins." Her eyes sparkle, half sarcastically. "They did things the sport had never seen. This one, they'd—" Tessa stands up and sits on her left foot. "They'd swap motorcycles in midair. It was terrifying. They brought me on tour whenever they could. Whenever it didn't mess with school. They were nuts about me staying in school, Brian especially. He and Mitch set up a college fund for me. That's how I got through UCLA with zero debt."

Jules raises her eyebrows. "So Mitch died—doing one of those tricks with Brian?"

"No," Tessa says. "The most flips anyone ever did in midair was two. A couple of weeks before my eighteenth birthday, Mitch makes an announcement he's gonna do three. Three midair rotations."

The Killer gets out of the secret elevator on the seventh floor and returns to Room 717. He's wearing plastic bags over his shoes, secured with rubber bands above the pant cuffs. He must have gotten them from a cleaning closet to avoid dripping more blood on the carpet. He goes to the bathroom in Room 717 and rinses his knife. There's blood on his coveralls and his mask. He gets into the shower fully clothed.

Jules says, "And Mitch—"

"He under-rotated going into the third turn. He landed on his back, crushed his spine from the midthoracic all the way up to C3. He was alive for about five minutes, after. Brian got to him, got to talk to him. I wasn't there—I was in school."

"God. Could he talk? Did Mitch say anything?"

Tessa doesn't seem to hear. "I begged Brian to quit. At the funeral. I literally got down on my knees, crying, screaming. He got on his knees, too, and he hugged me as tight as he could." Tessa doesn't seem to be in the ballroom anymore. Her voice is far away. She isn't crying or screaming; it's as if doing neither highlights how loudly, back then, she did both. She doesn't notice when Jules applies a last piece of tape and simply holds her hand. "He told me no, he needed to keep it up. Not only that, he had to do the triple rotation. He said he didn't have a choice." Tessa jumps like she hears a door slam and pulls her hand out of Jules's.

She considers the bandage for almost a minute. Nods her thanks.

Jules nods in return and says nothing.

The Killer sets his mask over the shower door. It hangs there like flayed skin. The bathroom window is open, and the pulsing-red sun is nearing the sea, turning the water violet, throwing soft golden light. A blob of Caucasian giant is all that can be seen. The Killer folds his rinsed coveralls over the shower door and shuts off the spray. There is a second pair of coveralls hanging on a hook, where the bathrobes usually are. The Killer's bare arm reaches around and pulls the clean pair inside. His arm is sleeved in tattoos—a melt of mauve and black ink, unidentifiable as any kind of design.

The same golden light bathes the ballroom. Its entire west wall is windows. They back the bandstand, ending at the two doors— storage room to the right when facing the bandstand, kitchen to the left—that split off to make the room's overall shape an octagon. Tessa is walking toward the kitchen with a clutch of bloody paper napkins. Jules is walking toward the storage room with a cheap folding chair in each hand. She got the folding chairs from the long table, where the representatives of Destin Management Group's fund-raising arm sat to write the descriptions of the silent auction items. Tessa was doubtlessly pissed that the folding chairs remained in the dining area.

Jules opens the storage room door. Her bloodcurdling scream fills the ballroom.

CAMERA 34, 33, 31, 12, 59

□ □ □ □ □ □ □ □ □

J ustin drops two clean plates. By the time they shatter, he's almost out of the kitchen.

Brian beats Justin across the ballroom, to the storage room, holding a soapy glass.

Tessa beats them both to where Jules is gaping at the storage room floor.

"It's cherries," Tessa says, laughing, and puts her arms around Jules in an anomalous show of affection, before Justin arrives and takes over. "It's canned cherries, Jules. A pallet must've leaked."

There are rooms in Manderley Resort that do not have security cameras. Not many, but a few.

Jules is laughing now, too. "Cherries?" she says, her nails buried to the cuticles in her husband's biceps.

"Cherries," says Tessa, grinning at Brian, who seemed primed, in running toward Tessa, to leap between her and any danger. It was a giveaway in his posture—canted forward, reckless but with a goal. It was in his face—panic, thick and animal. He's still trying to make it subside. He's breathing hard, shoving shaking hands into his jacket pockets. He remembers the soapy glass when his right hand won't fit. He looks at the glass like an embarrassment.

Brian grins back at Tessa but says, "Cherries? You sure?"

"What else would it be? Hey, Henri?"

Henri, also attracted by Jules's scream but disinclined to run, is in the doorway of the kitchen.

Tessa asks him, "Could you spare a sous-chef to clean this up? There's a mop spigot in here. It won't take five minutes."

Henri puffs up like a cranky bird. "We are all busy."

Tessa doesn't puff. She doesn't need to. Her voice does all the work. "This room isn't food storage. It's speakers and extension cords for the stage. I count at least two-dozen pallets of cherries in here. I understand you have a system for the pantry, but you can't put your overflow in with electrical equipment, and this is why." Her eyes, too. Her eyes can be depthless when she wants them to be. "It's your mess. Clean it up."

Her eyes were depthless when she stared past a straining neck, palmed a contorting shoulder blade, ran another hand down perfect vertebrae to a strong ass, and cupped. Stared at the ceiling, where she was seeing someone she wished were with her instead.

She looks at Brian. Stares, really. Her hips move like a clock's third hand. Brian looks back at her. He's put the glass as low by his side as he can, humiliated to be holding it. He licks his lips. Tessa bites her lower lip.

This has lasted three seconds.

"What else would it be?" Tessa says again, turning to Justin and

Jules. They shrug, disinterested in that particular question, but Jules's mouth is an intrigued little moue and Justin pumps his eyebrows at Brian, as if to say, Well, well. Brian doesn't notice. He's making room as a sous-chef squeezes by. The sous-chefs all look alike, which is counterintuitive, as all four of them have dyed hair and elaborate tattoos and strange piercings. Their efforts to appear distinct from one another have accomplished the opposite: they are a mass. And an individual split off from the group—receding, now, into the storage room—is androgynous, anonymous, forgotten amidst his tribe's collective desperation to be remembered. Running water is heard.

"Blood," Brian says. Does he say it so Tessa will turn to him again? If so, it works. "She thought it was blood. Looks like it."

Justin says, "And the cherries are clots and brains! Ehh-heh-heh-heh!"

Jules smacks his arm. She's snorting. "Shut up, Cryptkeeper."

"Nobody even remembers that show," says Tessa in solidarity.

"You do," Brian says. "You loved that show. You'd make me tape it and then watch it with you once the house was asleep."

Jules and Justin are quiet. Tessa turns her head, slightly but conspicuously, to regard the sun over the ocean. Brian taps the soapy glass against his outer thigh. There's the *tink* of glass against denim, the *swsshk* of a mop on sticky tile.

"Mademoiselle?"

Tessa says, "Yes. Henri, what's up?" and takes long strides to where he stands in the kitchen doorway.

"The phone," Henri says sullenly, "it calls for you." He releases the door when Tessa props it open with her boot heel.

She pushes the intercom button on the wall-mounted phone; it's right inside the kitchen, bright red. Tessa insisted on the kitchen phone being red, so as to cut through confusion in a real emergency. She said it would be a pity if Manderley burned down because the phone blended with the wall. "This is Tessa."

"The floor's clean down here, pumpkin. Thought I'd tell you."

"Excellent. Thanks, Del." Tessa checks her watch. "Where's Vivica? The big ballroom cleaning's tonight."

"I had her do a walk-through when she got here, and she found a stain on fifteen."

"Stain? Where on fifteen?"

"The carpet right inside 1516."

Tessa's brow darkens. "What kind of stain?"

"She said it looked like one of the electricians cut himself."

"The electricians weren't on fifteen today. Charles and I did room inspections yesterday, and there were no damn stains on the carpet." Tessa didn't approve of the white carpet. That was Charles Destin's choice. He wanted white everything. He said it would look rich. Tessa said it would cease to look rich the minute a guest spilled a cup of coffee, a glass of liquor, or an entire room service meal in his or her rich white room. Destin exercised his power of veto and told Tessa that spills were her concern, not his. He told her he pays her very well to clean up spills. He does pay her extraordinarily well. Tessa says, "We need Vivica up here. You, too. The ballroom takes precedence over the guest quarters, even the luxury suites. I can handle 1516 being out of commission, but a dusty piano?"

"I'll get Vivica right away."

"I'll get her." Tessa massages her forehead. "Please come get started. Okay?"

"Sure thing, Tessa. I'm on my way."

Tessa kicks the kitchen door wide.

"This is not me!" Henri shouts. "This stain, it is not of me!"

Tessa never yells. But here's her version. "It's not?"

"I stop giving samples to the workers when you say. I stop this even though they are virgin palates who can—"

"Henri, if you are lying . . ."

"I do not lie." He puffs up again. A wheezy fart amplifies across stainless steel appliances.

Brian uses the excuse of the glass he's still holding to edge past Tessa and rinse it, tray it, wash his soapy hand. "Is this what your average night's like?"

"This is slow," Tessa says. "I have to go to fifteen and check on a cherry stain—"

"This is not the cherries! Unless they steal! They steal the cherry coulis, mon Dieu!"

"I'll come with you," Brian says. "If that's okay."

"I'll be back in—"

"I'd rather come with you."

There's a pause. Then Tessa laughs lightly, her eyes closed. "It was a puddle of cherries, Bri."

"Not cherries! Zut, alors!"

Tessa points. When Tessa points, it is a signal to stop whatever one is doing. And if one can, to hide. "Henri, I swear to God, if you don't chill out, cherries are not the only thing that can be canned. Got me?"

Henri shrinks. His sous-chefs exchange disloyal sneers.

Brian holds his chin and aims an expression of glee at the ballroom. It is, I agree, a great deal of fun to listen to Tessa be authoritative.

"Let's go," Tessa says.

Jules leaves Justin by the dance floor, where the two of them were pretending to examine place settings while actually eavesdropping on the kitchen. Jules excuses herself by explaining she needs to check her underpants for "fear splatter." This makes Justin laugh uproariously. Brian, overhearing, grimaces in disgust. Jules crosses the ballroom in a southeasterly direction. Her body multiplies behind the champagne flute pyramid, then vanishes into the door marked "Ladies." She locks the door behind her. Her face changes, becoming a cartoon of fear: bulging eyes and all twenty-eight teeth. Her hands go to her hair and pull. She squeaks at the pain, careful to do it quietly. The ladies' room contains a sitting area with padded vanity chairs and mirrors framed in oversized bulbs. Jules leans over one of the chairs, braces her hands on the vanity counter, and breathes erratically at her reflection: she is of French Polynesian and British descent, pale, bleach blond, fine-boned, expertly contoured with cosmetics. She gropes an orange container from her blazer pocket and beats the childproof cap against the counter edge until it pops. Capsules erupt. Saying, "Shit, shit, shit," she dry-swallows two, sweeps those on the counter into a pile with her palm, and pinches them into the container a couple at a time. She combs the chairs, crawls on the carpet, recovering capsules as if they were pearls. She misses one behind her; she stands and steps on it. Her psychiatrist has told Jules on several occasions she must be patient—antidepressants aren't effective right away; take them daily at a designated time and sure, okay, here's some Xanax for anxiety. Jules's psychiatrist has also repeatedly told her it would be wise to inform Justin she is taking psychotropic medication and seeing a psychiatrist—keeping it a secret isn't good for the marriage—but Jules has told no one. Jules stuffs the pills back in her blazer. She then glowers at her reflection until it consents to smile, and it's a smile for a toothpaste ad. For any ad. Anyone would buy whatever she's selling. She leaves the restroom, walks to Justin on the dance floor, snuggles to him, and singsongs, "Skid-mark-free." He laughs again.

The Killer is leaving Room 717. He takes a left turn at the main elevator and presses a finger to his right hip pocket, where he's clipped his controller. When he opens the cleaning closet door, the shelves have already moved aside. He gets on the secret elevator, nudging Vivica with his shoes to make space. Vivica is dead, but she wasn't when the Killer left the secret elevator. Her bloody handprints are smeared all over the dull walls. Destin did not insist on white for the secret elevator. He insisted only that there be a secret elevator; he is paranoid he will die in a hotel like his father did, and he built Manderley the way he did so as to negate that possibility. The Killer holds one of the hotel's paper laundry convenience bags in his left hand, his knife in his right. The bag contains his blood-soaked coveralls. He presses the controller's button—the cleaning closet shelves slide over—and presses the button for the second floor with the tip of his knife.

"This thing takes a while, huh?" Brian is referring to the main elevator, outside of which he and Tessa are waiting, on the nineteenth floor.

"Don't get me started," says Tessa, then starts anyway. "Charles wanted a glass elevator because he liked *Charlie and the Chocolate Factory.*"

"You're kidding."

"Sadly I'm not." Tessa checks her watch. "He had it modeled after the illustrations in the book, but the fact that it's diamond shaped means there's a bunch of stabilizing cables and winches that make it a death trap unless it moves so slow, it'd practically be faster to take the stairs." Tessa watches the buttons for the floors light up as she speaks. "You said you wanted to talk to me, right?"

"Yeah," Brian says. "When you've got a free minute."

"This is as close to a free minute as I'm gonna get, Bri. We're less than a week from the party. I sleep here, when I sleep. Say what you need to say."

"When you've got a free minute," Brian says again.

"Same old Bri. Wanting all my attention."

"Oh, pot. Nice to meet you. I'm kettle."

A loud giggle bubbles over from the dance floor. Justin dips Jules almost to the gleaming wood. Henri is playing classic French croons, concertina piping through an ancient portable stereo.

"They're pretty great." Brian nods at Justin who is pulling Jules vertical again.

Tessa turns back to the elevator floor numbers successively lighting: 16 . . . . 17. She says, apropos of nothing, "They go to Justin's parents' place in Reseda for Christmas Eve. Then they go to Jules's parents' place in Ventura for Christmas Day."

. . . 18 . . .

"What do you do?" Brian asks her.

Tessa works on Christmas. She doesn't say so. She says, "Any year now," and presses the "Down" button again. Tessa works on Christmas, even if someone invites her somewhere. If someone invites her somewhere, she tells him to go see his family.

"I watch movies," Brian says. The pointed roof of the diamond-shaped elevator appears. "On Christmas."

Delores is in the elevator. Tessa pastes on a smile and says, "I work."

The Killer steps onto the second floor. He tilts his head and listens, standing inside Delores's office. The Killer can hear tearing sounds. Delores's office opens into the employee break room, containing a long table, a kitchenette, and employee lockers. Outside the break room is a hallway, off which is the housekeeping storage area. The secret elevator opens behind cleaning closets on each floor except for the first (the secret elevator opens directly into Franklin's office on the first floor), second (it opens into Delores's office), eighteenth (into the south wall of Room 1801, the nondeluxe penthouse), nineteenth (into the kitchen's walk-in refrigerator), and twentieth (behind my chair). The Killer puts

Delores is apologizing to Tessa—this is Delores's favored greeting to Tessa—before the main elevator's doors have fully opened. She sees the young man at Tessa's side and becomes guarded. Tessa introduces Brian. Brian smiles but doesn't offer Delores his hand. He slouches to appear smaller. His smile doesn't show his teeth, and he allows Delores a wide perimeter, but holds the elevator door open with his motorcycle boot. Delores scurries around him, as she does all men, like they might bite. Delores hands Tessa her clipboard, while Tessa puts her bandaged palm at the small of Delores's back and tells Brian to wait for her; this won't take long. Delores listens to Tessa's description of

Justin begins dancing with aggressive pelvic movements—in the vernacular, "grinding." Jules pushes him, gesturing at the three other people in the ballroom, who are ignoring Jules and Justin completely. Justin's posture becomes conciliatory, apologetic. His hands find Jules's waist, circle it, drop an inch or two so they skim the tops of her buttocks, and Jules pushes him again. Justin and Jules haven't made love in more than two months. Jules's psychiatrist has told Jules to tell Justin about her medications not least because a side effect of SSRIs is a waning sex drive, which a mate may take as personal rejection if he's unaware his depressed/anxious partner's neurochemistry is being adjusted.

down his paper laundry convenience bag on Delores's desk. He keeps his knife. The tearing sounds are coming from the housekeeping storage area, where Franklin is unwrapping miniature soaps, wetting them with a liter bottle of water, and glomming them into a large soap clump, which he presumably intends to leave for Delores to find. Franklin is on a ladder, his back to the Killer. The Killer watches Franklin, whose hair sticks up in odd porcupine spikes and whose eyes flash every time he tears through a soap wrapper.

what needs to happen in the ballroom tonight. Tomorrow the band will be setting up. This is the last opportunity to clean the bandstand without any instruments or equipment on it. The musicians will make a mess. Tessa will tell Vivica to join Delores. Delores tells Tessa she didn't see Vivica on the fifteenth floor. Tessa reminds Delores that 1516 is outside the main elevator's sightlines. Delores allows how that's true, and she and Tessa split up, Delores walking toward the storage closet. Tessa is returning to the main elevator, and to Brian.

Justin leans to Jules, probably asking—for what seems like the hundredth time—what the hell he's supposed to do, or what he's supposed to have done. Jules's peppy comportment slips for scarcely an instant, before she's grinning and waving at Brian, who, by the elevator, has been observing this tête-à-tête with curiosity—and maybe a glimmer of sad understanding. Brian waves back, and Jules snuggles to Justin again. Justin joins the farce, calling "Helloooo" to Brian, as if they're at opposite ends of an abyss.

Franklin thinks his prankster persona endears him to people. Franklin believes he's had an especially hard life, because he is gay. He majored in theater. He did theater in high school, too, but he also played baseball. He was a star catcher. This makes one want to laugh, but laughter is impossible, given the circumstances. Franklin came out to his parents when he was eighteen, and his parents reacted with nonplussed nonshock, and Franklin—channeling some character in some script—began a soliloquy about how their lack of acceptance shattered his heart, raped his mind, impaled his spirit with daggers the length of his long, hard life. None of this is in Franklin's personnel file. A more thorough background check became necessary for Franklin, due to his tendency toward pranks. He has established a shaky peace with his parents, who, when interviewed, turned out to be sedately liberal Episcopalians who owned a split-level in Pasadena, thanks to Franklin's father's success in advertising and Franklin's mother's greater success in selling Mary Kay cosmetics. It makes one thirsty to remember the taste of Franklin's mother's raspberry lemonade. It makes one nostalgic for summer, though it's summer outside.

The Killer is still behind Franklin, watching—perhaps enraptured by the glob of guest soaps that has grown to the size of a softball, or perhaps debating methods. More likely debating methods. An emotional reaction to this situation might be problematic, complex, and multifaceted. Franklin is unlikable. It is truly almost impossible to like Franklin. The only people who like Franklin are fellow narcissists.

Tessa and Brian are passing the eighteenth floor. "Tinted glass?" Brian says, knocking on the slate panes. "I noticed that coming up. What's it for?"

"The penthouses. Gives the highest-paying guests extra privacy." Tessa is reading her checklists. There are lists for housekeeping, kitchen staff, waitstaff, and admin. Tessa knows them by heart. She's reading them because she's nervous.

Brian leans on the railing, then stands straight. He shoves his hands in his pockets. There's the sound of flipping paper, a scratching pen. "Say, Tess?"

"Hmm?" She makes check mark after check mark, back-documenting the items she's completed since leaving her clipboard behind. "What?" she says.

They're passing the seventeenth floor. "This place have a pool?"

Tessa, surprised, looks up. Brian's smiling. Tessa laughs shortly, and nods. "Yeah. It's not in the building."

"Outdoor?" Brian whistles. "You went cheap with the pool?"

"I'll show you our cheap pool. You've never seen a cheap pool like ours, I promise you." Her eyes are teasing.

Brian makes a general gesture with his neck. "You like this job? You're happy with it?"

"It's good, yeah. The hours are only crazy during weeks like this. I get a lot of downtime." She sticks out her chin. "And I'm not risking my life every time I come to work." Brian is blinking, hurt. Tessa says more gently, "I get to do lots of planning, design. That's what I really like, the designing phase."

"You designed this place?" His eyebrows rise.

"No." Tessa is lying. Tessa smells a compliment coming and must block it. "I had input, that's all. I gave suggestions." Bullshit. She took architecture courses throughout college but chose to earn a business degree because it was more marketable. She's heart-stoppingly afraid of being dependent on anyone, ever again, after a childhood spent at the mercy of the foster system.

"You designed this place," Brian says in wonder.

"I helped. Some. Not much." Tessa flips a checklist over and—they are passing the sixteenth floor—draws a perfect sketch of the ballroom in seven seconds. "I thought of that." She points to the bandstand. "Making the room octagonal like that, so we could have storage and a kitchen on either side but keep the ocean view. It's not a big deal."

Brian takes a hand out of his pocket and touches the sketch. He caresses the lines like they are something else entirely. "Tess," he says, and rubs the side of his head. "Jesus."

"What?"

He leans against the railing again. "I thought I could—never mind."

"What?" Tessa says, stern.

Brian points at the fifteenth floor, which is coming into view. The door won't ding open for another twenty seconds or so. The main elevator really is ludicrously slow. The secret elevator is much, much faster.

Tessa's turning red. "What's—"

"When you've got time," Brian says, flicking a nail on the railing. "It's important, but it's not urgent. I've waited eleven years, you know? I can wait another couple hours."

"Wait for what?" There's a foreign softness in Tessa's voice. Hope?

The doors ding open. Brian holds them so Tessa can go ahead.

The Killer has lost patience. He is walking toward Franklin. Franklin's soap gob is almost the size of a basketball. This is Franklin's third strike. I instituted a strike system for him after he plastic-wrapped the electricians' porta potty seats twelve weeks ago. Destin told me to be lenient, but look at this, look at that damn soap ball— what a waste, what a child.

Tessa's walking with Brian toward Room 1516, and Brian's impersonating a butler named Jeeves—"Follow Jeeves, madaahme. Your quahtahs are ovah hee-yah." Tessa is trying not to laugh. Brian is saying, "Don't laaauf, madaahme. It's not dignifaah-yeed." Tessa blushes when she laughs. Tessa blushes when she comes. She only comes during oral sex, so it is a challenge to see her blush. Especially if one is not skilled at making her laugh. It would have been nice to know the key to making her laugh was to tell her not to laugh. Maybe the key to making her come is telling her not to.

It is pointless to speculate. It's a waste of precious energy.

It is incredibly painful, one assumes, to be yanked off a ladder from behind. Franklin lands like a dropped marionette. He yaps and jerks, sees the huge masked man looming over him, and manages to scramble a few feet before the Killer catches his elbow. And squeezes.

There are innumerable techniques for breaking human bones. Certain types of military training teach men how. Rangers and SEALs, primarily. There is no one on the first through fourteenth floors, save the Killer and Franklin, to hear Franklin shrieking, to hear the loaded pop of his right forearm, his right upper arm, his wrist concurrent with his left forearm (defense fracture), his—

"Can't wait to see a luxury suite," Brian says as Tessa takes a card key from her breast pocket. "A luxury suite in this hotel could fit two of my house."

Tessa says, "Your house is three thousand square f—" And she stops. And she slides the card key in. The lock blinks red.

Brian is very still beside her.

"Damn it," Tessa says. She shoves the card key in harder.

"Let me."

"I've got it." Her face is masklike and rigid. She will not hand over that card key for anything. It's a matter of pride now. Tessa is, in her backward way, nothing if not proud.

"Plee plee plee," Franklin says, like the sibilance at the end of the word is too much a task for his mouth. His jaw is broken. An educated estimate would claim twenty-two of his bones are broken. Certain tortures are conceived specifically to be bloodless. "Plee plee," he says, and the Killer looks down at him.

The Killer leaves the housekeeping storage area and enters the employee break room. Franklin attempts, once, to crawl. Two wet pops. The fractures feel like hot, broken glass trying to push through the skin. It's transcendent, the pain. It makes a man believe in God, but makes the man dislike Him. Franklin's holler reaches all the way, one guesses, to the seventh floor. There is no one there to hear it. There is no one until the fifteenth floor, where Tessa still has not succeeded in unlocking Room 1516. Brian has offered twice more to try his luck; Tessa has twice more refused. Despondent, she tries knocking. "Vivica?" she says.

The Killer picks up his coveralls bag, goes into Delores's office, and removes the piece of paper taped over the small television with motion-activated closed circuit surveillance. He watches the screen switch from Tessa and Brian at the door to 1516, to Henri conducting sous-chefs in the kitchen, to the ballroom, where Delores furiously dusts as Jules sits at a dining table and plays Words with Friends on her prohibited cell phone. To Justin, on the stairs, walking past the landing to the seventeenth floor and continuing down. He looks around as if terrified of being caught. He could almost be mistaken for an inept, inexperienced hoodlum seeking the perfect surface to deface with spray paint—"could be" because Justin has the same frosted tips, single earring, and loose clothes he's been sporting for almost a decade; "almost" because these features have begun their descent into ridiculousness, existing as they do beside Justin's burgeoning crow's-feet, a tiny but growing bald spot he's still able to comb over, and knees that pop when he's been sitting too long.

The Killer watches the television for a full minute, while Franklin begins to yell for help. It must hurt him, because three of his broken bones are broken ribs. The Killer turns off the TV and replaces the piece of paper taped over the screen. He takes a paperweight off Delores's desk—a bright red heart, tinted quartz, the size of a grapefruit—and the bag with his bloody coveralls, and walks out of the office, out of the break room, into the hall.

"Tess, for real?" Brian says.

"I can get it, Brian. Okay?" She has tried swiping the card key slowly, swiping the card key quickly, with extra strength, with no strength at all. The lock blinks red, red. "I've handled a lot of crap without you to help me, okay? I've gotten through so much crap, you wouldn't believe it. I've managed without you just fine. All right?" She slaps the door, hard, with her bandaged hand and tries swiping the card key quickly some more. Brian reaches for the card key, but she says, "No, I know how this works. You're going to ask how I'm doing and wait for me to say I'm fine, and then you're going to leave, and that's fine. That's totally fine. You thought you'd come visit. Great, Bri, fucking fantastic!" She slaps the door with every other syllable, saying, "What the fucking fuck is wrong with this thing!"

Brian grabs her. He pins her arms to her body and holds her. One's past experience may dictate that pinning Tessa is exceedingly dangerous, as at first, she'll merely use a hidden talent for contortion and escape. But if one catches her, she'll employ a knee to the groin and shout, as one writhes on the pillowy carpet, What part of the word "casual" is confusing to you?

She never once buried her head in the front of my jacket and said muffled words.

Franklin bellows "No" as if his jaw weren't broken. He screams like it's his only hope, and it is, and it's inordinately loud, and the sound reaches—probably—to the tenth floor or so, before the Killer's arm arcs downward with the paperweight in his right hand (he's holding his knife in his left hand, with his laundry convenience bag of bloody coveralls) and hits Franklin's skull on the left side. It is not a deathblow. The Killer can hit harder than that. Franklin is unconscious, but it's unlikely he's dead. The wound does not bleed much. The Killer puts the paperweight on the table where maids fold sheets, picks up Franklin in a fireman's carry, and goes to the industrial dryers. There are four of them in a rectangular alcove off the housekeeping storage area. Delores is only supposed to use the first dryer until Manderley officially opens. The Killer places Franklin in the fourth. Franklin's broken bones sound like a rock drummer's sticks counting down a fast song. The Killer shuts the dryer door and presses buttons. The dryer chirps. Whirs. And commences the sound of a too-heavy weight turning over and over and over.

The Killer turns around. Here are the washers. He goes to the first one and feeds it his bloody coveralls, then browses the housekeeping storage shelves: miniature shampoos, conditioners, bubble baths, and body washes. He picks a miniature box of Tide out of a stack, returns to the washer, shakes in half the powder, and places the rest on top of the machine, where Delores will not see it, as she is five foot one. The Killer is approximately six foot four. He shuts the washer door and presses buttons. Beneath the sounds of sloshing water and weight being thrown around, there's the rumble of despairing moans. The Killer picks up Franklin's basketball-sized soap sculpture, goes to a large trash can beside the washers, drops it in, and sits on the sheets-folding table. On the table's outermost corner, a copy of US Weekly vows in neon pink that modernity's substitutes for gods and myths are, in fact, only human. The Killer flicks open the magazine and reads.

CAMERA 59, 12, 6

□ □ □ □ □ □ □ □ □

I didn't catch that," Brian says when Tessa speaks, her voice stifled by expensive leather.

She turns her ear to his heart—"Why are you here?"—and burrows once more into his front, ashamed for having asked.

"To explain."

She shakes her head into his breastbone; his answer was insufficient.

Brian moves so he is no longer pinning her, exactly. He winds his arms around her back like vines. His hands disappear in her black hair, reappearing as protuberances in the thick sheet that reaches almost to Tessa's waist. Tessa has her arms around his waist. They are a match, physically. He is narrow. She can reach around him easily. He is not a dedicated weight lifter. He runs, like Tessa does, or plays some raucous team sport, like basketball, that involves ass patting and trash talking, and casual acquaintances he calls "friends." Excessive cardiovascular training in a fitness routine can undermine muscle development by metabolizing muscle protein. It is a matter of proportion. It is a question of how one wishes one's body to look. It's not vanity, per se. The protuberance of Brian's left hand undulates across Tessa's scalp. He is also stroking the small of her back. Tessa is shivering. Her nose is now at his neck. She is smelling him. His nose is at the part of her hair; he is smelling her, too. His eyes flutter, then shut tight. His voice is husky. "There are things you don't know. Things I didn't tell you, and I need to tell you. I swore I wouldn't, but—"

Tessa peels off him and takes a small step back.

Brian nods, shoves his hands in his pockets. "I have to tell you." He says this like Judas explaining why a kiss is necessary. "I have to." He reaches to Tessa's nonbandaged hand; she's still clutching the card key. He slides it from her grasp and turns it around, so that the magnetic strip will face the door when she swipes it. The strip must face the door for the lock to read it. There is a diagram on the card key illustrating this.

Tessa's face distorts in agony, mixed with anger.

"I'm nervous, too," Brian says, kindly.

"Why?" says Tessa.

Brian backs a step away. Another. He leans on the opposite side of the hall. "Because it's weird. We were kids, and now we're not." He looks down and sees an errant tuft of carpet that Twombley disarranged while sprinting to Room 1516. Brian tucks it smooth with the toe of his motorcycle boot. "We're grown-ups now. It's confusing."

"Why is it confusing?"

He smiles at her, but he sounds exasperated. "You want me to say it?"

"Yeah." Tessa crosses her arms. "Yeah, Bri, I want you to say everything. Eleven years without a word, and you show up tonight? Why now?"

"That's part of it."

"I'll bet."

Brian takes his hands out of his pockets and crosses his arms, too. They square off. He says, "I get it." His voice is firm. "I get it, Tess, I do—"

"You get it, huh?"

"Better than anybody else could." He points at her. This is a mistake. But, as with his previous mistakes, Tessa does not respond in her typical manner. She doesn't seem to grow, like a provoked cat. She curls in, like burning paper, and listens to him say, "You can be mad at me. I deserve that. I know I deserve that, a hundred percent. But do *not* for one second treat me like I don't understand getting left behind. I'm as much a pro at that as you are." He stows his pointer finger in his folded arms and says, as if regretful about being so stern, "Almost as much a pro. I had eight fosters and you had twelve before the Dominis."

"You had a brother die." She whispers it.

"So did you. Mitch was your brother. Mitch would've done jumping jacks on PCH at rush hour for you, Tess."

"You had a twin brother die. And you talked to him while he died. You held his hand." She chokes. "I watched it on TV."

Brian tries to shrug. But he fails, like his shoulder's too

heavy. "I'll tell you," he says. "But I really do need your undivided attention."

Tessa looks at him like he's an idiot. "Bri. You have it."

"No, you're worried there's a carpet stain behind that door. And that the bandstand's dirty and there's a maid you can't find." He sounds jocular again. "And your chef's a fuckhead."

"Hey, know what? These problems might seem insignificant to you—"

"No, they don't." He walks close to her, pries her arms uncrossed, and sets them by her sides. "They don't. I'll stick with you, help out if I can, and when you've got a few minutes, I'll—" He exhales with huge force at the ceiling, almost as though he's looking for someone up there. "I'll tell you. It'll take a few minutes. Till then, I'll keep you company."

"Like a guard?" She smiles. "You know how good security is in this hotel?"

"There's nobody here. Nobody. All these empty rooms, and you in that—" He wags his arm at what must mean the main elevator and gives Tessa a withering look. "I'm just saying, for this being the safest hotel in the world, I haven't seen one sign of security. Not one."

Tessa's smile deepens. "The best security is invisible security."

"But if security's invisible," Brian says, "how do you know when it fails?"

Hate is a warm, welcome sensation.

Tessa mangles responses and finally says, "Whatever. Fine." She turns to the door of Room 1516. "Vivica's our master stain surgeon. I'll take a look. Then we'll pop down to the second floor. I'm betting anything Viv took a fifteen after getting the cherries out." Tessa slides the card key. The lock blinks green. "Then we'll do a check on the progress upstairs. I have to pick a table setting tonight. I have to. One hundred seventy-five possibilities—it's gotten ridiculous. There, see?" She has opened the door and is pointing at carpet a half shade darker for being freshly dried. She bends and pats the fibers. "She's a wizard," Tessa says with no irony, while past the king-sized bed and its white duvet, past the fireplace that divides the bedroom from a sitting area, around the door to the bathroom and inside the deep clawfoot bathtub less than thirty feet from the entryway, Twombley lies in his black suit, his fair hair askew. He's the centerpiece of a crudely pretty Rorschach. I see wings in the gouts of blood that sprayed the tiles all around him. He's the caterpillar in the middle. He'll wake up any minute and fly.

"Remember the time you and Mitch—"

"Lorraine's bed." Tessa hides an incandescent blush.

"Had to be blue Kool-Aid," Brian says. "I said why not water, and you said, 'It's the Smurfs, Bri. We gotta drink blue Kool-Aid.' I scrubbed that comforter for a half hour."

"I did say I'd do it." She nudges his chest, unbalancing him. "Don't get all revisionist on me."

"Tess, you're many things." He stands and offers her a hand up. She takes it, and he pulls, too hard. She knocks into him, giggling. "But a stain wizard is not one of them."

Twombley was the only one who got away. McKeith and Rawlins were in front of him, on the twentieth floor. McKeith is facedown, the exit wound on the back of his head tacky and dark. Rawlins fell facedown, too, on McKeith's left arm. They look like lovers sleeping in on a Saturday. Since Twombley was behind the two of them, he dropped and played dead, but the ruse worked only because of the flash grenade, which caused confusion—for the assailants, and for the five security team members on shift. Addison was on the other side of the twentieth floor, so while he took the fourth or fifth of his bullet wounds, Twombley scuttled through the chaos and into the secret elevator. He didn't fire his weapon, or he fired it badly, or something. He must have hit "15" at random. He disgusts me a little, lying dead in a bathtub while Tessa and Brian laugh at fond memories.

The Killer flips *US Weekly* facedown on the table, to keep his page, when the washer's buzzing spin cycle clicks finished. He walks to the washer, removes his coveralls, and loads them into the first dryer. He goes to the housekeeping storage shelves and selects a box of dryer sheets. He steps toward the dryers, stops, turns to the shelves, and throws the dryer sheets back. He seizes a box of hypoallergenic, chemical-free dryer sheets. He walks to the first machine and tosses a hypoallergenic, chemical-free dryer sheet onto the lump of his wet coveralls. He shuts the door and presses a button.

Tessa and Brian are boarding the main elevator. Tessa presses the button for the second floor. She is asking Brian, "Why were we even in their room? We weren't allowed in their room."

"Lorraine was showing a house. She tried real estate for about six months, remember? She bitched all the time about it taking up her weekends."

"God, yeah. I must've eaten enough Lucky Charms on that bed to gag a yak."

Brian laughs, loudly. He bends with the strength of it. It looks cathartic.

The Killer has walked to the fourth dryer and opened the door. A hand flops out, limp, crimson, smoking. The Killer tucks it back in, closes the dryer door, but does not restart the machine.

"Corn Pops," Brian says, wheezing.

"That was your poison, not mine. And Mitch and his Cinnamon Toast Crunch."

"And you always took our toys! Those toys at the bottom of the—"

"You *gave* them to me!" Tessa is hopping up and down. "You *gave* them to me of your own free will, both of you!"

"It was ex*tor*tion." He points at her. "It was *larceny*."

"You were *willing victims*."

"God. God, yeah, we so were."

The Killer has left the housekeeping storage area and is crossing the employee break room. He arrives in Delores's office, removes the piece of paper that covers the small television, and turns it on. The screen flashes on Justin, who is exiting the stairs at the first floor and squinting at the foyer, its rich white shine. He walks on his toes to the manager's office, checking to see if Franklin's in, and smiles broadly when he sees this isn't so. Justin dashes across the foyer with the excitement of a schoolchild. The feed switches to Henri yelling at his sous-chefs in the kitchen. Henri is turning purple and using copious French profanity. His sous-chefs are all Californians. None of them speak French. They trade looks of derisive confusion, enraging Henri all the more. The feed switches to the ballroom. Delores holds a duster that rests on the end of a stick that can reach twenty feet above her head, to the bevels above the high windows. Jules is pocketing her phone, laughing at Henri's eminently audible theatrics. Her face lengthens, becoming gradually more disturbed at Henri's vocal volume and profane inflections. The feed switches to the main elevator. It is on the fourteenth floor, then the twelfth floor. There is no thirteenth floor. Brian's and Tessa's laughter has calmed. They're each looking off in an imagined distance. They share a past. They're watching it like a movie. Brian knew Tessa when she was young and innocent. If he was remotely decent, he guarded that innocence, as did his stupid dead twin brother, but then they abandoned her, both of them, so what right does he have to steal an eyeful of Tessa like the sight of her is a nutrient of which he's been deprived?

The Killer gets his coveralls from the dryer. He's hurrying. He doesn't run; he walks faster. He's careful not to make noise. Justin's right downstairs. He remembers his knife and the heavy quartz paperweight, and—he pauses, his masked head tilts—he goes back for *US Weekly*. He checks the TV. Brian and Tessa are down to the sixth floor. They are fidgeting. Tessa is fixing her hair, releasing its thickness from the knot at the nape of her neck, so that all of it tumbles around her face, setting off her bright eyes, and she plumps it with her nonbandaged hand. Brian takes off his motorcycle jacket and puts it over his arm. He has underdeveloped arms. He should lift weights. He is risking osteoporosis, like an old, frail woman. The Killer turns off the TV, reboards the secret elevator, et cetera, and Brian says, "You look good," like that's not the most obvious thing in the world to say, and Tessa says, "Thanks. You, too," offhandedly, and upstairs, in the kitchen, Henri has calmed enough to give his sous-chefs what he calls "une tentative finale" to craft the cherry coulis, reassigning flavor profiles and giving instructions in a mixture of French, and English so heavily accented that it might as well be French. The sous-chefs exchange low, anxious mumbles, trying to decode what their mentor is imploring them to do, as Henri has turned unctuous with desolation, certain his minions will fail him. Henri is a fuckhead, but so is Brian.

upstairs, in the ballroom, Jules continues to be relatively worthless, shadowing Delores as the poor maid tries to dust and forming theories. "Do you think they were ever a thing?" Delores doesn't answer. "No," Jules answers herself. "No, I doubt it. He and his brother were pretty much the only family Tessa ever had, but"—she reaches to a table, folds a napkin into a rose, and holds it up—"I don't think it was ever sexual." Jules then folds the napkin into what looks like a vagina. "But it is now." She titters.

---

downstairs, in the lecture hall, Justin says, "Hey, sexy," his voice deeper than usual. "Thanks for the video today." His mistress says, presumably, that he is welcome. She's a flight attendant named Charlene. Justin calls her Charlie or, more often, Sexy. Their dalliance began nine weeks ago. It's been eight weeks since Jules started seeing a psychiatrist. It is legitimate to wonder, in one's duller moments, whether Justin's affair caused Jules's mental problems or Jules's mental problems caused Justin's affair.

the Killer dismounts on the seventh floor, walks quickly down the hall, enters Room 717, and tosses his knife and clean coveralls and the paperweight on the bed. The knife puts a tear in the white goose-down comforter, and a few feathers fly up; the quartz makes the springs squeak and creates a deep valley in the mattress; his coveralls flop half on the bed, half on the floor. He unbuttons the front of his coveralls. He sits on the toilet and opens *US Weekly*. There is the plunking sound of a leisurely turd.

Brian's hand ghosts the bottom of Tessa's back as she precedes him out of the elevator, onto the second floor. Tessa's saying, "Hey, Viv?" She doesn't seem to feel Brian's hand. He must not quite be touching her back.

"Do you smell that?" Brian says.

"Yeah. Somebody microwaved their dinner too long."

Brian sniffs, disturbed. Tessa doesn't notice, as she is describing the layout to Brian. "We figured the business types and conference-goers would be inspired being on the same floor as the real workers in the hotel, so we've got eight seriously lavish conference rooms behind us and to either side. For the huge-deal CEOs, there's a high-ceilinged lecture hall off the lobby." (There, Justin lazes in a back-row business chair. He says, "Return the favor? What do you think I am, a freak?" and chuckles at an expected response. He says, "I don't know—I've only got about five more minutes," and takes a pair of clips from his pants pocket. They're chip clips, for holding bags of pantry foods shut. He's using them to clip his iPhone to the seatback in front of him. He puts a Bluetooth in his ear—"Better talk dirty so I finish fast"—so he can use both hands to pleasure himself, which he is now doing. I fervently hope he does not put the chip clips back in their designated kitchen pantry tub.) "I'd show you the space, except catering's using it as a staging area for the party's lobby décor, so it's full of tables and extra seating and textiles and trays, and Justin promised he'd fillet anybody who went in there and screwed with the supplies, so—" Tessa's tone and the rate of her words are painstakingly casual, as are Brian's assent to them, his nods.

But when Tessa stops chattering, he says, "That smell's . . ."

"What?" They pass the housekeeping storage area.

"Nothing," Brian says.

Tessa walks into the break room. She frowns. "Vivica?"

Brian's hands are out of his pockets. He frowns, too, and sniffs.

Tessa walks to Delores's office, but sticks only her head in. She believes it's important to respect others' workspace. "Viv, are you—?" Tessa snaps her fingers—"She's in storage"—and passes Brian in the doorway. "I bet she has her earbuds in, which is against—" A forbearing smile is on Tessa's lips, ready to deliver a lecture about using personal cell phones and all other devices while on the clock. But the housekeeping storage area is empty. The alcove that houses the washers and dryers is not fully visible, so Tessa goes to check it, saying, "Vivica, really, I need you up—" But Vivica isn't there.

In the secret elevator, Vivica's dead eyes stare at one of her smeared handprints.

"Hey, Tess?" Brian is kneeling by a spatter of blood on the floor. It's the size of two postage stamps, and the shape of Florida.

"Franklin," Tessa says to the blood. She takes a roll of toilet paper off the housekeeping shelves and holds down the outer corner with her thumb, winding a thick white wad around the thick white wad of her bandage.

"Who's Franklin?" Brian kneels and stops Tessa from wiping up the tiny puddle. "Hold on a second. Back up. Who's Franklin?"

"The hotel manager," Tessa says, allowing Brian to continue holding her bandaged hand above the stain.

"Your boss?"

"He wishes. Why?"

Brian appears to do difficult mental math, but he does it looking around at the space. He looks at the bloodstain. "How do you know this is his?"

Tessa realizes what he's getting at. She smiles—amused. Charmed, goddamn it. "It's fake. The blood's fake. Franklin likes to play practical jokes."

"Yeah?" Brian says, still holding her hand. "Like what kind of jokes?"

"The sick kind. He promised to stop, but I think he kind of can't help it." Tessa laughs at Brian's plain worry. "Okay," she says. Dipping a finger in the red, she raises it to her mouth.

Brian catches her wrist. "Tess, Christ, don't—"

"It's fake! Franklin messes with Delores all the time. She's his favorite target. Look at the soaps, the empty water bottle on the floor, the ladder right there. He was sticking the soaps together. He's done it before."

"And to give his prank a one-two punch, he squirts some fake blood on the floor." Brian brings her dripping fingertip to his nose. He smells it. "Smell it," he says. "Don't taste it. Smell it."

Tessa does. Her lip curls in faint revulsion. "Right. So?"

"So, they don't usually bother to make fake blood smell like blood."

Brian releases her hands, steals the toilet paper, and wipes her fingertip clean while Tessa says, "Fine. One of two things happened. Either our head of security caught Franklin at it and intervened—"

"Intervened?" Brian echoes. "And caught him how?"

"I don't know. That's not my department. I'm design and logistics." She steals the toilet paper back and wipes the stain, though Brian protests. "Franklin's right now having his ass handed to him. Hopefully getting fired, though that'll make the next few days a living hell for me, finding a replacement."

"What about the smell?" Brian says, standing when Tessa does. He watches her toss the bloody paper in the trash.

"Ha!" she says. She reaches into the garbage can, most of her top half disappearing. She lifts out the soap ball. "That creep is fired." She drops it, and a duo of thuds suggests it bounces in the bottom of the can.

Brian repeats, "What about the smell? And you said one of two things happened."

"Someone cut themselves," Tessa says, reorganizing the soaps on the housekeeping shelves. She spots the collapsed stacks of dryer sheets and fixes those. "Vivica. She came down for a snack, was checking on—I don't know, something—in this room, she cuts herself, overcooks her food—"

"You're reaching," Brian says.

"What else would it be?"

The buzz of fluorescent lights fills a telling silence.

Brian says, "That's not food. It's meat, but it's not." He blows all his breath at the floor and forces himself to look up. "On the circuit. When there was a crash and gas spilled and a guy got burned— big-time burned; we're talking ass grafts to the face—this is how it smelled."

Tessa looks sick, but she stands up straighter. She turns and leaves the housekeeping storage area for the employee break room. She does so professionally, shoulders back, expression controlled, until she's no longer in front of Brian. Then her forehead crimps, and she presses on her mouth. Tessa is an ambulant contradiction. She is at once strikingly strong and heartrendingly vulnerable. The paradox makes a natural protector desperate to protect her. The best security is invisible security. The most thorough safety is safety one's object of protection doesn't know about. She shakes her head at a dirty dish in the employee break room sink, rinses it, and sets it in the drying rack. This seems to focus her, and she rounds the long break room table to stand in front of the lockers. Employees are assigned a pad-lock. Tessa turns her combination.

Brian bangs his forehead on the housekeeping storage area's wall, once, and goes to follow Tessa. He pauses at the table where the maids fold sheets. Runs his finger along the edge. His finger comes away flecked red.

He looks around the room, his eyes landing on the dryers.

Tessa pulls on her padlock, but it doesn't pop open. Franklin cut off all the padlocks with bolt cutters, on orders from his phone contact, at a quarter after five o'clock today. He then replaced the employees' padlocks (labeled with employees' names) with other padlocks. He then hid the bolt cutters in a conference room on the second floor. Tessa tries her combination again.

Brian is opening the first dryer. He wears the grim resignation of a man who feels foolish and yet knows he is right. The dryer is empty but still warm. He touches the ridges inside and spins them. He scowls, shuts the door. And looks at the rest of the row.

He moves to the second dryer. He looks markedly different—threatening, worlds apart from the golden-retriever-like persona he's been using on Tessa this afternoon. His lips pucker and his eyebrows angle and he opens the second dryer. It's empty, cool. He checks the third, fast: empty.

Brian inches sideways. He's shaking his head. His lips are moving in false, rapid-fire consolations that what he knows is inside isn't inside. He's reaching for the fourth dryer.

The Killer is still on the toilet, on the seventh floor.

The other Killer is still playing solitaire, on the twentieth floor.

CAMERA 6, 13, 4, 5, 12, 33

☐ ☐ ☐ ☐ ☐ ☐ ☐ ☐ ☐

Brian grips the handle of the fourth dryer. If he finds Franklin's body, he might not scream. He might hurry to Tessa, shush her, drag or carry her to the foyer. Maybe—barely—he could do this before the other Killer notices, summons the secret elevator to the twentieth floor, boards it, and presses the button for the first floor.

The other Killer has abandoned his game of solitaire. The red of his cards is so vibrant against the thin gray rug that the colors throb like strobes. The twentieth floor was designed to be boring—no, it was hardly designed at all. It's a monitor bank on the north and south side and thin carpet and wraparound tinted windows and space and space and space and a conference table and a coffee station and, now, four dead bodies. The other Killer stands at the secret elevator, his finger poised over the "Down" button. He watches Brian.

In the employee break room, Tessa checks her padlock's underside and sees her name is not on it.

Brian hears swearing and a loud rattle of metal. His hand retreats from the fourth dryer, and he runs. "Tess?" he says, arriving in the employee break room.

Tessa is checking all of the padlocks for labels, finding none. "I am going," she says, "to murder that rotten little sneak the second I see him, I swear on my life." Brian is set to ask a question, but Tessa says, "Franklin locked up our stuff. I was going to use my cell and call Charles and fill him in on how Franklin crossed the line and is *fired*." She screams the word.

Brian goes near her, but does not touch her. He's smarter than he looks. "Landline's out, right?"

Tessa says, "Right" through her teeth.

Brian perches on the back of a break room chair. "I don't like this."

The other Killer is terrible at solitaire. He cheats, so he always wins. He's dealing a new game, his motions like those of a grandfather clock, which will count seconds as long as it has to, and not a moment longer, and not a moment less.

Tessa and Brian are arguing. Brian is asking her why he smells burned flesh and keeps finding red stains, and Tessa is cutting him off by saying she doesn't want to hear about how his deathsport (she says it like that, like one word) has made him an expert on the smells of burns and blood. She is endeavoring not to cry, but this time, she does not allow Brian to hold her. She says something regarding the stairs.

Henri is turning his music way up, to motivate his cooks.

The other Killer, on the twentieth floor, is wearing the same mask and coveralls as the Killer, on the seventh floor. This makes it difficult to distinguish between them. The other Killer, as he plays solitaire, often rests his masked head on his fist. When he does this, he resembles Rodin's famous sculpture, *The Thinker*. The Thinker is—still—playing solitaire, and the Killer is—again—sitting on the bed in Room 717.

US Weekly sprawls, forgotten, beside the toilet.

Brian insists on preceding Tessa down the stairs to the foyer. He enters the stairwell in a stance of intense suspicion, his head snapping upward at the echo of Justin's dead sprint past the eighteenth floor, up one more flight, to the ballroom (where Justin tears through the door, hearing the manic squall of a concertina, perceiving an opportunity to be of use, and Justin's very excited about this because now he can save Jules's ears to make up for betraying her trust), and Brian signals Tessa to wait, wait a second, until the door from the stairs to the ballroom slams, the specter of far-off music hushes, and Brian decides, incorrectly, that silence means they're safe. He signals Tessa to come on.

Brian moves like an athlete, but an athlete in an effeminate sport, like gymnastics. His body suggests a complete willingness to take a blow or a wound or any discomfort, really, for Tessa, his arm to his side and in front of her, like a mother in a minivan braking suddenly and acting as a human seat belt for her child. The hesitance in his sideways arm suggests he feels stupid. He doesn't trust his instincts, not enough. He has seen some hell; he has walked through it. But it requires many prolonged sojourns in hell to learn that instincts are the animal inside that wants nothing but to survive. To propagate.

Henri's French accordion ballads blast on. Justin is touching Henri's shoulder and yelling. Justin's mouth shapes, "Turn it—down!"

Jules has cranked the volume dial to the left. "They need the musique!" shouts Henri, though his sous-chefs rub white-sleeved wrists on their ears.

"He's always in here," Tessa says. She has broken her own rule and is standing in Franklin's office. "I'm telling you, security busted him. He's being fired right now." She wilts against a filing cabinet. "A thousand more things for me to do."

Brian's hands are in his jacket pockets again, chastened. There is no evidence of foul play in Franklin's office. "How'd he get hired if he's such a crap employee?"

"He knows a guy who golfs with Charles's uncle." Tessa has slid a piece of paper from Franklin's printer, has clipped it to her clipboard, is writing items down. "Actually, he fucks a guy who golfs with Charles's uncle."

"Charles," Brian says, nodding, distracted.

"Yeah." Tessa is too distracted to note he's distracted.

The intercom barks: "Zut, alors!" and "Tessa, come in, Tessa." Jules is sort of laughing.

Tessa goes to the intercom on the wall two feet to Brian's left and hits a button. Brian doesn't move, as most people would when Tessa looks severe like this. "Talk to me."

"We need you in the kitchen. Henri's gone whatever's French for 'loco.'"

"Right up." Tessa walks past Brian. He follows her. She stops in the middle of the foyer, where chandelier light burnishes the marble. It burnishes her, too—the curtain of her hair a long copper river, the line of her body a black slash in the white room. "Brian, I can't do this. With Franklin fired, the opening's in meltdown, and I can't call Charles to tell him about it. So I need you to—"

"I'll stay." Embarrassed. Indifferent to embarrassment, or as close as he can manage. "I won't get in the way. I'll quit bugging you about what I came for, I'll make an appointment to talk to you later, when you've got the time, but"—he shoots defiant distaste around the gleaming first floor—"I'm staying."

"Why?" Tessa pretends this question is perfunctory, an annoyance. She does want to get upstairs as quickly as she can, but she also wants . . . Her body seems to change its mind millisecond by millisecond, limbs angling toward Brian and at the same time away.

Brian puts a hand to the small of her back and guides her toward the main elevator. He hesitated for a moment. He looked guilty. He looked afraid. He is fantastically readable, like Tessa. Most people are fantastically readable. That's why masks are a great idea for killers.

"I'm learning about hotels," Brian says, pressing the "Up" button. "You know how I love to learn." He leaves his hand at the small of her back a few seconds longer than necessary. Not that his hand at the small of her back was ever necessary. He smiles. At her, and then at the floor. Then at her, and he keeps smiling at her. Tessa tries to mirror Brian's sentiment, his light heart, but she has no talent for denial. The elevator arrives; they board. There is quite a long silence.

Then Tessa says, "Troy shouldn't have pulled you out of school."

"Mitch wouldn't have gone without me."

"Mitch shouldn't have gone, then."

Brian looks out of the glass elevator. They are passing the fifth floor. "Mitch hated school. When Troy took us along, summers, you saw. Mitch just lit up. Then Troy got the idea for the Domini Twins, and that was it. It wasn't even a question." He prods her with his elbow. "There are more kinds of education than what happens in a classroom."

"Like the kind that teaches you how charred flesh smells?" Tessa regrets it the instant she says it. But she doesn't take it back.

Brian watches the seventh floor pass. Room 717 is around a corner. The door is closed anyway.

Tessa hugs her clipboard. "Was Mitch—did he get burned when . . ."

"No."

Tessa watches the seventh floor become the eighth.

"There wasn't any pain," Brian says. "There wasn't any physical pain."

Tessa's eyes fall shut. She's very tired. She slept two hours last night. "I'm sorry. I am."

Brian is stony. He watches the ninth floor pass. "For what?"

The tenth floor passes.

"How about you tell me what you're sorry for," he says. "For bad-mouthing my career every chance you've gotten tonight? For calling me stupid, or—"

"I never—"

"For saying it's my fault he's dead?"

Tessa backs away from him. Her shoulders hit the glass. She mutely shakes her head. She shakes.

Brian watches the eleventh floor. The twelfth. He could be searching the carpet for bloodstains.

Tessa's voice is too soft to hear.

"What?" Brian says, watching the fourteenth floor. There is no thirteenth floor.

"Look at me."

Brian watches the start of the fifteenth floor.

Tessa hits the "Emergency Stop" button on the elevator. It rings up the shaft like an alarm clock. Jules, Justin, Henri, and the sous-chefs are in the kitchen, arguing about noise levels. Delores is the only person in the ballroom. She is the only person upstairs who would conceivably hear the alarm, but she has earbuds in. They are plugged into her iPhone, which is in her apron pocket. She hates French accordion music.

The Killer hears the alarm. He gets up from the bed, leaves Room 717, follows the hallway, and stands at the main elevator's doors. He looks at the buttons above the doors, sees the button for the four-teenth floor is illuminated. The Killer enters the stairwell.

"You never think about yourself," Tessa says. "You never have."

Brian reaches for the elevator buttons, but Tessa bats his hand.

"That's all I'm saying. You loved school. You were on the honor roll every semester. Look at me, Brian."

Brian acquiesces, because he can't not. Tessa's face is inches from his. Muscles in his neck clench. His fists dig and dig in his jacket pockets.

"I never made it a secret how I felt about you on those things." Tessa sounds angry. Or, she would, to someone who doesn't know what she sounds like when really angry.

"Motorcycles," Brian corrects. "You can say the word, Tess. They're called motorcycles."

"Now, Mitch?" Tessa says, like she didn't hear. "Mitch I shut up about. He was going to do what he was going to do. He always did. It drove me crazy, and it drove you crazy. Remember?"

"No. I don't."

"Yes, you do. You tried to talk him out of it. You tried to talk him out of riding back when you were both too short to reach the clutch pedal, but he taped hockey pucks to his boots. Remember that?" Tessa foils Brian's attempt to look at the floor by grabbing his chin. "And when you saw that, you taped hockey pucks to *your* boots so he wouldn't be ripping over the hills all by himself. And when he started trying tricks, you did them, too, and you were better at them than he was, and so you said, 'Let's do tricks together,' and you did that so you could make him take it slow, cycle up through the less dangerous stuff first—"

"I liked stunts. I liked doing them."

"But you never loved doing them. Not like Mitch did." Tessa is still holding his chin. She puts her thumb in the middle and strokes an indent there. "You did this the day you tried your first jump with him. I was watching. Have you forgotten I was there? Mitch botched his landing. You nailed yours, but you turned to see if he hit his, and you spun out. Mitch sprained his wrist, but you landed on your chin and skidded through the dirt. I held your head while Mitch ran for the house. You came to and you told me—remember?"

He reaches up and holds her hand holding his chin. "Yeah, Tess. I remember."

"You said, 'Mitch needs to quit this before it kills me.' You laughed, but I was crying so hard, I almost threw up. So you sat up. And you hugged me. You told me you were fine, everything was okay. And you bled so much, you needed a transfusion at the ER." Brian tries to hug her now. Tessa wriggles free and puts a distance between them. "You never thought about yourself, not once. Not until he died and you decided to stay on the circuit when I really needed you."

"Tess," Brian says.

"What?"

Brian points at the segment of the fourteenth floor that is visible to him. "Who's that?"

Where the main elevator has stopped, Tessa and Brian are about two-thirds on the fifteenth floor and one-third on the fourteenth floor. This means, when Brian asks, "Who's that?" he's referring to the Killer's black boots. When Brian asks, "Who's that?" the Killer's black boots move, calmly walking to the left.

Tessa says, "A member of the security team, doing a check." She twists a hank of her hair into a knot. "Probably."

Brian flattens his belly to the elevator's floor. "Where's—there, hey! He's wearing a mask."

"A what?" Tessa also lowers to the floor. "Bri, if you're making this up . . ."

The Killer has paused at the door to the stairs. He and Brian are four feet and two glass panes apart. Tessa appears next to Brian, and the Killer looks at her.

Tessa shouts, "Franklin! You're so incredibly fired!"

A second passes. Then the Killer shakes his head at Tessa. Slowly.

"It's—that's Franklin," Tessa says. "Gotta be. Or—security's running a scenario."

The Killer taps his wrist, where a watch would be. He then opens the door to the stairs and lets it fall closed behind him.

"What scenario?" Brian says.

Tessa stands and hits the "Emergency Stop" button. The elevator rises. Tessa gasps. The Killer is on the fifteenth floor. Brian stands and gets in front of her as the Killer's neck sinks backward, watching them rise. Tessa's and Brian's necks sink forward, watching him recede.

"They ran a scenario last week," Tessa says, "where there was a bomb in the lecture hall. They cleared us all out. No one told any employees about it. Charles didn't even know about it. We thought it was the real thing." She watches the sixteenth floor's empty halls. Then the seventeenth floor's empty halls. "They're making sure we take the proper steps, that's all."

"And what are the proper steps?" Brian asks.

"Form a large group in an open space and wait for the notification that the scenario has been run to its conclusion," Tessa recites verbatim. Love blooms through me like a bright red flower. This is intolerable.

"What if it isn't?" Brian says.

"Isn't what?"

Brian gives Tessa the stank eye.

She gives it back. "Isn't a training exercise? Then Bri?" She claps her hand on his shoulder. "It's been great knowing you."

He doesn't laugh.

Tessa does. "Chill out. Honestly, you haven't met the guards here. They're the most intense bunch of suits that ever existed. They take it personally when stuff gets by them." She blows a strand of hair out of her eye, comfortable now in her own explanation. "That mask. Franklin wore it to scare the staff on Halloween." She scoffs. "They could've at least come up with something original."

Brian jumps when the elevator dings at the nineteenth floor. Delores is on the bandstand; she's sweeping in preparation to mop.

"See?" Tessa says, reading his relief at this tidbit of normality.

The elevator doors glide open. He follows her into the ballroom.

The volume of Henri's music shoots to a deafening level. Tessa and Brian cover their ears. Tessa says, "Del! Delores!" as she and Brian skirt the bandstand, but Delores can't hear. Delores, oddly, favors heavy metal. Tessa jogs toward the kitchen door, bursts in unnoticed for all the noise, crosses to the portable stereo on a shelf near the pantry, and only when she's hit the "Power" button do Justin and Henri stop yelling at each other and look at her. "What the hell," Tessa says, "is going on up here?"

Brian, per his promise to stay out of the way, is lurking unassumingly by the dishwasher. He peeks underneath it and taps its controls like a friend.

"I told him," Justin says, stepping away from Henri. Justin looks as angry as he ever does, his forehead a lightning storm. Jules's forehead is confused: her husband's sense of righteous offense is out of proportion with the crime. "Have at him."

Henri's cheeks are fading from plum to a uniform maroon as he says petulantly, "They need—"

"The musique?" Tessa says.

Henri's lower lip quivers. He knows that Tessa is kind, but not nice. She is accommodating, but not a pushover. He has pushed her, and she will not go over.

She turns to the stove, where the sous-chefs are feeding Jules spoons of cherry coulis experiments. "Sous-chefs go hang out in the ballroom," Tessa says. "We're waiting on an all clear from security, and then you can go home."

"Mais non!" Henri throws his hand towel, as his sous-chefs flip the burners dark and set down spoons. "You stupide children, you shall remain here with me until—"

"Henri—"

"Stupide! Stupide!" he shouts—not at her, but at the sous-chefs hanging up their white smocks. Tessa blinks on a pellet of Henri's spit as he shouts, "Cochons de lait! Putains!" He moves to intercept his assistants as if Tessa's not standing five feet ahead of him. He knocks into her. Tessa totters on her boot heels.

Henri's coat makes a farting sound as the back of it splits. The white fabric is tissue in Brian's grip. Brian places Henri against the wall, like Henri is a troublesome robotic knickknack marching off the end of a mantel. He holds Henri there by the front of a cherry-stained smock. The sous-chefs hesitate by the walk-in freezer. The walk-in freezer locks. The walk-in refrigerator does not, because the secret elevator is hidden behind the shelf that holds the juice concentrate.

Tessa has regained her balance. Brian seems to realize his own obviousness. He holds Henri against the wall, huffing a hard breath in annoyance at himself. Jules and Justin both have their eyebrows high up on their heads, and they blow on spoonfuls of cherries periodically, like all of this is an excellent show, complete with food.

Tessa tells the sous-chefs, again, "Go to the ballroom, guys. I'll tell you when it's time to leave. Start bright and early tomorrow." She looks at Henri and says with a level of calm he should recognize as dangerous, "Shall we say seven?"

Henri sticks his nose in the air.

"Seven," Tessa tells the sous-chefs. "Go have a seat. Don't mess with the place settings, no card games."

The sous-chefs mutter, leaving.

Tessa goes closer to Henri. She looks at Brian as if to say something, but Brian shakes his head. Tessa was ready to say, "Let him go," and Brian was saying, "Don't tell me to do that, because I won't do it." They are painfully transparent.

Tessa points at Henri. "You're a brilliant chef, but you should keep in mind that there are chefs younger than you, less choleric than you, who would eat rat droppings to work in this facility. I'm thinking of a dozen names right now. I'm thinking of their phone numbers, because I've memorized them, because your brilliance is not worth what I have to do to keep you in check." Tessa goes still closer to Henri. Brian lets Henri go, because Henri is crying quietly. Henri does this often; he's faking it. "Stop crying," Tessa says, "or I'll fire you right now. I don't give a fuck what it does to the opening." Henri's trembling lip drops. "You can go home," Tessa says, "or you can stay here. But you play your music at the volume I indicated with a fluorescent green piece of tape to mark where it's not splitting everybody else's ears. If you decide to stay, you're going to take an hour and eat. You haven't eaten all day, except sampling, and all the sampling has been cherries. Your blood sugar's going nuts. That's why you're being such a pill."

The four sous-chefs have settled at a table near the bandstand. One of them moves a place setting's shrimp fork inside a wineglass, but his companions nag at him until he puts it back. The same sous-chef then takes a cell phone out of his pocket and fiddles with it. The other sous-chefs ignore this, eager to see him get in trouble. Delores departs the bandstand, holding her broom, and enters the storage area where, presumably, she is filling the mop bucket, as running water can be heard.

Henri is now sitting on a stool by the dishwasher. Tessa has gotten him crackers and cheese from the walk-in refrigerator. She keeps Tupperware full of snacks specifically for Henri, for times like these. Henri is diabetic; he ought not to skip meals. She pats his back and makes the sober suggestion that he apologize to his sous-chefs. Henri gets up, toting his Tupperware in both hands, his gait mildly unsteady, since notification of low blood sugar can make the effects more drastically felt.

Brian, Justin, and Jules all stand by the stove. They have all three tasted all four varieties of cherry coulis. They have each chosen a favorite, which they now eat. Actually, Brian let Jules and Justin pick their favorites first, and he took one of the two remaining. Brian asks, "When does Tess get a break?" Jules and Justin laugh. Jules says, "Sorry. Sorry, you didn't mean that to be funny." Justin says, "If you can get her to leave the hotel for five minutes, you'll go down in the annals of myth." Jules says, "Forgive him. He talks like that sometimes." Their silverware scrapes the bottoms of the steel pots. Jules says, "Did you two ever . . . ?" Brian licks his spoon and frowns, perplexed. Justin says, "Sleep together. My wife is asking if you and Tessa ever slept together. Because that's completely appropriate, honey." Jules says, "Oh, what? I point out the elephant in the room and I'm a jerk?" Justin says, "No. You poke the elephant in the eye and you're a jerk." Brian says, "Yeah. We slept together." He plugs his mouth with cherries and garbles, "She was eight and I was ten."

Tessa guides Henri to the table where the sous-chefs sit, like she's guiding a little boy into his first day of kindergarten. She confiscates the sous-chef's cell phone without a word, leaves the cooks to talk, and walks toward the storage room. Tessa pushes the storage room door wider, as the doorstop for that room, according to Delores, "sucks." Delores, looking up from steering the mop and bucket, yanks out her earbuds. Tessa shakes her head in what would be a bosslike manner, except she's grinning, and then Delores is laughing, and then they're both laughing. "It's off," Delores says, pulling her phone out of her apron pocket and touching the screen. "It's—hey, wait a sec." "No exceptions," Tessa is saying, reaching for the phone but not taking it. Delores gives it willingly and says, "I got a text. Take a look." Tessa reads, scrolling down with dabs of her index finger. Henri is apologizing between crackers, speaking mostly in French, but his sous-chefs are used to this. Most of them know "I'm sorry" by now, as well as "The flavor profile of cherries is a whore of shit, a whore of shit."

Justin and Jules gawp at Brian as he laughs through a swallow. He seems to debate, to decide. He waves his spoon in the air like a silver flag of surrender and says, "She wouldn't talk. That's normal in the beginning, but people started getting weirded out about it after a few weeks. Me and Mitch, we didn't—well, we faked like we didn't care about her, but we did by then. She'd smile when she was playing with us. She'd even giggle, but get her around an adult and she'd clam right up." Brian stirs his saucepan. "Her teacher at school called Lorraine in. And Lorraine told Tess—at the dinner table, in front of me and Mitch—'If you don't start talking, I'm not keeping you. I'm not gonna send you back—I'm gonna send you to an institution.'"

"God," Jules says, "what a bitch!"

"You can't imagine," Brian says. "So after dinner, when me and Mitch and Tess go to the park like we always do, and I'm pushing her on the merry-go-round, I say to her, 'Tess, you know, you can talk to me.'" Brian chuckles. "She looks at me, like—like, she still does it. A minute ago, when I wouldn't drop that chef's shirt so he could knock her over some more. It's a look like, Do you think I'm the dumbest person alive or what?"

"Exactly!" Justin says, laughing.

Brian puts his saucepan back on the stove. "But that night—Mitch could sleep through anything. Identical twins aren't—we were pretty damn close, but we weren't identical in every way. A pin drop could wake me up. So that night, when my door opens, I sit up straight. It's Tess at the door. She shuts it behind her, comes in the room, and she sits on the floor between my and Mitch's bed, her back to this little wood dresser. Then she pats my mattress, like, Lie down, weirdo, what am I gonna do to you? So I do. And then she whispers to me, super-quiet, 'Why did the rabbit cross the road?'" Brian crosses his arms, like he's embracing the memory. He gives Justin and Jules a minute to guess, but they don't. "I said, 'To get to the other side?' and Tess whispered, 'Because he was stapled to the chicken!'"

It has been deniable, up until now, that Brian is good and decent and precisely what Tessa needs. But now he is smiling down at his folded arms, the boyishness in his grin set against—or amplified by—the crinkles his laughter cuts into his face, crinkles that are like a prophecy of a happy future. It is easy, undeniable, to imagine these crinkles beaming at Tessa over their joined hands. Gold bands on their joined hands.

Unless he dies tonight.

"After that, she started coming into our room every night, and her and me would talk while Mitch snored like a dying buffalo in the next bed. And me and Tess would figure out one thing for her to say in school. One thing at school and one thing at home. Then add another thing, and another, and eventually . . ."

"She was fine," Jules says.

Brian nods, and picks his saucepan off the stove to finish. "Got cold too easily, though. I must've given her every scarf and mitten and hat I ever owned, but they were never enough."

"And your bed," says Jules.

Brian says, "Sorry?"

"You gave her your bed. You got on the floor instead of her. Didn't you?"

"She told you that?" Brian says. He colors and looks at the kitchen door, either wishing Tessa would appear or thanking his stars she doesn't. Maybe both.

Justin puts his arm around Jules. "My wife's a good guesser."

Justin's hand strokes Jules's upper arm like a gentle child would pet a frightened animal. If he did that when they were alone—but he sees no reason to, and nor does Jules, since no one would be there to watch. Jules and Justin are at their best when they have an audience—a common problem among millennials, who were raised by television and movies, as well as among natives of Los Angeles, who grow up understanding that behind the curtain, is another curtain. Jules and Justin have fought fiercely to construct lives that put them onstage as often as possible, with as large and varied an audience as possible. They have an incredible array of friends, "friends," and people they've friended. They only know how to act when they're acting.

Brian stacks their three pans and goes to the sink. Justin and Jules try to argue against his doing their dishes, but Brian's saying, "Tess didn't like her room much. It faced the woods, and the coyote calls freaked her out. I slept fine on the floor." He rinses. "I'd set my alarm for a half hour before Lorraine woke up, take Tess to her own bed. Lorraine would've gotten the wrong idea for sure. Or she'd have pretended to, if it gave her something else to rag on Tess about. I swear Lorraine wanted a girl just to call her ugly once a day." He loads a tray a tad roughly and smacks the dishwasher's "Start" button. "Anyhow," he says, hosing the sink, "Lorraine never knew. And Tess quit coming to our room at night when she was about thirteen. It—" Brian shrugs. "You know, it would've been kind of strange then, I guess."

The kitchen door swings open. Tessa stands in it, holding up Delores's cell and setting the sous-chef's confiscated phone by the dishwasher. "The drill's over. Security just texted."

CAMERA 34, 33, 12, 4

rian dries his hands and tosses the towel beside the sink. He walks to Tessa, takes Delores's phone, taps the screen alight and reads, "'Attention, employees. Scenario complete. Manager and maid in protocol debrief. Proceed as normal.'"

Tessa doesn't say, "I told you so." But her face does.

Brian, for once, isn't looking at Tessa. He's looking at the cell phone. "Is this how they always notify you that you can move around again?"

Now Tessa's face says exasperation. "No, usually they call the room where the employees are grouped. If we all followed protocol."

"And if you didn't?"

Justin takes the cell phone from Brian so he and Jules can read it. Justin says, "Then they get the lowest-ranking member of the security team to round up the ones who didn't follow protocol so the head of security can lecture them to follow protocol." Justin sighs. "Poor Viv. Fuck Franklin, but poor Viv. It's like detention."

"The phones are out," Tessa says, because Brian's still skeptical. "So they texted."

"Except," Jules says, also skeptical, "we're not supposed to have our cells on us."

Tessa shakes her head at Jules. "Doesn't apply to Delores. The head of security overruled Charles on that one."

"Why?" says Brian.

Tessa lifts flat hands, mutely claiming ignorance. But Tessa knows the answer. The answer is that Tessa's infinitely visible to Charles whereas Delores is not. Delores is the ideal person to act as a clandestine liaison for security. This is why she has the television monitor in her office, as well as an iPhone in her apron pocket, though she is by no means exempt from a rule that states employees are under no circumstances permitted to use earbuds while on the clock.

In addition, Tessa finds Manderley's level of surveillance excessive. She thinks Charles Destin is paranoid and megalomaniacal—which is not untrue—and that he hired safety operatives who revel in playing God with those they claim to be protecting—which is false and harsh and an outright bitchy thing to say—but she said this to Jules in confidence, or what she thought was in confidence, because Tessa's aware of roughly a quarter of Manderley's surveillance. It's not that she isn't attuned to danger; it's that she is overconfident in her ability to defeat negative circumstances by sheer dint of will. Or, in Tessa-speak: "Look, Charles thinks this is a game. And what you and your team mostly do is cry wolf. But if a wolf comes at me? Last thing I'm doing? Is crying about it."

Justin says to Brian, "Don't worry about it, man. Security has it down. They've taken every precaution in the book." Justin hands the cell phone to Jules. "They've written a whole new book of precautions."

"Yeah." Brian shoves his fists in his pockets aggressively, scanning the ballroom. He inspects the mural on the ceiling, and his eyes bounce from cherub to cherub, as if he's counting them.

On the twentieth floor, the other Killer—the Thinker, the Thinker—returns to his game of solitaire. He was busy with his phone, composing two text messages: one to Delores, signaling the all clear, and one to the Killer, telling him Henri was bound for a dinner break. The Thinker has the latest-model cell phone. He leaves it on the security counter. It's on vibrate. He resumes sitting cross-legged on the floor, his chin in his hand.

The Killer, in Room 717, picks up a matching phone from the bedside table and reads a text message. Leaves Room 717. Remembers his knife.

Tessa is speaking to the sous-chefs. Henri has finished his crackers; he shakes his head when Tessa asks him something. She says something stern in reply. He goes with his sous-chefs toward the main elevator. He takes the crackers with him.

Jules is handing Delores her cell phone. Jules's medication seems to have taken effect. Her body possesses the loosened, laid-back jointlessness of someone who's either just received the best massage of her life or who has been sipping fine brandy by the fire for too long. Or who took a double dose of Xanax. She drapes an arm over Delores's shoulders, raises a finger, reaches in her back pocket, produces a glossy piece of paper, and unfolds it. It's a knitting pattern. Both Delores and Jules enjoy knitting. Jules is terrible at knitting, but she's aware she's terrible. She gives out her projects as gifts. She always safety-pins a card to the shapeless bag or unraveling sock. The card always says something like, "For you: my epic fail." Delores, who can spot intoxication at a thousand yards, shrinks beneath Jules's half embrace and waits for it to be over.

Brian has been telling Justin, in the kitchen, where they're propped against the door frame facing each other, "This isn't right."

"What?" Justin says.

"First thing you learn when you do jumps? The safest trick is the simplest trick." Brian nods at Delores, who's receiving her phone. "Where are these guys, anyway? Where's headquarters?"

"For security?"

"Yeah."

"Twentieth floor."

"I want to talk to them. For five minutes—hell, for one minute."

Justin is shaking his head. "None of us has clearance. Only Charles and other members of the security team can access the twentieth floor. That's the first thing *we* learned." Justin's stance is placating, slightly forward, arms a relaxed fold, to counter Brian's anxious uprightness. "Brian, listen, Charles hired them first. He installed them first. The twentieth floor got finished before the rest of the hotel had walls. We don't even know how the hell they get up there, dude. The stairs and elevator dead-end at nineteen. And they can run a scenario—any kind of whack-a-doo scenario they want—at any time." Justin was a surfer. Sometimes he tucks back long hair that isn't there anymore. "But that's why this is the safest place in the world."

"And you saying that?" Brian says. "Is why this might be the most dangerous place in the world."

The Killer is on the secret elevator. He steps on Vivica's forearm and bumbles his balance. He kicks Vivica's forearm, picks up Vivica's body and tosses it, twists and crushes it, until it folds like a box with broken corners—rigor mortis has only started to set in. The secret elevator door opens, and the Killer presses the controller button on his hip, but he does not open the cleaning closet's slatted door on the fourteenth floor. He stands close to the slats and waits.

Henri despises the break room. He considers it an insult to his dignity to eat in a room with taupe tile, eggshell white walls, and a view of either three-dozen light brown lockers or a fridge/microwave/coat-hooks combo.

Because Henri despised the break room, Tessa—when wooing Henri to be head chef at Manderley—took him on a tour of the luxury suites, and told him to choose the one he liked best. She assured him that if he accepted the position of head chef, the suite of his choice would be the last rented to guests, and that if no guest had rented it, Henri could cook in the suite's kitchen and dine in the suite's dining room on his dinner breaks. Henri toured the luxury suites like a shah in the market for a new hearth rug. He had no idea there were penthouses in the hotel that made the luxury suites look like Quonset huts. He still does not know this. He is stunningly unobservant about anything but the finer points of food and the slights incurred by his own ego.

He now bids his sous-chefs a desultory au revoir, and exits the elevator on the fourteenth floor. He turns and walks toward the closed cleaning closet. The main elevator lowers with excruciating slowness. The Killer, behind the cleaning closet door, does not move. Henri turns right, bears left, and unlocks Room 1408. He goes inside. The sous-chefs' observing faces disappear.

The Killer opens the door to the cleaning closet, exits, presses the controller button on his hip, and the bloody mess of the secret elevator vanishes behind linens and bottles. The Killer goes to the door of Room 1408. He takes out his card key. It will unlock the door. It will unlock any door but the deluxe penthouse, Room 1802. He's not aware of this. No one, except one person, is aware that no one, except two people, have access to Room 1802.

The Killer doesn't put his key in the lock. He wavers, seeming to consider.

Tessa is examining place settings. Again.

Brian is watching her from the kitchen doorway, halfheartedly trying to converse with Justin, who has enlisted Jules to help him finish the rest of the dishes left behind by the sous-chefs' frantic flambéing. Brian is asking Justin where he used to surf; Justin must have mentioned it.

Jules holds up a finger to her husband and squeezes around Brian. Justin tells Brian, "Laguna. You ever surf?" Jules goes to Delores, who is in the storage closet, presumably dumping the mop bucket (tumbling water can be heard).

"Some," Brian is saying. "I'm not very good at it."

Tessa is moving a water glass. She puts a hand to her head as though to soothe an ache.

Brian says, "I'm rotten at it, to be honest," as Jules squeezes past him again, into the kitchen. She wedges a doorstop and goes to the portable stereo. She turns the volume down—to the level marked with a tiny neon green Post-it—before switching it on.

Delores remains inside the storage room. Her tapping foot is visible. She is doing nothing, which makes her nervous. Jules must have told her to remain in there.

Jules whispers to Brian. She indicates Tessa, who isn't far from the dance floor. Tessa doesn't seem to hear the music. But she must. It's not deafening, but it fills the ballroom. It's a French tenor over lachrymose accordion. It would remind a child of the dinner scene in *Lady and the Tramp*.

Brian shakes his head and turns to whisper to Jules. But Jules keeps walking to the dishwasher. She trays the cookware her husband has rinsed, grinning like the Cheshire cat.

Brian probably wanted to whisper to Jules that Tessa doesn't dance. Since he can't say it, though, since Jules is too far away, he misses the opportunity to give himself a spoken reason to not walk toward Tessa.

Brian walks toward Tessa.

Henri chose Room 1408 because, like every luxury suite on the hotel's west side, its west wall is entirely glass, offering a view of white sand and bright blue water, and now, a sliver of sun playing Narcissus with the ocean, its last effusive vermillion spilling down the horizon line. The sight is enough to make one sick with longing.

The Killer unlocks Room 1409, on the other side of the hall. He sits on the bed and takes a Ziploc bag from the left hip pocket of his coveralls. The bag contains carrot sticks. The Killer feeds a carrot stick under the chin of his mask. A loud crunch is audible. He takes his phone from his right hip pocket and taps a text message, which makes the Thinker's phone vibrate six inches from my face. The Thinker grunts, throws an ace he'd hidden up his sleeve for absolutely no discernible reason, and comes to the security counter, where he taps the text message open. It reads: "Tell when chef dun cooking am hungry." The Thinker is either staring unbelievingly at his phone, or he's a slow reader. Probably the former. He types a reply—"Fine"—and claws his phone angrily from the security counter.

Brian and Tessa are dancing. He is speaking, and she is listening. She is glancing at the tables. She looks ready to cry. This is the second time today Tessa has looked ready to cry. Most people who know Tessa— even those who know her very, very well—have never seen her cry.

Henri opens the fridge in 1408. The Killer eats another carrot in 1409. The sous-chefs arrive in the break room and hurry to get their coats and open their lockers and take their unlocked belongings, including cell phones. (The sous-chefs only recently began working at the hotel. What with everything else Tessa's had to do, she hasn't assigned them padlocks yet. She was reminded, early this afternoon, to assign them padlocks tonight. She forgot.) They use the stairs to get to the first floor because it's faster than the main elevator. They want to get away from the smell of Franklin, crisped in the fourth dryer; as sous-chefs, they're more sensitive to aromas than most. They gabble out the hotel's front doors, their shadows long in the light of the chandelier, blending into the navy blue of early night. They split at their cars. Their headlights give the hedge maze eight large, yellow eyes. They drive out of the lot one at a time.

Brian is not much of a dancer, but neither is Tessa. Jules and Justin are not subtle people; they're leaning around the kitchen's door frame like a sitcom cliché. Delores hates men, but she's smiling, watching Brian and Tessa from the storage closet's doorway. The ballroom's chandelier flips on, a sudden and spectacular brightness, making clear how bruiselike the dusk had turned the nineteenth floor. The hotel's lighting system is designed to sense darkness and illuminate it. Delores, Jules, Justin, Brian, and Tessa all flinch like they've been caught doing something unbearably private.

Henri is not cooking anything especially ornate, for him: a potage, for which he slices celery and onion and sautés them in butter before adding spices and heavy cream. He lets it simmer on low. He tenderizes a chicken fillet and butterflies it, stuffing the breach with Emmentaler and a thin slice of ham, and slides it into the oven under foil. He cuts a fresh peach and then speaks threatening French at a handful of cherries, which he pits, halves, and drops into a saucepan with some brandy. He puts the saucepan on the stove. A vivid blue flame licks the pan's underside as Henri flicks his wrist, quivering the contents, letting them gel but not too much. There's a *brrr* from the pocket of his chef's coat. He removes the pan from the heat, takes out his prohibited cell phone. He answers, which means it could be only one person.

"Clauthilde, ça va?" he asks, concern softening his usually shrill vocal timbre. "Ah, ne t'inquiète—non, non, je ne fais rien. Dis-moi." Clauthilde is Henri's daughter. She's a graduate of the International Culinary Center. She's currently a sous-chef in Lyon, working under a mad genius whose standards are impossible to meet. One wonders if she appreciates the irony of calling her father to ask for advice; her side of the conversation is, of course, inaudible.

Henri's steps seem to glide to the dining area as he listens, his obesity at last countermanded by the grace often gifted to fat men. He walks this way only when talking to Clauthilde, and he talks to Clauthilde only in the strictest privacy. He sits in the chair nearest the bay window, leans back, and crosses his legs. I speak perfect French, but the first time I heard him give his daughter this speech (she calls to hear it at least once a month), I thought I'd translated incorrectly.

"My little love," he says, smiling a sad, wise smile at the glowing ocean, "the chef did not mean what he said. He does not mean what he does. It's a sad thing to be the slave of your art, but it is the only way to truly create. Making the world new requires leaving the old world behind and drifting alone in a space devoid of perspective. It drives men—pardon me, people—to terrible extremes. Extremes of beauty, of ugliness. It is not a life I wish for you, but you tell me you are determined to know. This torture of composing flavors that tongues taste and throats swallow with perhaps a polite nod, never knowing the creator's heroic battle against insanity, his—or her—daily struggle to be more than merely *good*. This man who throws your dishes and calls you his fool, you may decide he is a monster, and I hope this for you. Or you may decide to hear instead his passionate invitation to court greatness, with all the suffering this implies, with no assurance whatsoever that greatness will embrace you in return. These are your choices."

Across the hall, the Killer waits, sitting on the bed, tapping his fingers on his knee.

Henri slaps his knee at something Clauthilde says. "Oui, oui! C'est vrai!" He laughs, shaking his head at the ocean, "You will fall in love with this man, I think. I will escort you down the aisle to him in the same church we . . . Ha! You deny it!" He takes the phone from his ear, chuckles, and slips it back in his pocket. He finds it endearing when Clauthilde hangs up on him. He returns to the kitchen and shakes the saucepan over the flame again, humming the "Wedding March."

Tessa has turned off the music in the kitchen. Brian is pressing the "Down" button by the main elevator. "He wants to see the pool," Tessa tells Jules and Justin. She sounds completely done in.

"Are you okay?" says Justin, scouring the sink.

"Honey," Jules says to him, "go ask Delores what she thinks of the champagne pyramid."

Justin says, "Delores? Delores looks at me like I'm gonna—" Jules looks at him like she's gonna—"I'll go see what Delores thinks of our pyramid." He flaps his hands in the air to dry them, expediting his exit.

"It looks great," Tessa says, wiping the counter with a dishrag. "The pyramid, you guys did an amazing—"

"Tessa?"

Tessa sets down the dishrag.

There are the hums of the kitchen fluorescents, the chug of the dishwasher. There is Justin, in the ballroom, indicating the champagne pyramid on the far side of the silent auction table and asking Delores how she likes it. There is Delores regarding him peripherally, consoling herself, it is plausible to assume, that if Justin, this seemingly innocuous man, becomes suddenly violent, she, Delores, has a loaded revolver in her apron pocket.

Brian, at the main elevator, seems to be preparing himself. Idiomatically: "psyching himself up." He takes deep breaths in and lets them out slowly. Brian uses breaths quite often to make himself do or say things he's reluctant to do or say. I bet he does yoga. That would correspond to his sad, skinny little body, which I could break in half like a chopstick.

Could have. I could have.

"I can't do this again," Tessa says.

"Do what?" says Jules.

Tessa shakes her head. "You wouldn't understand," she says like she honestly wishes Jules would. Tessa passes Jules, the heels of her boots clacking toward the kitchen door.

Jules says quietly, "You decide what you can't do."

Tessa stops in the doorway. She smiles the complete antonym of a smile, and then points at a table in the southwest quadrant of the ballroom. "This one."

Jules contains her surprise. Tessa means the place setting. It's the simplest place setting. It's almost stark: plate, fork and knife left, spoon right, water glass at two o'clock. A napkin in the shape of a sailboat. "You got it," Jules says.

Tessa proceeds toward Brian. He smiles tightly at her once she's at his side. She smiles tightly back.

"That's a nice bracelet," he says.

Tessa says, "Thanks," and raises her left wrist. The frail gold ripples like a thread of water. She looks at the hollow elevator shaft.

"I noticed it when we were dancing. Was it a gift?"

"Yeah. Good guess."

"Barely a guess. You wouldn't buy yourself something like that."

"It's been eleven years. How do you know what I would and wouldn't buy?" Her tone is playful and sharp. Playful to cover the sharp.

"Who gave it to you?"

"An acquaintance."

"Close acquaintance?"

"Sometimes."

Close acquaintanceship apparently means knowing how many tastes Tessa's chemicals can call to a tongue's encyclopedic memory. Such as a busy afternoon arguing with the army of interior designers, arguing during ovulation—the flavor like oysters from a restaurant tucked in the back roads of the Amalfi Coast. Tessa might have heard the acquaintance's vow to take her there someday, but she might not have. She might have been asleep or she might have been faking.

"Sometimes?" Brian says.

"Sure. Busy guy."

"Busy with what?"

"Likes to stay busy. Former Navy SEAL, former Rhodes Scholar. Gets things done."

On a night when a storm tears its fingernails down the sky, she might tear her fingernails up an acquaintance's shoulders. Having bathed prior, Tessa finds her gustatory balance favors sweetness, the tang of excellent wine, a wine served with dessert, the type of dessert served on a tiny plate, one or two bites of it at most. There, on the plate, this is a pity; it's an odd little nadir of despair, but Tessa is the taste writ endless, until she says, "For fuck's sake, give it a rest."

"A SEAL and a scholar," Brian says. "Rare combination."

"Rare but real." She bites a nail, catches herself, and stops. "He's OCD as hell, though. Talks like a robot. Like a robot if Sartre got shit-faced and built one."

Tessa took Intro to Philosophy in college. She got an A minus.

Brian's grinning. "He work here?"

"I can't answer that question without proof of your security clearance."

Jules is diagramming Tessa's chosen place setting so she and Justin can duplicate it exactly on 175 tables. Justin is getting started on the table nearest the one Jules is diagramming. His hands and elbows move with impatience, and he glances at Jules with his mouth in a stiff line: he thinks the diagramming is unnecessary, and he believes Jules is doing it to get out of a few minutes of manual labor, and he's right. Delores has procured the window-washing equipment. The three of them will be occupied for the next several hours.

Brian's laughing. The elevator's arriving. The doors open, and he and Tessa board.

Brian says, "He's one of the guards, isn't he?"

Tessa presses the button for the first floor. "Security specialist," she says, breaching protocol. "I'm sure you have a girl in every thunderdome."

Brian slumps. Now they both sound done in. "That was Mitch, not me."

"So you're a virgin? Wow, Bri, congrats."

"You can really channel your inner Lorraine when you want to, you know that?"

This wounds Tessa. She tries not to show it. But it shows: her composure is too firm.

"Sorry," Brian grunts.

"Stop it," Tessa says, the shake of her head and the veer of her body like an attack in a fine fencing match. "Did you come here to have this out?" Brian's "No" gets lost under Tessa's "Fine, let's have it out. Let's both say what the other one did wrong. I'd love that, personally, because I have no idea what I did wrong. You were my family. You were my best friend. You and Mitch, but you more than Mitch." She jolts, then presses on with a grimace of pure horror. "Yeah, I said it. You more than Mitch. Mitch wanted to play, all the time, even when it was time to grow up. He wanted to play with his toys, and you went along with him, to take care of him, keep him safe. But *he* didn't want to be safe. *I* did!" She stands as tall as she can. "You decided I was worth your time. When I was eight years old and a messed-up, mute nothing, you decided to bother with me. And ten years later, I asked you to do one thing. I asked you to put your damn toys away, because Mitch dying was the worst pain I thought I'd ever go through." She draws away from Brian, like he's cold. "Except then you told me you were going back on the road. And that I had to look out for myself. And then you did the stunt that killed him, and I was watching on cable at a party, and you landed it perfectly, and

I went and got so drunk, I was throwing up for two days after." She's crying. Tessa's actually crying. "And I kept waiting to hear from you, but I didn't. I never did, not until today, and I don't know what I did wrong, Brian, what did I do?"

Brian goes to hold her. Tessa shoves him. The fourteenth floor appears.

Henri removes his chicken cordon bleu from the oven and plates it. He streams the soup into a shallow bowl and adds green grape slices and almonds for garnish. He changes the oven's setting to "Broil," moves a rack to the top tier, and slides in a cookie sheet containing the halved peach with cherry coulis brimmed where the peach's pit would be.

The Thinker, who microwaved a Smart Ones frozen dinner (Twombley's, the beef stroganoff) and folded the mouth of his mask to slurp plastic forkfuls (he has been eating right behind me for the past four minutes) taps at his phone.

The Killer receives the Thinker's message, jumps up, and minces excitedly out of Room 1409. He still closes the door with stealth. He unlocks the door to Room 1408. Brian and Tessa don't see him. He's around the corner from the passing elevator. They're too intent on each other, anyway.

"It was nothing you did," Brian says. "It wasn't you."

"It's not you, it's me," Tessa mocks. She's wiping her eyes and nose, furious with herself for crying.

"It wasn't either of us." Brian inhales deeply. Exhales. "It was Mitch."

"Oui?" Henri says. "I help you how, Monsieur Franklin?"

Henri takes his plate and bowl to the dining area. The dining area is open, visible from the living room and kitchen. This is why it is inferior to the dining area in the penthouses. The regular penthouse, Room 1801, has a dining room around the corner from the kitchen. It is a separate space. The kitchen in Room 1801 is likewise divided from the living room by a breakfast bar and a tastefully placed fainting couch, its foot pointing to a tucked-back staircase, which ascends to a spacious bedroom. In the deluxe penthouse, there is, upon entering, the kitchen to the right, the living room to the left, and straight ahead, a winding staircase that leads to a sumptuous, panoramic view of the ocean and the interstate, Los Angeles's smog turning improbable colors in the far distance. The bed is a Tempur-Pedic king and a half.

Henri favors an austere place setting: crystal water glass containing light ice and Pellegrino to the left of a wine goblet, silver ice bucket with a chilled chardonnay ready to decant, a single fork, a single spoon, a good knife.

The Killer, in his haste, forgot his knife. He waits until Henri has set his dinner to the most flattering angle.

"I dine now," Henri says as the Killer approaches. "You make funny at me when I fin—eh!"

The Killer throws Henri far from the table. Henri tumbles over the living room sofa. The Killer takes the knife out of the place setting, being careful not to upset any other aspect of the place setting. He goes to Henri, who is spinning in an attempt to get up, like a round beetle flipped on its back. The Killer grabs Henri's thick, dark, curly hair and draws the blade across his throat slowly enough to relish the act, but quickly enough that he can drop the bleeding-out chef, speed-walk to the kitchen, discard the knife in the sink, wash up, take a new knife from the wooden rack beside the blender (Manderley Resort fully stocks the penthouse and luxury room kitchens;

the regular rooms do not have kitchens, they have only coffeemakers; breakfast on the nineteenth floor is delicious and not at all affordable), and situate himself in the dining chair, napkin in lap, steam still rising from the cuisine, the first forkful of which—he chooses a bite of cordon bleu and half a broccoli floret (Henri steamed some broccoli as a side)—he pulls the chin of his mask away from his mouth to eat. The Killer nods, approving.

Blood from Henri's carotid artery sprays the living room like a leaking fire hose. He reaches for the wound with the raw human instinct to stanch the blood flow. He makes no sound, as his vocal cords have been cut. Henri falls on his left side. The oven dings. The Killer's head tilts. He goes to the oven, cracks the door, searches the counters. He puts on an oven mitt, moves the peaches to a lower rack, and sets the oven dial to "Warm." He is returning to the dining area, when he retraces his steps and looks in the freezer. A pint of top-quality Belgian ice cream, vanilla flavored, stands alone on the shelf. The Killer all but skips back to his seat and resumes eating. Henri gurgles his last.

"What?" Tessa said—twice—to Brian's obscure confession that "It was Mitch."

Brian said, "I have to tell it all at once. I can't—I can barely do it at all, but I know I can't do it in pieces. The pool's private, right? Nobody will interrupt us there?" Tessa managed one nod, and now they ride the last few floors down in silence. Brian appears ready to jump out of his own skin and run away. Tessa seems to wish she could dissolve into the elevator's glass wall. She cleans her eyes and cheeks of tears, but more keep falling. When the elevator descends through the foyer's ceiling, she jabs the intercom button, dialing the extension for the ballroom.

"The lobby chandelier's dusting up again. Del, do it the easy way, please. No ladders."

Jules's voice rejoins tinnily, "Roger that, Captain."

Brian points at the speaker. "Those two seem happy." He says it like it's a test.

Tessa doesn't answer, except to look at Brian with a cocked eyebrow: Really?

Brian nods. Tessa passed.

The elevator settles on the first floor and dings open. Tessa walks. Brian follows. They pass the check-in counter, moving westward. They pass the information desk. They are bound for the large door opposite the hotel's main entrance. They are walking away from a parking lot full of vehicles that could take them far from Manderley.

Jules speaks to Delores, presumably informing her of the need to dust the foyer's chandelier. Justin's acquired a cart to hold the dishes no longer required in the more florid place settings.

The Killer is eating his soup second. Philistine.

CAMERA 7, 64, 7, 4, 12

□ □ □

Tessa and Brian appear on the dunes. Her right boot heel gets stuck in the sand, and she lurches. Brian reaches out to help her, but she slaps his hand. He says something. He says something else. Tessa ignores him.

The rear façade of the hotel is virtually identical to the front, though it seems flatter, duller. This is because no one who exits the hotel from the west would possibly bother looking at the hotel itself. The view is too fine. It's the well-worn panorama on millions and millions of calendars, screensavers, and posters with inspiring quotes: sky meeting sea in a melted crayon box of colors and a sugary foreground stretching infinitely to either side. It might still strike some as boring, as any other beach. Except there is the pool.

What most would guess to be part greenhouse and part rock formation—a mound of rough boulders and smooth glass, the limestone winking in the dregs of gone sunlight—stands short and stunted and lovely in the most natural of ways. Tessa is saying something, probably telling Brian about how she scouted locations for Manderley, about this cave and how shore accretion as a result of elsewhere's erosion had exposed it, about how she took one look at it and knew.

Only the sound of the ocean can be heard. It's a beautiful sound. It's the sound of life. The sun has set, and the waves are red. It is nine twenty-five p.m.

Tessa holds the pool entrance open for Brian. He walks in.

"My God," Brian says.

Outer Santa Barbara has suffered terribly from the accretion and erosion of its shore. This limestone cave may have once been the habitat of sharks, orcas, rays. It was dry when Tessa scouted it. It now glows green from moss that is nurtured by the hot humidity in the greenhouse. The mosses eat bacteria. Water tumbles down striations of rock through a pump system that pulls water straight from the Pacific. The pool is self-sustaining, self-cleaning, mostly self-lighting. Exactly one thousand round ten-watt bulbs are strung above the pool, woven into a net beneath the glass ceiling, like tiny moons. The pool is roughly fifty yards by ten, sparsely surrounded by comfortable chairs and a few granite tables with benches, but Tessa bends and unzips her boots, steps out of them, and sits at the edge of the deep end, dangling her feet in the water. The deep end is very deep. Twenty feet.

Brian sits beside her. He leaves his boots on, his feet out of the water. "It's kind of dangerous, isn't it?" he says, looking at the daggers of rock.

The answer is: Yes. Yes, it is dangerous.

Tessa says, watching her bare feet glow green, "Talk, Brian."

The Killer is spooning ice cream onto the peaches. It's dark in Room 1408. He doesn't turn on any lights. He shuts off the oven instead and crosses the hall to Room 1409. The Thinker told him to, by text message. Room 1409 has a north-facing window. Looking up from, say, the pool, one would not see a light on the fourteenth floor if the light was in Room 1409.

The Killer props pillows against the headboard and loses patience with using a spoon to slice the peaches. He retrieves his knife from the end of the bed and slices his dessert with it instead. He looks like a child trying to transcribe an addition problem with an enormous novelty crayon.

Jules and Justin are still changing place settings; only now they're on opposite sides of the ballroom.

Delores is—where is Delores?

Brian has been staring at the water. At Tessa's feet, like soft green animals in the water. One of Brian's knees is flat to the limestone floor. His other knee is bent, a notch for his elbow. He's angled toward Tessa. He is, it looks like, sitting comfortably. But his demeanor makes one wonder if there has ever been a man more acutely uncomfortable in the history of time.

"You remember—," Brian says. It comes out craggy, and he clears his throat. "You remember when Mitch broke his leg?"

"Which time?" says Tessa.

"Oh yeah." Brian laughs, airily. "No, the second time. While we were on the road."

Tessa nods.

Brian puts his head to his upright knee. "Tess, look. Tess, it's something I really can't explain. I can explain part of it. I can explain what happened. But—I've never tried telling somebody what it's like, being twins. It's not like you're *a* twin. It's like you're both. You're never alone. It's impossible to really be alone. And that's so great, but sometimes, you just want to be you. You want to want what you want." He laughs again. "I knew I'd cock this up."

Tessa says, "I do get it." She's looking at him like he's certifiable. "As close as anybody can, I get it. When Mitch broke his leg the second time . . ."

Brian's mouth assumes the shape of an awful taste. "The doc prescribed him painkillers. It was a bad break. He was in pain, and he ran out of painkillers. He refilled the scrip." Brian peeks at Tessa out of the corner of his eye. "How many blanks are you filling in?"

Tessa's pale.

Brian takes her hand, and she lets him. "Mitch wanted to stay on the circuit, even injured. He was riding injured. It was aggravating the leg, but he wouldn't listen to me. He wasn't feeling the pain, see. He figured he was fine."

"He seemed fine. Whenever I saw him—"

"Whenever you saw him, he'd cut his doses. He got good at it really fast. I've learned since that it's pretty easy with pills—to figure out how much you need to be normal, how much you need to fly, how much isn't near enough anymore." Brian lets go of Tessa's hand. His teeth are bared, as if he's under the ministrations of an invisible torturer.

Tessa takes her feet out of the water, making a *woosh-patter* sound. She moves closer to Brian and cups his jaw. "Say the rest."

Brian's voice is steady, but it's too hard, brittle. It wants to break. "It's pretty easy with pills. It's a lot tougher with heroin."

Tessa's hand drops from Brian's face.

"There's every kind of drug you can think of on the circuit. Plus about fifty you can't. You know—you knew Mitch, how he was. He found something he loved, and he wouldn't give it up. He couldn't. I'd talk to him about rehab, and he'd laugh at me—not in a dickish way, in a sad way. He'd say he had it under control, but he knew he was lying. He knew what he really meant was more like, 'There's no point, Bri.'" Brian's throat squeaks on his own name. His head falls forward to Tessa's shoulder. Before Tessa can reach out, he's sitting straight again, straighter. Speaking more quickly. "When he announced he was doing the triple, I tried to talk him out of it, Tess. I tried. You have to believe me. I even went over his head, I went to Troy. I told Troy about the drugs, but he brushed it off. Said Mitch was gonna make history. The promoters said the same thing." Brian looks nauseated.

"Slow down," Tessa says.

"I can't. I've gotta get this all out, or—I didn't understand why, what this bug up his butt was about the triple. I asked him, I said, 'Mitch, do a fucking double,' because that was high-risk enough. A *single* is high risk. But Mitch told me he'd been offered fifty grand, so he had to do it. And that made no sense. I knew his finances were a mess, but I was covering him." Brian's mouth opens to say more, but his voice stalls. It croaks. His words won't come out.

Tessa says, "What can I do?"

Brian closes his eyes, takes her hands, and places them on either side of his throat. He holds them there. "Our bank accounts were separate. But I forgot we set up your college money in a joint fund."

Tessa transforms, slowly, into a close imitation of Munch's *The Scream*.

Brian doesn't see the transformation. He doesn't want to. "I forgot until Mitch under-rotated on the second turn going into the third, and I could see, and everybody could see, how he was going to land, and it occurred to me right then—Oh yeah. Tess's college money." Brian opens his eyes and takes in Tessa's profound and boundless horror. Brian takes it in like he deserves it, because, "I should have thought of that earlier. I could have told him we'd make it up. I'd make it up. But he didn't want me to know, cuz that was the worst thing either of us could have ever imagined doing. We promised you. We told you you'd go to college on us. We swore it, and Mitch was so proud we could do that for you. The day we showed you the paperwork—remember? Your seventeenth? You and me and Mitch at the Lone Spur Grill. You cried, and you never cry." Brian takes a handkerchief—a handkerchief?—from his jeans pocket and dries Tessa's face. "Mitch told me that night—before he fell asleep, he told me he was going to marry you someday. And then about a year later, he's dying on a dirt ramp because he drained your college money down to nothing. He drained it to nothing, and then he borrowed to put it back and he drained it again. And he's dying, and he's looking up at me, his big brother—by eight minutes, but still his big brother—and he's telling me, 'Make it up, Bri. You gotta make it up, okay?' And he keeps saying that and saying that, and I'm telling him I will but he needs to hold on, we'll make it up together. But then his breathing gets short, and before it gets so bad he can't talk anymore, the last thing he says to me, the very last thing is—'Don't tell Tess.'"

Tessa makes an appalling noise. A child in a sadist's strong grip might make this noise. She covers her mouth with both palms. Tears fill and flood. Her complexion is hectic with color.

Brian is nodding at her, but he keeps talking, like his words are rocks and speech is their momentum down a hillside. "The promoters didn't even wait till after the funeral. They quoted me a hundred grand to do the stunt. The day before the wake, remember? Remember that call I got when you were helping me pick out what he should wear?" Tessa looks down at the glowing green stone. "I wanted to tell you. Tess, you can't know how badly I wanted to tell you." He takes her shoulders. She stares at the stone. "You were the only person who felt him being gone like I did. You were the only other one who knew how good he was, how he wasn't just some fun-time jerk. He was more than a party; he was good. I knew—Mitch didn't know, but I knew—you could handle hearing it, the whole truth, and you'd come out the other side still loving him, exactly the same as before, better. Tess, you've gotta look at me for this last part. I swear on Mitch's grave, it's the last time I'll make you look at me ever again, but please, please do it."

Tessa does. It's the whole world's misery. Asking why, why it has to be this way.

Brian reels. He holds the angle of her neck. He says, "When you got down on your knees, grabbed the sleeves of my best shirt, and begged me—right after the funeral—to stay with you, and help you, and take care of you, keep you safe . . . there aren't words in any human language for what was going on in my mind. It was like Mitch was on a loop in my head—'Don't tell Tess. Don't tell her.' So I said I was leaving but I'd be back. I had to do some stunts, I had to do the one that killed Mitch, but I'd visit." Brian finally breaks. "And you looked just like this, and I almost told you, I came so close, you can't even—so when I landed the triple and paid off Mitch's debt and had enough for your first semester, I decided I'd keep going, go a little longer without seeing you, make enough for your sophomore year. Then I went a little longer and a little longer after that, but you have to understand, it never got easy. It should have, but it didn't. It got harder and harder. The longer I went, the more sure I got that the next time I saw you, I'd tell you everything. I'd tell you Mitch loved you, and so did I, and we had about a dozen drunk conversations where we fought about who should be with you when you were grown up, and Mitch always won by telling me I could keep it together without having you to keep it together for, but he couldn't." Brian's and Tessa's commingled sobs fill the pool with ghostly echoes. Brian talks through his and says, "So I stayed away half because I thought of you as his, and half because he used the last breath in his broken body to tell me not to tell you he was weak." Brian wills himself calm again, brushing Tessa's hair back from her moist cheeks and staring at her with the focused heat that they've both been trying to throw ice water on all evening. "But he was weak," Brian says. "And so am I. So I'm here. If I'm too late, then that's okay. That's what I deserve. But you have to tell me I'm too late."

Tessa does not excel at playing dumb. "Too late for what?" She sniffs. Pillows her lips together.

Brian spares a hand to plumb his jacket pocket. He produces a glossy sheet of paper folded in quarters. It is doubtful this one contains a knitting pattern. He unfolds it and shows her.

Tessa is no longer playing dumb when she says, "I don't understand."

It's the cover of this month's *Travel* magazine. Charles Destin and Tessa posed for the photo together in the center of the maze. Destin is giving her a rose. Tessa's smiling down at it. Destin looks like a great big phony clowning creep, and Tessa looks bottomlessly sad, because she looks almost happy. She felt accomplished that day, having impressed the reporter, who later rated Manderley at five stars.

"This Destin guy." Brian says. "I didn't snoop or anything. I just did some careful Googling, but he's got a reputation I'm not crazy about." Brian folds the photo again. He watches his hands fold it. "I trust your judgment, though. You talked about that security guard to spare my feelings, maybe—to not let me know you fell for someone. But I can handle it if you have. You just have to tell me. Or, you don't even have to tell me. You can tell me to get out of here if you want me to go."

Tessa has evidently reached a point where so many emotions are occurring at once that selecting a reaction is impossible. It's easy to identify with such a state. She stands and walks a short distance from Brian. Brian is putting the photo back in his pocket, but he changes his mind. He crumples it and pitches it toward a trash can ten feet away. He misses. The balled-up paper bounces off the can's rim. Tessa picks it up and drops it in, as though gratified that her standing and walking served a purpose. She looks around the pool like she'll never see it again, taking in details: the jasmine vining up and through the latticework on the greenhouse's glass, rolled and stacked towels so white, they throb in their seashell-shaped basket. She pats them. She smells a jasmine blossom.

Tessa turns, crosses her arms, and says, "The photographer who did that cover said a romantic shot would sell the hotel to a wider client base."

Brian's brow crinks.

"I'm not with Charles," Tessa says. "I'm not with anyone. The head of security's a convenience. He wants more, but I don't, and I made that clear to him from the beginning." She gestures at Camera 64. "You can wave at him if you like."

Brian stands, hastily, wiping his tears on his sleeve while shouting, "Jesus fucking!—Tess, you let me say all that when he can—"

She yells over him, "There's no audio surveillance anywhere but the lobby—"

The most thorough safety is safety one's object of protection doesn't know about.

"And his team's watching sixty-four screens at a time. They're half-staffed because we're not open yet, and you and I were facing mostly away from the camera while we were talking. If you're saying what I think you're saying, then you need to get in the habit of giving me at least a little goddamn credit."

Brian's mouth works. He laughs, helpless. He takes a step toward her.

"Stay right there," says Tessa, quiet and deadly, pointing at him.

Brian freezes.

"I get it," she says, her pointer finger accenting "I" and then the pair "get it." "I do. But it's still eleven years. It's eleven"—she points—"goddamn"—she points, and points again—"years."

"I know," Brian says. He tries to inject huge, incontrovertible sentiment into these two words, but—

"Do you?" Tessa's eyes are round and shining. "Because this isn't fucking automatic. Okay? This isn't an auto-forgive."

"Tess?" He takes one step. "I know."

Tessa looks ready to run, but she's not sure which direction. "Great, then you're going to be really specific, right now—what you're saying, exactly, about what you want and what you feel and all that girly stuff, or I am out. I'm done. I can't do it again. If all you're doing is wondering what I'm like in bed—"

"You're not with anybody?"

"Did you hear anything else I said, Bri? I can repeat it."

Brian smiles, not all at once. It's like a sun rising. Outside, the sun has set completely; its final hints of light are gone. The ocean is almost black. Inside Manderley, while the light was fading:

Delores got the fifty-foot ladder out of maintenance storage and cleaned the chandelier in the foyer.

The Killer received a text and took the secret elevator to the first floor; he watched Delores from Franklin's office.

Jules and Justin fixed place settings. They had a tiff about the only dish cart being near Justin. Jules moved closer.

Now:

Delores is riding the main elevator past the eighteenth floor. Her feet shift; she hums. She's anxious to get back to cleaning the ballroom's windows. She finds childish delight in using her long-handled squeegee. The ballroom fills her view right as Justin picks up the vase and throws it with all his strength straight at Jules's head. Delores closes her eyes and plugs her ears and sings "My Country 'Tis of Thee" twice before she looks again, listens again, breathing through her nose to will herself calm.

The Killer is in Franklin's office. He swivels on the office chair, enjoying the break from his duties as well as the three-thousand-dollar "seating experience" Franklin insisted upon to counteract an acute case of sciatica. He opens desk drawers idly, hoots when he finds the scotch, pours a glass, and toasts the security camera to provoke the Thinker's envy, but the Thinker's occupied with his cards. The Killer stands and takes his drink into the secret elevator. Vivica's eyes are milky and opaque.

Jules drops a salad plate. She yowls, "Cock-sucking slut-fuck retard—" et cetera at Justin, seeming, in that second, to truly believe the broken dish is his fault. Justin takes this for about twenty seconds; then he picks up a Swarovski vase centerpiece, slings his arm back, and throws it with all his strength straight at Jules's head. She ducks. The vase shatters onto the table behind her. The petals and bits of crystal look like purposeful décor. Jules and Justin stare at each other, their jaws agape.

Brian walks toward Tessa.

Tessa says, "Did I stutter? I said get specific, right now."

"I am." He hasn't stopped walking.

"Brian—"

"Don't be afraid of me. Don't think I'm going to hurt you. I'm not. Not ever again." He reaches her, but he doesn't reach for her. "I'm going to take care of you."

Tessa tries to back up. She hits the latticework. The jasmine reports that she is trembling. "Define 'take care of,'" she says. "Define it specifically."

Define "take care of." To watch over. To concern oneself with. To worry about, even when the object of one's care isn't interested in one's care. Tessa wants freedom, independence. No woman truly wants independence. She wants the freedom to choose her own master. This is also what men want. The origin of all human conflict is, possibly, disagreement about who ought and ought not to be one's master. The origin of all human happiness is, maybe, mutual agreement on the subject.

Brian reaches for her—for her waist, a hand on either side. "Take me somewhere I can show you."

Tessa's hands, on his either arm. "Show me here."

He looks smarmily at Camera 64. "Plus," he says, and winces, "stone floor?"

Tessa explodes into laughter, and so does he. She takes his hand and pulls it toward the door. Brian looks back at her boots. He smiles, boyishly. It is an encouraging sign that Tessa feels she will not need her boots where they are going. They are going over the dunes. Their mouths don't move; they're not talking. They've had enough talking. They are entering Manderley, crossing the foyer. Tessa is pressing the "Up" button on the elevator, and then they are waiting.

Delores is sitting at the table where the vase landed. She's alone in near-perfect quiet, her eyes roaming shattered dishes and pebbles of expensive glass like they're terribly familiar. She begins to pick up the pieces, but then she laughs a cruel, disturbingly sexy laugh and puts her earbuds in. She takes a pack of Marlboros and a lighter from her apron pocket. She lights up, puffs, and looks out the north-facing windows. No doubt finding streaks. As she stubs her cigarette into a cracked water glass, she begins humming along to "Enter Sandman." En route to her squeegee, she steps on a shard of the salad plate Jules dropped—it's the size of a small pie slice. She puts it in her apron pocket, with her gun.

The Killer arrives on the nineteenth floor via the secret elevator. He's in the walk-in refrigerator, behind the juice concentrate. He hits the controller button; the shelves slide. He moves to exit the walk-in refrigerator. Stops. He surveys the shelves' contents. Opens drawers, poking choice cuts of meat with his knife, not finding what he's looking for. He exits the walk-in refrigerator and enters the kitchen, passing shining steel surfaces. The pantry door is ajar. He sticks his head in and emerges with a box of Cheez-Its. He opens the box, cuts the inner bag with his knife, and feeds the savory orange squares under the chin of his mask. Eventually he ambles to the ballroom door and looks in, at Delores.

Jules and Justin are in the main elevator. They said nothing to Delores; she passed them with a wide berth. Jules and Justin say nothing to each other. Jules reaches for her Xanax automatically, stops herself, and scratches her nose. Then she holds her nose, cupping it, glad it's still there. She's aware that the prettiest crystal is the most breakable, that

Brian and Tessa are still holding hands. Their hands are twining. Their hands are fairly writhing. His thumb digs at her palm. Her palm shakes. Tessa's other hand touches her own lips. She touches her own right breast, above the nipple, and flutters her blouse. I look at the security counter. At the override system: a sixteen-inch screen with no keypad or other its destruction is the most complete, that splinters of it could have torn her skin like a razor on a ripe plum. Justin blinks every five seconds, as if he's focusing on blinking at a set interval of time, as if focusing on how many seconds have passed were a marvelous alternative to thinking about how he could have disfigured his wife not two minutes ago.

obvious access. The screen is dark now, lifeless. But if one were to input the correct authorization codes, everything in Manderley, including the elevator, would suddenly be under the complete control of one man and his dexterous finger. There's a pencil. It's ten inches from my face, on the counter. I could almost scream; I almost do. I would, except—

The Thinker has tired of solitaire. He is standing at the wall that faces east. The walls on the twentieth floor are all glass, but tinted glass, and the eastward view includes the hedge maze, crescent-shaped driveway, a road, desert, mountains, river, and sky. Now, in the dark, these things are dim outlines. The Thinker stands with his hands behind his back. He is not tall, but neither is he short. Not fat, not thin, not muscular, but not skinny. He is average, whereas his accomplice is very large. He is the brains, whereas his accomplice is the brawn.

It is rare for a man to have both. It is not necessarily vain for a man to consider himself rare, if it is the truth.

Jules and Justin disembark on the eighteenth floor. He unlocks Room 1801, the regular penthouse. They enter, the door shuts behind them, and Jules sucks in a breath to say something.

"Don't," Justin says. "Let's—don't."

Jules trails him to the spacious living room, where Justin plucks the remote from a cherrywood end table and points it at the television. Jules steals it from him.

"We have to. We need to talk about it," she says, sounding meek.

Justin walks to the stairs. Under the stairs is a bookshelf, and behind the bookshelf is the hollow maw of the secret elevator. Jules catches Justin's arm. He shakes her off, but he stays there, one hand on the railing. "Not tonight."

"When?" says Jules.

"Tomorrow."

Justin walks upstairs to their nondeluxe bedroom. Jules lets her hand fall and holds the railing where he held it, feeling the warmth of him and thinking—it's a legitimate assumption—about tomorrow. Justin will wake before her; he always does. Jules will meet him at whatever stunning experimental breakfast Henri prepares. She and Justin will ooh and ahh, relieved there isn't time for solitude and reprieved from the pressure to talk about it; they will be afraid because there's plenty of space—there's so much space in the world—and the two of them and their struggles and their failings are so small, and the end of their marriage will make not a ripple in the greater ocean of human events.

Jules puts the remote control back on the end table. She squares it to a perfect right angle before sitting on the sofa, pressing the "Power" button. The flat screen blinks on, already set to her desired channel. Jules curls up, pops a pill, and watches E! News.

Brian has been watching Tessa's free hand. Tessa's free hand has hit the "Up" button four times, and each time, her free hand returns to a spot above her left nipple, which she touches like it's simply something to touch. Brian's shifting where he stands, as if the fit of his pants is becoming uncomfortable. He looks around the foyer. "So, is there a ton of video surveillance in the hotel?"

"Some," says Tessa. "Not in the rooms, not in the elevator."

The best security is invisible security.

Brian repeats, "Not in the elevator," and massages her nonfree hand.

Tessa presses the "Up" button. Twice.

Delores doesn't hear the Killer letting the kitchen door swing closed behind him, the *rap-rap rap-rap* it makes when it flaps against its rubberized frame. He doesn't make a sound coming closer to her—

"I'm scared," Brian says, "that it's going to be weird."

Tessa nods. "Me, too."

"We've never even kissed." The pointed bottom of the diamond-shaped elevator appears. He squeezes Tessa's hand.

"I know," Tessa says. "What do we do if it's weird?"

"I don't know." The elevator dings open. He and Tessa get on. Tessa swipes her card key in a special slot. "What's that for?" Brian says.

"The elevator won't stop at the penthouse level unless the guest swipes their key," she says. She says it breathlessly. "It's a security measure." She's turned toward Brian.

He turns toward her. He still has her hand. He puts it where his pulse beats visibly in his neck. "If this is weird, I say we just—"

"Keep going," Tessa finishes for him, and laughs.

He laughs. "Yeah, exactly. Don't be a quitter."

"Never," Tessa says, and strokes down his front, to his chest. He shivers. "I'm like the rabbit who wanted to cross the road."

"Staples. That's determination, Tess."

She crooks her finger: C'mere.

He leans.

But Delores cleans a mean window. The Killer makes a reflection, approaching behind her back. So Delores turns with her oversized squeegee right when he's in range of its length and smacks him with the wet end across his mask. The Killer gurgles a syllable— Gluh!"—and catches his mask and straightens it before it falls off. In doing this, he drops his knife.

Delores catches him again on the reverse. The Killer sputters. Delores is saying, "Franklin, I told you if you kept messing with me, I'd make you real sorry," but this slap of the squeegee makes the Killer's mask fly all the way off, to his right. He chases after it as Delores says, "Hey, who're you?"

CAMERA 12, 56, 62, 63

□ □ □

The drawbacks of video surveillance are two-fold: one, even if a fabulously wealthy properties owner claims to be dedicated to security, the budget for actual cameras will be finite and, therefore, the number of angles available to team members will be limited, which means that if, for example, a remorseless psycho killer is briefly unmasked, it will be a matter of luck if his face is clearly discernible; two, though the preening, spoiled properties owner requests all security feed be backed up for six months on an online storage site before the images are disposed of, he is ignorant of how vulnerable online storage sites are to external penetration, meaning the head of security might decide instead to erase the feed at six thirty a.m. and six thirty p.m. every day, choosing these times because shifts change at six a.m. and six p.m. and at those hours, when the shifts cross, team members discuss scenarios, breaches, so on, which the feed helps to illustrate.

Brian's lips meet Tessa's very softly. Both Brian and Tessa remain very still. Only their facial expressions betray change, betray a sense of surprise. Very positive, pleasant surprise. It's Tessa who moves first, but by nanoseconds. It's hard to guess, unless one really watches. Unless one can't look away—not even to such arresting images as Jules in a lacy white negligee, climbing into bed beside Justin, not even to Delores dropping her squeegee and ripping into her apron pocket for the gun—from Tessa's arms wending around Brian's neck so he'll come closer, and their lips becoming not less soft, but less scared. "Not weird." Tessa groans it, and Brian says, "Hmm-mm" with a downward vocal timbre that means he meant, No, not at all. He takes advantage of Tessa's speaking mouth being open, and he presses it wider with his kiss. And Tessa makes fists in his motorcycle jacket. And her eyebrows rise, and her hips rise, and Brian's hands find her hips like his hands are heat-seeking and her hips are hot.

The Killer picks up Delores's dropped squeegee right as she takes out her revolver. He hits her wrist with the squeegee's handle. Her shot sails far wide, to the window wall behind the bandstand. Cracks cobweb out from the bullet hole in the glass.

Brian sets Tessa's ass on the railing. He touches all along the sides of her body like he wants to take it slow. Their mouths are not taking it slow. Tessa's body isn't, either. Tessa's bare feet are pulling Brian tighter to her. He stops kissing her, with an evident struggle on his part, and his parts, and he says, in the second and a half he succeeds, "I love you. I—," but Tessa says, "I know, shut up," and renders him silent, or silent of recognizable linguistic phonemes, as Brian has dared now to put a hand under Tessa's skirt, and his kiss-muffled ululations at this are almost as shameless as hers.

Delores drops her gun, and the Killer runs at her. Delores bends with astonishing speed for a hausfrau. She picks up the squeegee and jabs. The Killer grabs his stomach.

Tessa's hand moves to Brian's jeans. Brian's hand moves to the front of his fly, where Tessa's unzipping it. He puts both her hands back around his neck. She grins and says, "What're we waiting for, exactly?"

Brian kisses her. "A bed."

"Why?"

He nibbles at her neck, moving her shirt's collar aside for better access. "I don't know, shut up."

Delores goes for the gun. The Killer catches her in a tackle as she grabs it. It skids across the ballroom, hops onto the dance floor, and spins to a stop at the base of the bandstand's stairs. The Killer drags Delores by the hair, toward where he dropped his knife. Delores shrieks, reaches in her apron pocket, pulls out the shard of broken salad plate, and stabs it into the Killer's hand. The Killer howls through his mask and drops Delores's hair. Delores is up and running for the gun. The Killer is running after Delores.

The main elevator is passing the eighth floor. Brian is unbuttoning Tessa's blouse. She is saying, "Slowest damn elevator in the world," and Brian is smiling, minutely, before he sees a lacy white bra supporting a small breast. He turns serious, palming it. He nods and, all at once, lifts her off the railing so her bare feet are on the floor, pulls her black underwear around her bare ankles, and ducks under her skirt, the actions so quick, Tessa doesn't have time to react, until she reacts by hollering at the glass ceiling and trying to make fists in the glass walls.

The Killer tackles Delores. She hits her head on the dance floor. She moans, facedown. She's inches short of the gun. The Killer thrashes up Delores's body, seizes the revolver, and flips its chamber open. He sprinkles the bullets and tosses the gun; it bounces once before landing in the storage room. The Killer pulls Delores's scalp backward to beat her skull into the floor. But Delores rears like a bucking mare and throws an elbow into the side of the Killer's head. The Killer rolls off her. Delores stands and runs for the kitchen, dizzy, her limp more pronounced.

The elevator is on the ninth floor. Tessa balances on one foot, ass on the railing. Her other foot has stepped from her underwear and hangs over Brian's shoulder. Brian's neck and head are cloaked in her skirt. Tessa says his name. His name rises in pitch. It's as if Tessa is birthing him. One might prefer to think of the tableau as something ludicrous—like Tessa birthing Brian—rather than to admit the two of them are birthing something noble and lovely and sacred. Something that will last, so long as the two of them are not hacked to pieces tonight.

Jules and Justin decide to make love.

Jules and Justin are asleep.

Delores slaps the kitchen door open. She yanks a trash can over behind her. It's large and gray and rubber and full of disposable accoutrements slick with cherry coulis. She runs for the walk-in refrigerator. The Killer slaps the kitchen door open, but he doesn't see the trash can and goes flying over it, like Superman, his hands splayed out, and Delores is digging in her apron pocket for the secret elevator controller she has never used. She was told never to use it except in an extreme emergency. This qualifies as an extreme emergency. The Killer lands and skids through red-gobbed paper towels and chunks of waxed paper. Delores finds the controller and presses the button. The juice concentrate moves, too slowly. Delores shuts the door to the walk-in refrigerator and pulls on a shelf crammed with tubs of peppers and fresh fruit. She grits her teeth and makes a sound like a creature giving birth.

Tessa makes a similar sound, in the main elevator. Brian's head, under her skirt, moves both gently and powerfully at once, like waves.

Red and green peppers fall to the walk-in refrigerator's floor. The Killer shoves at the door. He's unable to open it, but he is able to reach inside through a gap. He is slicing at the air with his knife. The juice concentrate has moved mostly aside, but Delores isn't looking in that direction. Delores is instead snatching a pair of kitchen scissors off a nail; the scissors are there to open plastic pouches of refrigerated material. She raises the scissors and strikes toward the Killer's exposed arm. The Killer sees this and flounders to pull back. He succeeds. Delores turns. Delores screams.

Tessa is getting close. The elevator is coming up on the twelfth floor. Tessa is trying to hide the fact that she is weeping. She is wiping her temples free of tears. The tears are on her temples because she is staring up at the ceiling as if she sees God in that apex of glass. She has hiked her skirt high enough so she can look down and watch Brian's efforts. She begins to breathe erratically. She says Brian's name, twice. Her pussy shoves at his face like she can't help it. She can't help it. Brian keeps his pace steady but hikes her skirt higher. He ups the pressure of his tongue. Tessa screams.

Vivica takes up a small rectangle of space inside the secret elevator, her shins flat to the floor, her back atop her calves, her arms in a tangle around her chest and head, bringing to mind Madonna's "Vogue" music video from the early 1990s. The repeated sight of a disturbing image might numb one's capacity to forestall insensitive associations. Delores has not seen this sight repeatedly. Delores is screaming. The Killer is bashing at the walk-in refrigerator door, and the shelves are heavy, but so is the Killer. Delores puts her fingers to her mouth, then in her hair. She doesn't want to get into the elevator. The elevator is painted in blood. Delores makes a sound between her teeth—"Nnnnn, nnnnn"—as she steps in overdelicately, avoiding Vivica, packing to the opposite wall, pressing the button for the lobby with a shuddering fingertip. Delores gawks so dedicatedly at Vivica that she doesn't notice the Killer finally barreling into the walk-in refrigerator, or the hideous purpose in his lunge for her, or how close he comes to preventing the elevator door's sedate slide shut. She says, "Nnnnn, nnnnn," and picks up the intercom phone receiver. She says, "Nnnnooo!" when she finds it's been disabled.

The Killer bolts across the walk-in refrigerator, the kitchen, and the ballroom, toward the door for the stairwell (beside the main elevator); he pulls and pulls at the door for the stairwell, before remembering this door requires one to push. The Killer flies down the stairs, passing the eighteenth floor. He hears the main elevator ding open there. He pauses, but only for a second. Delores has obviously made him angry. Delores is obviously going for the lobby. The staff's cars have not been disabled, because it didn't seem possible that anyone would get to the parking lot. The Killer runs down the stairs, incensed, his coveralls stained and sticky.

The secret elevator, Delores inside it, is passing the seventh floor.

She is no longer saying, "Nnnnn." She is no longer looking at Vivica. She's undoubtedly smelling Vivica. She is holding the kitchen scissors so tightly, her knuckles are bloodless, and she watches the seam of the elevator doors like an enemy.

Tessa leads Brian out of the main elevator by the hand. Outside the elevator, she pushes him against a wall and kisses him. She sucks his tongue into her mouth, greedily. She takes a card key out of her blouse's breast pocket and leads him to Room 1802, the deluxe penthouse. She leads him, but this time not by the hand. Brian walks awkwardly. His erection looks enormous, but only in proportion to his overall body size. It's an average erection. While Tessa puts the card key the right way around, Brian pushes her into the closed door with his pelvis, filling his hands with her hair so he can lick the nubs of bone in her neck; he fits his teeth around one. "Hurry," he says. She does. The door to Room 1802, the deluxe penthouse, explodes open with the force of their combined weight. The doorknob makes a slight dent in the wall before Brian slams it shut.

Tessa does not notice the dent in the wall: next, the seas will boil.

Tessa's grasping at Brian's pants. "Bed," he says, "where's a bed?"

Tessa says, "Why?" but yanks him by the shirtfront toward the spiral staircase in the middle of the lavish entryway. Brian pulls her down in the middle of the spiral staircase and rips her bra in half so he can tongue Tessa's left nipple.

"Bite it," she growls. He does. She curses, loudly. Brian picks Tessa up and carries her upstairs. It's easy to carry Tessa. Tessa's thin. It might seem romantic that he's carrying her, but it's not; it's easy. True romance is predicated on difficulty. Protection is fantastically difficult.

It's dark. "Where's the bed?" Brian says.

Tessa tugs him by the belt loops.

The secret elevator—with Delores inside it—opens into Franklin's office. Delores has the scissors raised. There's no one in Franklin's office.

Delores tried her cell phone in the secret elevator, but there was no reception. She takes cautious, soundless steps. The Killer is racing down the stairs. He is passing the ninth floor. Delores is entering the foyer, looking around, seeing no one. She is tiptoeing underneath the chandelier she cleaned less than an hour ago, beginning to walk faster. The Killer is passing the sixth floor. Delores digs in her apron pocket and takes out her car keys. She can see her car in the parking lot. She's in sight of the main doors, and the parking lot is well lit. Well-lit parking areas are safe parking areas. The Killer is passing the fourth floor, putting on speed. Delores can hear him, which is why she hurries, running for the main doors, twenty feet away. Now fifteen, ten. The Killer passes the second floor.

The Thinker stands up from behind a reception sofa. He does not move quickly. He doesn't need to. Delores rebounds off the locked main doors. She drops the scissors. She has hit her head. She reels. She bumbles right into the Thinker, who puts his hands around her throat and begins to squeeze.

Tessa bumps into the bed. The mattress pushes the backs of her knees to bend, and she sits easily. She is eye level with Brian's pants, and he lets her pull them down this time. He steps out of them, then a pair of boxer briefs, and Tessa's lips swell around his penis as she takes it into her mouth. Brian hisses, allowing her mouth to work awhile before he puts a thumb to her chin and bends, too, kneeling at the bed to undress her. He doesn't do it slowly, but he doesn't hurry, either. When she's naked, Tessa pushes Brian's jacket off, then his T-shirt, and then they stop. They eye one another like curiosities.

When the Killer comes tearing across the foyer, knife high, Delores is slapping at the Thinker's mask. But the Thinker keeps his masked face remote enough that the edges of Delores's short fingernails scrape the tip of the Thinker's rubber nose and that's all. The Killer arrives at the pair of them and throws Delores into the bellhop counter. Delores casts out a hand to catch herself and smacks the bellhop's bell as she rams into the counter hard enough to break all the ribs on her right side. A tinny *ping* sounds through the foyer.

The Killer and the Thinker look at each other. An observer might find the image surreal. As if a funhouse mirror stood between them, altering the average man's stature to gigantic, or the gigantic man's stature to average.

The Thinker walks away, to Franklin's office, and to the secret elevator. He boards and presses the button for the twentieth floor.

Tessa touches the side of Brian's face.

Brian puts his hands on Tessa's knees. He kisses her left knee. He leaves his lips there and puts his head sideways. Tessa touches a scar on the top of his bicep—a burn.

Brian puts his chin on her knee. He smiles. He stands and sets his palms softly on her upper arms, pushes her onto her back. She is on top of the comforter. Tessa frequently espoused to me the belief that it is in poor taste to make love on top of the comforter, as that is how hotels obtain a reputation for being unsanitary, with black-light detection of semen and vaginal secretions on the bedding, so on. One might scold Tessa for scolding on such grounds—might tell her she's cold, removed, cruel. It would seem advisable to withhold the criticism that she is incapable of love, for two reasons: one, it would turn her off, immediately and irrevocably, for hours or maybe days; two, if one met her after years of hard work in difficult fields that prohibited romantic attachment, prohibited romantic but not sexual attachment, that unprohibited sexual attachment resulting in two sons and an ex-wife, a family that feels strangely like a footnote, like something that—beside the moment of meeting Tessa—becomes an asterisk corresponding to an afterthought at the bottom of a page, because meeting and getting to know and falling in love with Tessa was like having a monster inside wake up and make one suddenly aware that air could smell like flowers, whereas air when one was asleep, as one was during one's whole life before meeting her, was only a bland and unremarkable means to keep breathing. In such a case, it ceases to matter after a while whether the other person feels similarly. It stops hurting—much—so long as she consents to allow one to wait for her in Room 1802, the deluxe penthouse, where one turns off the camera feed when one knows one will be with her there, turns the feed on again when one is not, in case someone else is with her there, as now, when—

The Killer walks to Delores, who is groping for the kitchen scissors she dropped. She reaches with her left arm, so as not to move her right side. Reaching with her left arm makes her move her right side. Delores wails like a woman in labor, but she keeps reaching. The Killer steps on the scissors when she reaches them. He grinds his heavy boot onto her fingers. Delores wails but will not let go. The Killer puts all his weight on her hand, and Delores wails more loudly as bones in her fingers pop like a pinecone in a campfire. But the Killer is standing on one foot. Delores sweeps her right foot around in what must be an excruciatingly painful maneuver, into the back of the Killer's right knee. The Killer falls like an awkward child on an icy sidewalk. His tumble to the marble and his loud, deep cry of pain happen in concert with a warbling quasi cheer from Delores, who is moving. In spite of unbearable pain, she moves and gets the scissors, and she isn't foolish enough to climb the Killer in search of a kill strike. She instead jabs the scissors' blades into the Killer's left shin, and he yells and she yells, and she moves higher on his shin and stabs him again. And maybe Delores knows this is the extent of her hope. It's quite possible she added up the scenario of locked doors to a second killer to her vicious injury and arrived at the sum that the likelihood of her survival was next to nothing. Perhaps she is thinking of Tessa, or of Jules—certainly not of Brian or Justin or any other man in the hotel—and has decided that she, Delores, can increase their odds of survival by hobbling the Killer. Or maybe she does believe she'll live. It's conceivable she believes she'll live, but I doubt she does. She's a realist. It took her four tries to make her husband stay away. It took shooting off his testicles. Delores poises the scissors above the Killer's testicles.

And the Killer swipes sideways with his knife, a kinesthetic sequence that is the unquestionable signature of Navy SEAL training, hilting the blade into Delores's neck. The Killer braces his foot on Delores's chest and pushes. The knife pulls horizontally out of its puncture, which is not a SEAL move. It's not even a SEAL flourish. Navy SEALs have a deserved reputation for being masochists. Some masochists are sadists, but by no means all. When sadistic Navy SEALs are denied the pleasure of killing for valid US military missions— say, through a dishonorable discharge—they often become mercenaries.

Honorably discharged SEALs often find high-paying positions as experts in security.

"I'm going to take care of you," Brian says. "I'm going to take care of you, Tess." He is holding her ankles, massaging her ankles. He says, "I'm going to take care of you," in syncopation with a steady, slow rhythm. Tessa's knees are in her armpits. It looks uncomfortable. She doesn't—but does but doesn't—sound uncomfortable. "I'll take care of you now, I promise."

The secret elevator arrives at the twentieth floor. The Thinker exits. He presses his controller, and the wall closes behind him, blocking the meaty stink of Vivica. The Thinker puts his controller on the floor, beside his playing cards and his phone, and paces. He looks cursorily at the security team members scattered across the space. The twentieth floor has no exit other than the secret elevator. In the event of a bomb threat or accidental fire or any scenario wherein the lower floors would require evacuation, the security team would coordinate the evacuation from the twentieth floor, handling their own exodus last. This procedure was outlined to each security team member during the hiring process. The entire security team is composed of former Navy SEALs. It is extraordinarily difficult to kill a Navy SEAL. One must, it could be claimed, be a Navy SEAL to kill a Navy SEAL. One must be a Navy SEAL with a very smart accomplice in order to neutralize a former Navy SEAL and former Rhodes Scholar and his entire night-shift security team.

The Killer is very, very angry with Delores. But Delores is dead. There is nothing the Killer can do to her now, except inflict postmortem injuries. The Killer sounds like a deep-voiced child throwing a tantrum. But instead of beating a floor, or hitting a pillow, he uses his knife on Delores. Instead of pitching toys in every direction, he pitches Delores's hand, then her other hand, then one foot, and then the other.

"You're safe with me," Brian says. Tessa's quickening. Tessa's probably blushing. It's impossible to tell when the image is green, white, and black. "You can come," Brian says. "It's okay. You're safe. Come for me." The secret to making her come is to tell her to. Apparently.

A rich man builds a hotel by the sea. He names it after the setting in a classic horror novel. He does this because Destin, Sr., used to read novels into a cassette recorder and leave the tapes for his son when he went away on business. Destin, Sr., stopped this practice when Charles turned eight, but Charles Destin continued listening to the final recording—hearing his father intone, "Manderley, Manderley, 'Last night I dreamt I went to Manderley again'"—until the cassette wore out, years after the death of Destin, Sr., by a household bomb in a third world hotel. Charles Destin, damaged from the loss of his father as well as from a lifetime of having whatever he wanted whenever he wanted it, confided these details in therapy. Therapy is supposed to be confidential, but I bribed Destin's psychiatrist. One should never take it for granted that the man one is ostensibly protecting isn't the man from whom others need protection. I can picture Destin in any of his twenty pairs of lambskin slippers, lounging in his den and conceiving some cosmic comeuppance for his father by butchering the innocents in Manderley. Or perhaps it's much more rationally capitalist. Perhaps Destin thought, after too much fine wine one evening, that it would build immeasurable cachet if his hotel were to, shortly before its grand opening, suffer a tragedy in the tradition of cliché horror.

"Holy—," Tessa says, and laughs like a purring cat. "I'm keeping you." Brian has slowed but has not ceased moving. He hasn't come yet. He's a freak. Tessa is rolling them over. "Bri, do me a favor?" He blinks up at her, through what must be an ego-annihilating focus. "Be selfish." He nods. Tessa never gets on top. Tessa is working extraordinarily hard, and the key to making her come again is—evidently—to make her work hard, and to ogle the gyrations of her breasts, and to touch them and then her thighs and to beg, to beg, "Faster, yes, Tess, Christ, faster," and to continue one's shouts in the affirmative so that even as she comes, she keeps moving, selflessly, for you.

Or, another rich man envies the rich man his hotel by the sea. His primacy in the property management industry has suffered as a direct result of Destin's ascendancy. Cameron Donofrio finds the hotel's grandeur kitschy and overdone. He drinks too much fine wine one evening, and decides that not only is there a way the hotel could be branded a failure before it ever opened, but there is a way this could be accomplished artistically. Theatrically. He hires the theatrically minded hotel manager to commit acts of minor sabotage, and separately hires a pair of assassins to brutally murder the entire staff in one endless summer night.

The Killer—the Killer is throwing organs out of Delores as if she were a toy box, and—

Or, a terrorist cell committed to the unraveling of global security sets out to demonstrate its prowess by undermining the claim that a particular hotel is invulnerable to outside penetration. It chooses a hyperviolent modus operandi to instill fear in the populace.

No. Terrorists operate in volume. They fight systems and so purport systemic slaughter, but almost always on a large scale. And they need the message to be clear, lest their agenda get lost in the ghastliness.

Or, any number of international enemies of the head of security decide to exact revenge by destroying his reputation with a concentrated, localized attack on the hotel that he has been tasked with making impregnable.

No again. If it were about me, they'd have tied me up and forced me to watch the anarchy descend. They don't know I'm alive.

The Killer and the Thinker are mercenaries. Their methodical exactitude, their emotional remove, their adeptness and skill— nothing else fits. Killers for hire. Their names, which are not their names, are whispered in a vast, hateful underbelly of the world that operates with cynically perfected efficiency. Too many ends are too ideally realized by means of murder.

It's de rigueur, after a decorated career in special forces, that an invitation is at least casually floated to join their ranks. A man might pull up a stool in a high-end Los Angeles bar, strike up a conversation, subtly imply the ops are rare and the salary huge, and leave a card. One might, if one were human, consider it for a single idiot second before asking the bartender for a match and watching the card curl into an ashtray. One could still smoke indoors back then. Though I never did.

So, the Killer and the Thinker's price had to be astronomical.

For the detail, the maximization of grotesquery, the hourly labor for staying all night. Further evidence that a man with astronomical resources was behind the order. Charles Destin or Cameron Donofrio?

Whoever it was, after the contract is in circulation, bidding begins. The team that executes the plan must be small and very experienced, because I made it a point to know every possible danger. Charles Destin told me he had enemies. He described corporate rivals, jealous husbands, and tennis opponents he defeated in tournaments. I took it for granted such men would use civilized means of murder. But civilized men can pick up the phone and call savages, and leaders of nations do it all the time, but Manderley is not a nation. It's a posh hotel, built for business, for relaxation. For trysts.

Brian bucks. His neck knocks backward. He yelps with no dignity. Tessa pulls on his buttocks with avarice. She is patient. She milks him. He stills. Rolls to his left, on top of her: They are exhausted. They kiss exhaustedly. They don't talk. A minute later, snoring— Tessa's—can be heard. Brian smirks. He moves. Removes himself regretfully. He turns the comforter down and rotates Tessa so her head is on the pillow. He spoons her. Less than a minute later, a harmonic octave of snoring—Brian's, the fucker—is audible.

The Killer droops. He looks at what he has wrought. He examines the foyer with a nod of satisfaction. Then he peers at his lacerated leg and stabs what once was Delores one more time. He turns away from a stunning, repellent, viscerally offensive mess, and tracks blood across the floor. He tracks blood up the stairs, and down the hall of the second floor, to the laundry room, where he strips off his coveralls and pours into the washer the remainder of the detergent he left atop the washer, before pressing buttons. He goes to the fourth dryer and opens it, to check in on Franklin. The Killer slams the dryer door, turns a dial, and the dryer rattles to life. There is something wrong with it. It was not, evidently, designed to roast hotel managers to death.

The Killer is bleeding, but not too much. His shins are not fractured, but he's limping. Delores might have severed a few fibers of muscle when the scissors whickered off bone. He goes to the employee break room and takes the first aid kit from a cabinet beside the refrigerator. He cleans the lacerations, and applies bandages and gauze. He has numerous scars. He is an enormous man. He is conclusively a man, and favors tightie whities. This is strangely rewarding.

Then, the duo that wins the contract has to become intimately familiar with the workings of Manderley's surveillance. They must know when staff change occurs. They need to get an access card to the twentieth floor. The most efficient method for doing all of these things is to pay off a member of the security team. The most torturous part of all of this is not knowing why, and knowing it's almost impossible I'll ever know why. But the second-most torturous thing to endure is duplicity on the part of people to whom loyalty is supposed to be sacrosanct.

Tessa doesn't like to be held in her sleep. Usually.

Jules and Justin do not snore. The Killer tends his wounds.

The Thinker, by now, is completely sick of solitaire. Which is why he's collating his deck and building a house of cards.

It is eleven o'clock. The security team intended to run a scenario tonight. A fire drill. When all civilian parties in the building were asleep, security was going to set off the fire alarm and watch to see if employees followed protocol. The protocol for a fire drill is to descend the stairs in an orderly fashion, forgoing the elevator, and exit the lobby level. It is a basic protocol, admittedly, but it's shocking how often civilians, when confronted with imminent threats, forget instructions and panic. Delores was not one to panic. Security was going to wait until Delores left to set off the alarm. Delores would be leaving about now. She didn't like her home. She preferred her workplace, a bygone habit from a time when a malicious abuser awaited her in his wingback chair, smoking cigars and spitting in a saucepan. This is in Delores's file.

Delores's head is on the mantel in the bright red foyer; it's turned so it can stare at her body on the floor. The fourth dryer tumbles and tumbles its load in the housekeeping storage area. Henri lies facedown on the plush carpet of Room 1408, the carpet dark with blood, the blood discernible in night vision's green, black, and white. Likewise Twombley's blood, in which he bathes, in the bathtub of Room 1516. The security cameras switch in and out of night vision automatically, sensing the amount of light available.

Vivica's eyes are like a somber summer day, covered in fluffy white clouds. Where do they come from?

Where does memory come from? How does time pass, what is it? Is it the cinematic flash to running down the stairs in the house back in Indiana? The white walls scuffed by spirited boys? The revisited sense that the carpet there was not plush but it was thick. It was much too thick, and natty and dull. The railing's surface with divots like healed acne, imprinting onto a smooth hand, an innocent hand, connected to an innocent body intent in its footy pajamas. The smell of syrup, vanilla, nutmeg. Bacon to counter the sweets. Sunday breakfasts. First one down the stairs got to lick the bowl of muffin batter. The secret was to decide, before sleep, "Wake up the minute the bacon's on." The secret to anything is to decide. Anything is surmountable. Anything. Anything but death, but if death is not foreign, if death is not exotic, if death isn't—but death is. Death always is. It's the unknown country. It's the tenant of tall shadows. It's the dark. It is the Thing humanity has tried to vanquish with cities, with lit-all-night streetlamps; with medicine and surgery, religion and mythology, art and demagoguery, and yet—yet, yet, death looks at these measures and feels the briefest, barest confusion. It carries on with its business. It's the boogeyman. It is there in the operating room, and in the pill proffered afterward to ward off infection. It's in every religion, myth, painting, song, poem, novel, and film, and in every speech by every fool who ever tried to argue that anything is surmountable. Death is not, because death simply *is*. If death simply *is*, how can it be argued that anything matters? Tessa once said, answering that very question, in bed, after saying the subject was a stupid waste of syllables, "Because if nothing matters, then everything does." She said it with a rude brusqueness, like a self-evident fact. Like the maxim she lived her life by. And perhaps, perhaps that maxim is what makes her slightly other, mildly apart and above. Only mildly, slightly, because the difference in her can be a deficit as well as an attribute. She can hear the words "I love you" and reply, "I don't love you. I don't think I ever will. If you want to keep doing this, that's fine, but it won't ever be anything more for me." The viciousness! The courage! What *is* that, what *is* it? Brian has it, too. It is—it is an insouciance vis-à-vis death. An equanimity about the value of life in the midst of death, but not an acceptance. Not at all. Death is not something many people think about—at least outside of religious dogma—and of those who think, few are capable of arriving at a conclusion that is anything but cynical, and so what Tessa has somehow done—and Brian, it seems, has done it, too—is

to refuse to arrive at a conclusion, but instead to insist on honesty
and forthrightness at the expense of sweetness. But not of decency.
Never, ever that. It is idiotic folly, says the part of the mind that has
known death uncommonly well, walked with it through war zones,
swum with it in black coastlines, jumped with it out of Black Hawks.
But another part of my mind watches time pass, hours of it, here
on the twentieth floor, where the Thinker's house of cards rises to
a skyscraper. He estimates its stability has reached its limit, and he
then begins construction on a maze in front of the tower, laying the
cards horizontally with the precision of a kinesthetic sage. This is
the part of my mind that watched the Killer finish taping his bandages, dry his coveralls, put on his coveralls, clean his knife, search
the employee break room refrigerator and find Vivica's huevos rancheros in a shallow Tupperware bowl, microwave it, eat it, board the
secret elevator, skipping the stairs in consideration of his limp, arrive
at the seventh floor, enter Room 717, set the clock radio's alarm for
two a.m., send a text that made the Thinker's phone vibrate, and fold
his hands across his stomach for a nap. As I watch these men in masks,
the part of my mind thus engaged wonders, if it possessed Tessa's and
Brian's insouciance, what might have happened at five oh two p.m.,
when Addison pointed to the monitor showing the secret elevator,
and to the two men in it whose heads were bowed so all that could be
seen were the parts of their hair. One man was enormous; the other
average. Like Bowles and Petrovski. Bowles and Petrovski carpooled.
Bowles had a hard time keeping his schedule straight; Petrovski was
going through a divorce. Addison laughed at how they'd come to
work when they weren't scheduled to, and the team returned to its
meeting, prepped to take the piss out of Bowles and Petrovski when
they arrived at the twentieth floor. The head of security was running

behind, too. I'd been screamed at, minutes ago, by Charles Destin. I was conducting the meeting distractedly, and yet another distraction in the form of my two worst employees botching their schedules annoyed me into the human fallacy that petty concerns render death inert. Death is not ever inert. The two men in the elevator were not Bowles and Petrovski. The Killer and the Thinker knew Bowles's and Petrovski's builds, and that their own builds could effectively deceive the security team. The large man—the Killer—wields a brutal and accurate knife, and the average man—the Thinker—can fire eight calm, considered shots through a silencer in the time it takes five former Navy SEALs to reach for their weapons.

The Killer's knife throwing is exceptionally accurate, but not perfect. He was aiming for the neck, and he hit it, but he hit the back of the neck. He hit the space between the second and third vertebrae. His first victim fell into a chair, spine neatly severed but no major arteries hit, barely bleeding, head coming to rest on the counter that faces the bank of security monitors, eyes wide open. Such an injury would result in death if the victim moved even an inch the wrong way, and the chair into which the victim fell is on wheels. One of the sixty-four monitors (eight rows, eight columns, a third of them motion-activated and two-thirds fixed on pivot points crucial for security protocol) shows the twentieth floor. The other members of the security team, not including Twombley, were shot. They, including Twombley, are obviously dead. The Killer had another knife, a larger one he preferred, which is why the Killer's Navy SEAL field knife remains lodged in the back of my neck.

The Thinker stands from a Manderley of cards it took him two decks to build. He pokes the foundations with his toe, curious how much force it would require to knock the tower down. It does not take much. The Thinker faces the east wall. The bank of security monitors is on the north wall, in front of the windows, and beneath them sits a countertop for the security team members to set their cups of coffee on—or, in a pinch, their inert skulls—and in front of the counter sit the chairs, on wheels, which in most scenarios do not seem highly dangerous.

In the center of the counter, there is a blank black monitor, framed in more white Formica and angled at forty-five degrees. The override system. It's a touch screen. It's been called an excessive and absurd measure, but only behind my back. It's absurd now only because with the press of a few buttons the entire hotel and everything in it—light switches, doors, even the faucets—would be under my control. Beside the override monitor, ten inches in front of my face, there is a pencil. I thought, as Delores ran, as the Killer followed, as the Thinker left the twentieth floor for the first time all night and went to the foyer and flanked her expertly—I did consider worming my head along the counter (if simply the act of moving didn't sever my few vital nerves that remain intact), seizing the pencil in my mouth (assuming I could angle my head), and, using this makeshift appendage to activate emergency override protocols, manipulate some minor aspect of the foyer to help Delores escape (the Thinker locked the main doors manually with chains and a padlock).

It would have been an impractical act. I would not have positioned my head exactly right afterward; the Thinker would have noticed I'd moved. I'd be dead now. It might have bought Delores a few seconds. Survival is about what *is*, not what might be.

It is only when the Thinker goes to the east and looks out, as he does now, that it is possible he will see the head of security blinking. It is therefore advisable to stop blinking.

Tessa, in her sleep, will sometimes cuddle toward an erection if one is pressed against her. Tessa appears to be doing this now. Normally, if Tessa does this, and it wakes her companion—as it does, now, Brian—and if her companion wakes her in response—as Brian does, now, playfully grazing his lips across hers—Tessa will grunt in disgust and turn away, citing a dire need for sleep and a supreme distaste for her (and for her companion's) foul breath.

She will not open her eyes dreamily, and gaze upon her companion like he is a dream, and kiss him. But she does so now, to Brian.

It is one thirty a.m. Veterans of special ops units are well acquainted with one thirty a.m., and hours like it. Particularly special ops veterans who cut their teeth on the skirmishes of the mid-to-late eighties, fights that weren't supposed to be happening, wars that were never sanctioned by the general population or the politicians elected by the general population. They were like extramarital affairs. They happened in hours easily unaccounted for—hours that are cold, dark, and beautiful—the same as an affair happens on lunch breaks or supposed late nights at the office. The soldiers tucked dog tags under undershirts, so the metal wouldn't wink back at the stars, alerting an enemy who had to die silently. It isn't true that soldiers are brainless orangutans, swinging dicks knocking down dictators. Nor is it true, either or often, that these men, while floating on an inflatable raft in calm waters, waiting for the order to fall backward into the tiny waves and swim over a mile to shore, contemplate the night sky, or what they are about to do, and their position in time and space, and their personal philosophy, and karma. Most of the men are contemplating something, but typically it's a girlfriend back home, or a wife, or their mother. Most men, when faced with death, think of a woman, one woman. It is wise for the lieutenant who forms the combat unit to promote to CO the one man who does not think of a woman. It is preferable that he think of philosophy and karma. It is ideal if he grew up poor—not destitute, but definitely poor—and if he is too poor to afford college, yet wants to go to college and has an excellent mind. He's barely nineteen, but he has shown unparalleled discipline and persistence in training. He's in special ops because the pay's better. He's trying to make enough money to send not only himself, but his little brother and little sister, to college. But the little brother joins up, too, and gets killed in an on-base Humvee rollover. The little sister, shortly afterward, gets pregnant and then gets married. He watches the stars, waits for the order, and thinks—even now, before his siblings' misfortunes have come to pass—that one thirty a.m. and the hours like it are the hours of unfairness. They invite, in his fellow soldiers, diaphanous recollections of a woman—*the* woman, whether mother or lover or whatever she is—and turn her into something other, something much more than what she is. This is what the CO thinks: that loving a woman this way is foolish. And he thinks he'd give anything to forget what these hours can do. He believes the rich and the lucky are impervious to one thirty a.m. The rich and the lucky, in the mid-to-late eighties, are rationalizing a dominance he will only watch grow over time. But the coup will be: he will join that dominance. Not the highest echelon; that is closed to him. That is a precipice for men and women born to obscene, situational, circumstantial wealth, wealth once-earned but now merely passed on to the lucky. He will become, instead, the man who watches over them, making sure they live to love their luck. He will be an individual security attaché for a while, after an honorable discharge and a stamped recommendation letter from an admiral and excellent SATs get him into Columbia, followed by

Oxford, followed by the realization he'd make far more money in the security sector than he ever could as a philosophy professor. (It will haunt him, how he abandoned academia for money, but not much, no. He is a pragmatist; he is not emotional; he is not sentimental, until he is, when—) Then he is approached about interviewing for the head of security position in Destin Management Group and—he meets Tessa.

I didn't care about the interview. I didn't want the job. I was a private consultant, coordinating the protection of actors and pop stars, heiresses and tycoons. The money was profane, and I never had to meet the people I was protecting. I designed routes for limousines, rewrote schedules for meathead bodyguards, and taught defense techniques. I had a reputation—made from a decade and a half alternating between the CIA and the Secret Service—and I was coasting on that reputation. I was bored, but I didn't know it. I was sitting in a room with six other interviewees, a room with smooth black walls and a bowl of floating white flowers in the midst of a dozen high-priced chairs, a Monet (not a reproduction) behind the receptionist's elephantine desk. Water poured down one black wall but didn't pool anywhere. It recycled invisibly back to the top. No magazines to read, no clock. Modern decorating aesthetics equate beauty with empty space.

I was offended, sitting there, that six other interviewees were vying for the position. Destin Management Group had gone through some trouble to contact me. My number was unlisted, my address classified. I am offended, still, at the memory: we sat in that black room in our black suits with our black ties and shoes, profiling one another out of habit. Seven men contacted through unofficial channels. We were called that way, placed that way—in a room with nothing to read and no clock to hear ticking—to communicate to us that not one of us was special.

But one of us had brought a book. I remember it had a black cover, a black cat backlit in green. One of us was reading while the rest envied him his book, yet the rest of us recognized this as an enormous error—his reading, not our envy—because there was certainly a camera or two or five trained on our behavior, on our watchfulness, and this man leisurely flipping pages was failing the test. A man across from me smiled at our peer's obvious failure. But a smile, too, was a failure. We were all so alike. We were virtually identical. Standing out in any way was an error, for safety is the provenance of ghosts, and though the water wall's trickle provoked the need to urinate, only I sat patiently, not moving, while one by one the others visited the men's room.

"Anybody know if they're interviewing somebody right now?" said the man across from me, the one who'd smiled.

Another of us responded; another joined in. I said nothing. I knew that the current head of security for Destin Management Group was watching us. I knew, because it was what I would have done: observe who can and cannot be still and attentive and unmoving and quiet until such a time as action is called for.

We weren't waiting for the interview. This was the interview.

I truly didn't want the job. It meant a bump in pay, but not one worth the fantastic amount of work it would be to set up the gratuitous safety measures legendarily demanded by Destin at all his many new properties—paranoid son of a murdered diplomat, spoiled child with a god complex—but I wanted the offer of the job. That was all I wanted.

She appeared at the receptionist's desk, and my breath stopped.

Suddenly, she was there. I would never describe the feeling, both because it would sound like it always sounds when someone describes the sensation of love at first sight, and because I had no one to describe the feeling to: it was a hollowing out all through me, and yet a filling up. It was the end of a wait I'd never known I was enduring. It was senseless. It made perfect sense.

The walls were black, and so was Tessa's hair, and so were her clothes, her boots. I would learn she had ten of the same black skirt and blazer, twenty white blouses, four pairs of the same black-heeled boots. Her black hair glowed darker than the walls. Royal blue in it, thanks to the room's shadows. Like fine, clean water in a mountain's valley. Like a lake it would be fatal to try to reach.

She smiled at the receptionist, setting a file on the desk. She whispered, "He's the one," and she winked at the receptionist and disappeared again. I would learn there was a hallway Tessa had designed in the administration wing of Destin Management Group headquarters, to make such subtle entrances and exits possible. I would learn she'd wanted to major in architecture, but Destin's offer of a guaranteed job after graduation swayed her, because she had a horror of ever returning to the destitute dependency of her early childhood. I would learn it was my file she'd set in front of the receptionist, as I was called moments later and led to a back room, where I sat opposite an aged but fit man who gestured to a monitor beside us, to a specific monitor on which my fellow interviewees were being dismissed. And he said to me, with no facial expression to speak of, "Tell me what mistakes these men made, and what mistake you made."

I stated baldly that I had stared at Tessa in blatant distraction after he'd selected me as his successor. I acknowledged my own mistake, one I would repeat. And repeat.

I listed the other applicants' bathroom breaks, conversations, smiles, the book—how these errors demonstrated a need to be occupied and moving and active with something other than the task exactly at hand.

He nodded. Then he said, "Do you want the job?"

"Bri?" Tessa whispers.

"Yeah?"

"You love riding."

He kisses the underside of her neck, where the skin is so pale one can—up close—trace the veins under Tessa's skin. "It's not that I love it," he says. "It's in me. I've been doing it so long, it's part of me. It's how I got somewhere." He kisses her lips. Tessa's been tasting them as he speaks. "If you absolutely need me to quit riding, I'll quit."

If Tessa had absolutely needed anything, I'd have given it. I wouldn't have paused to ask myself what I was sacrificing, what was being lost. But Tessa didn't need anything from me. Not a damn thing. She was helping launch Destin Management Group to a height that dwarfed Donofrio Properties, spat on it from the troposphere of success, and she was doing it the fair way, by being simply better, by working harder. Destin Management Group built an office complex for an animation company in Palo Alto, and while construction raged like a competitive sport, walls and plumbing and electric and the highest-tech technology in meeting rooms resembling a sketch from *The Jetsons*, Tessa was called away from a problem with the unisex bathrooms to the coffee bar, where the animation company's CEO was livid over the design of the cups and saucers. So Tessa took four hours to call the coffee bar manager, get the number of the distributor through whom he'd ordered the dishes, call that number, and climb the levels of speakers' importance until she was joking good-naturedly with the CEO of *that* company. She talked him into marshaling his designers together and creating for the office complex an exclusive set of cups and saucers. When the animation company's office complex was toured by a journalist, he ordered a coffee at the coffee bar, and used a paragraph of precious space regaling his readers with the fascinating, tilted, off-kilter design of the dishes from which he sipped his soy chai latte. Tessa's job was to make an infinity of infinitesimal decisions like that, and to make the right decision, every day, all day. And the head of security watched her do this, from banks of monitors in close little rooms. He would take coffee breaks and bring her coffee, to which she said thank you, but then she would sip, set down the cup, and forget about it. He would see the cup from a monitor. It was torture. But it was also bliss, because she didn't have a boyfriend, no husband, not even a father, and so it stood to reason that she was profoundly alone, as the man who watched her was alone, and *that* made it stand to reason that Tessa—given enough time and attention, enough focused prodding—would come to love the man who watched her. She had come from nothing, as he had. She'd come from a larger nothing than he had, and the sense of this, followed by the confirmation of it when he read her personnel file, was arguably what made him love her with such abrupt completeness. She lived in a humble apartment, but he owned a house in Malibu. She had made good her escape, but dared not enjoy it yet. He could teach her. He could save her.

"You love riding," she says again. She winces. "How many motorcycles do you have?"

Brian winces, too, and says, "Eight."

They laugh. They hold each other in the middle of the bed. A shape under the comforter. Tessa's leg, rising around his waist, and the shape of Brian's arm, stroking that tear-jerking home country of high on her thigh, to her buttock, to her hip and the lowest part of her back.

"Keep one," Tessa says. Her laugh muffles as Brian kisses her hard on the mouth.

He says, "Two. I never ride one of them. It's Mitch's."

"Two." Tessa kisses him. She does it like she's serious about progressing beyond a kiss. Though that is a guess. That is not based on experience. Experience would suggest that sex was utilitarian for Tessa. Boring, really, most of the time.

"You love working." Brian pins Tessa under him to say it, pins her hands by her head. "Keep your job, but scale it back." He says it roughly. He's holding her wrists rather roughly. "Take a vacation. Take a big vacation, soon, so we can go somewhere and try and kill each other with sex."

Tessa says, "'Kay," and rolls him over, under her, but he rolls them again, to the edge of the bed, where they teeter, giggling. He sounds like a girl; he practically is. He has the ass of a twelve-year-old girl, and he was the one *Tessa* thought of when *she* contemplated the dead morning hours, happening upon a cold cup of coffee she'd abandoned in another building project in another part of coastal California. Brian was why she looked sad when she brought the cup to her lips, needing the jolt to stay awake, needing to stay awake to make more decisions, put out more fires, do more work, more, more work. It was Brian she didn't want to go to sleep and dream about, so she'd take the cup to the nearest microwave and nuke it, drink it, make sour faces at it. She didn't have a boyfriend, husband, not even a goddamn father, but she had a soul mate, somewhere, missing her, needing her. Those two elements—missing and needing—multiplied together and then taken to the power of the years they'd been apart, resulted in a string of digits that stacked to dwarf the love of a man who thought Tessa would come to need him because she no doubt wanted to forget her humble beginnings, when the truth was that Tessa wanted to remember them. She wants to revel in them; she wants to return to her beginning, and be brand-new. She sounds brand-new, like a child. Happy. Brian's tickling her.

The Thinker leaves the east window. The monitor for the twentieth floor shows him sitting at the slop of his playing cards, gathering them together again, sighing and dealing his fifty-first game of solitaire. There is a salty, wet drop on the security counter, under the inert skull resting there, sideways. There is no way for the skull to lick the teardrop without alerting the Thinker to the body's continued functioning (though the body has urinated and moved its bowels in the chair with wheels, by now, but bladder and bowels let go in death, and so the smell blends with the three other bodies that are actually dead).

There is a running time clock on each security monitor. It is one fifty a.m.

It is not impossible to recuperate from severe spinal injuries. It's also not impossible that the Killers want to leave a survivor, to testify to the Killers' cunning and ruthlessness. Probably only one survivor. Probably leave only one, knowingly.

Jules and Justin are sleeping.

Tessa is tickling Brian now. He's ticklish in his armpits.

It is easy to be motionless when one is paralyzed, and in three hours, when the security team arrives for shift change, the Killers will have left. And my team is trained to check vital signs before moving a body, no matter how apparent it is that the body is dead, and they will find that my body is not dead, and they'll get my body on an ambulance, to a hospital, through physical therapy, into a wheel-chair, onto crutches, off crutches. Tessa will visit. She'll be trauma-tized. She'll be inconsolable, because Brian will have died for her, heroically, taking a knife to the heart as she ran and, against all odds, escaped. I'll console her, despite my condition. I'll be the only one who can understand.

Seconds are not sloppy, necessarily. Some things are better left over; everyone knows that. Lasagna, for example.

Tessa and Brian are talking. They are saying the fastest way is to go to city hall on Monday. He is saying, haltingly, Kids—I don't, and she is saying, Me either, and he is boneless with relief. He is telling her the two of them, knowing what they know, seeing what they've seen—she is finishing for him: What if something happened to us? He is holding her so tight, so tight, and in years and years of profes-sionally spying, hearing conversations meant for two sets of ears, an exchange such as this, a sight such as this, is embarrassing to observe. It does not belong to anybody but them. No part of it can be bor-rowed for one's own use. It can't be projected upon. It could only be observed in the hours of total, utter unfairness, hours of beauty; it isn't fair, not at all. I never had the remotest chance at all.

It is two a.m.

In Room 717, the clock radio suddenly blasts the bridge of "Born to Run" by Bruce Springsteen. Clarence Clemons was a wizard with a saxophone, truly. I'll miss the sound. It is premature to think what one will miss, when one is not dead yet. There has been remarkable medical progress in the realm of severe spinal trauma.

The Killer sits up on the bed and stretches. He arches his back. He's probably yawning under the mask. He moves a dial on the clock radio, and it quiets. He turns on the bedside lamp and taps his phone alight, then types a text message.

The Thinker's phone buzzes. He stands and walks toward the bank of monitors on the north wall. He stops directly behind the seemingly dead body in the chair with wheels. If the Thinker nudges the chair, it could easily roll. If the Thinker moves—but he doesn't; he watches. His mask makes it impossible to decide whom he's watching.

Justin and Jules are sleeping.

Tessa and Brian are holding each other, so tight; it is not any-one's moment—even with the Thinker watching—but theirs. They are kissing again, but without the hurry of before. With an altogether different heat. Hate is natural, and self-hate is natural, but the two combined are an unnatural sensation: to despise Brian or to despise the desire for the Killer to kill Brian? One or the other, not both.

The Thinker types a text message, and the Killer's phone lights but does not buzz. The Killer reads it, goes to the bathroom—the stiffness in his shin a bit worse—and urinates, checks his wounds, fills a short glass with water and drinks it by folding the chin of his mask. He takes his knife from where he left it on the nightstand.

The Thinker, turning from the monitors, bumps the chair. The angle of vision changes, panic red and fiery, but say nothing, do nothing; you are dead. The angle changed about the width of a hair. You are not dead. There is no method to estimate the pressure or direction of body weight now loaded against the chair on wheels. There was no method for estimating this before. There's no moving any muscle of the body. There's no God; don't pray.

Please. Please, God.

CAMERA 63, 62

□ □ □

Tessa and Brian communicate with tongues' calculated laziness. Tessa must be overly warm—which never happens—as she pushes the covers down. Brian kicks the covers lower, and there, now, is all of them. It is embarrassing. A naked body is embarrassing. So is a dead one. Two naked bodies pressed together are doubly embarrassing. It's a matter for philosophers, but then again, it's simple. It reflects unfairness—deadness does; nudity does. It's not fair that we are at once so vulnerable and yet so aware. That walking (the Killer walks, limping, out of Room 717 and toward the cleaning closet/secret elevator) this life with almost the same pure physicality as the orangutan (though with less hair to guard against cold and thinner skin that tolerates less injury) but a mentality that places that body in a continuum of thought, feeling, endeavor. It is unfair. She is so soft. She's an ideal contrast to a hard, muscular body, but that isn't what she wants. She wants Brian; it's plain from how she kneads his arms from shoulders, to elbows, to slightly higher than wrists and then reaches under his arms to knead his buttocks, lower back. Buttocks again. And Brian has a softness that is more conspicuous, somehow, than hers. A flexibility. A comfort in his muscles' tautness that lets the tautness keep a disproportionate mobility. He does not, as would be understandable, mount Tessa now, and make all his anatomy a show of hardness to contrast with her softness. Rather, he counters what Tessa is doing to him—the kneading—with caresses to the border of her scapula and the long line of her intact spinal column.

The Killer boards the secret elevator.

Jules and Justin are sleeping. They are still asleep when the bookshelf downstairs slides aside and the secret elevator opens into the living room of Room 1801, the regular penthouse. There are many reasons it will be distasteful to watch Jules and Justin get butchered. The main reason is there's no chance whatsoever the two of them will live. They simply won't. They are defenseless, sleeping, as the Killer climbs the stairs toward them, disappears from that camera, and appears on the one upstairs. They are on their designated sides of the bed—he on the left, she on the right, if one is facing the bed—and they have lived lives in which their knowledge of their own vulnerability is startlingly limited. Justin's parents run a successful travel agency. Jules's parents are artists—painter and photographer; they collaborate occasionally—whose livelihood does not depend on their art, but on inheritance from industrious ancestors. Jules and Justin had bad skin and broken hearts in adolescence, but then the pimples cleared and they found each other in grad school. Justin's parents bought him a motorcycle for a high school graduation gift. They made him buy the helmet so he would feel a sense of responsibility.

He rode the bike for a few months, then lost interest. Justin has long eyelashes and a touchy disposition that he thinks makes him sensitive to others' feelings, but it does not. It makes him sensitive to his own feelings. He married Jules because she's hot. He introduces her to people as "my hot wife, Jules." Jules, it could be asserted, listens to Tessa's problems with such a ready ear because Jules herself has had so few genuine problems that hearing Tessa talk is like listening to a pioneer woman tell about doing laundry with a ribbed board and a rock. Or an Amazonian hunter who eats his kill's heart as a gesture of respect. Or an elderly couple wealthy enough to live on a cruise ship complaining that the bingo room is open only until midnight. It could be said, if one periodically entertained unkind thoughts about Jules, that Jules befriended Tessa in the first place because she found Tessa's difficult past exotic. These unkind thoughts might be substantiated by Jules's end-of-the-day recitations to Justin about everything Tessa told her. Everything. As Jules has begun to develop problems of her own, her recitations to Justin have begun to include problems for Tessa that actually belong to Jules: Tessa's got a secret shoe stash that's bankrupting her; Tessa takes her top off at the beach purely to reassure herself her tits still draw stares; Tessa's seeing a shrink and it's not helping at all. It comforts Jules to give Tessa her problems. Jules comforts herself by pretending Tessa wouldn't mind: Tessa never tells Jules to keep secrets. But some things are implied. Some things are just decency. Decency is made exponentially more difficult when one has never really been tested. Jules and Justin love to tell people how Tessa delivered them from certain ruin when their catering business was failing, but Jules's and Justin's parents would have bailed them out one way or another. Jules's and Justin's parents gave Jules and Justin a house for a wedding gift. They've never existed without a safety net. They are nice people. It's not that they're not fundamentally decent people; it's that one cannot know, because they've never known hardship. It is easy to be nice when being nice is easy, but niceness is the first thing to go when an unexamined life becomes even slightly difficult. People begin failing tests they never realized they're taking. People get pills; people get mistresses. They get angry at grand injustices they created for themselves, and they created those injustices in an effort to ignore the fundamental, foundational injustice that being alive means living in the shadow of death. It strikes them—these blessed children—as horribly unfair. The Killer walks closer and closer to the bed.

Brian isn't being as gentle now. Tessa is baiting him brutally, with a fingernail down the ridges of his back, a lick to his mouth and an evasion of hers, a laugh, as if patting a dragon's nose. Brian stops. Suddenly. He looks at her quite seriously. He looks very young and very sad. Tessa starts to match him, younger and sadder. When they match perfectly, Brian fits them together. It's all visible, as the covers are down. It embarrasses.

The Killer makes no sound. Justin's eyelids snap open, seeing what his ancient, primitive instinct sensed and woke him to see. He scrambles out of the bed on his side. "What the—? Who the fuck're—?" He grabs a lamp by the base and tries to brandish it, but the plug holds inside the outlet and he almost falls backward. The Killer has stopped at the foot of the bed, intrigued or amused or both, as Justin bends and yanks the lamp's cord with the noise one makes during a tough tennis serve.

The sound wakes Jules. "Whuh?" she says, falling out of bed like a klutzy sleepwalker, "Babe-uh?" She blinks at the Killer and shakes her head, chemically incapable of anxiety when it might for once be beneficial.

"Come on!" Justin shouts. "Come on, freak—let's go!" Justin rushes forward with the lamp in both hands, feigning insanity or truly finding a temporary form of it. It might work on a burglar or a hophead.

The Killer waits. Justin swings the lamp around. The Killer catches it with one hand, waits. He waits until Justin sees the knife in his other hand. At the same time, as if on cue, the Killer nods and Justin shakes his head. The knife pistons up-in so fast, Justin seems to understand he's been stabbed only when he hears his own offended grunt. He looks down at the handle in his heart like it's a harmless new addition to his body—a freckle, a callus. At worst a sliver.

Jules stands straight. Sober in a heartbeat.

Justin coughs a mouthful of blood. Lifts a fist and punches the Killer's mask with a force no greater than a slap.

Jules shrieks and tries to run, but the Killer moves, taking Justin with him. He uses Justin's struggling body like a portable wall to railroad Jules back on the bed, where she whirls, tumbles, and yanks an end table drawer open. She throws the Bible. The handset of the cordless phone. A book, a cup of cold tea, a clock radio, the sound system's remote control, more. They all miss the Killer, but the clock radio hits Justin in the back. He's holding on to the Killer's coveralls, aspirating blood as the Killer watches him die.

The room is a shambles. Both lamps are broken, water glasses spilled, a bodice-ripper romance paperback stomped under the Killer's boot. Jules sinks into a corner, screaming. The Killer slides Justin's body off the knife. Justin flumps to the white carpet, making a high hissing noise that indicates his lungs can't get any air. The Killer is walking past him, toward Jules. Justin grabs the Killer's foot. The Killer turns back to Justin. Jules screams.

The penthouses, both of them, are soundproof.

It's abnormal. Neither of them gets on top. They stay face-to-face on their sides, and the movement is scarcely happening. Overlying this is screaming that Tessa and Brian can't hear. Tessa and Brian aren't here anymore. It's bizarre. It's as if they see El Dorado in the banality of the other. Humiliating, shameful, a body is a shame. An inert body is a shame. It can do nothing but think. It can only wonder at a healthy penis violet with blood and a blooming rose of softest-soft flesh fitting together like a childish idiom—a lock into a key, puzzle pieces, a tunnel taking the train chugga chugga woo woo—delighting in the childish, in the simplification, because the mind within the inert body understands, now, when the epiphany no longer matters, that this process, which I have always mistaken for simple, is not. This process is everything else, except for simple. *That* is shame, a shame, *the* shame: whom can an inert body tell? Whom could they tell, these two who are anything but inert? Tessa can't keep looking at him; it's too much. Her head drags backward, and she mews at the fourth post on the bed. But Brian follows—shame! humiliation!—and he's showing her he understands: It's too much, but keep looking at me. Keep looking, Tess.

This is why sex isn't meant to be watched. It's meant to be participated in, not watched, unless it's staged to be watched, as in pornography, which is banality resigned to itself, and therefore not embarrassing beyond one's being privy to the size and shape and color of a stranger's sex organs. Tess, keep looking—this is what Brian is telling her, without telling her aloud—and he is not saying it to anyone watching. He is unaware that anyone is watching, which is why he's able to do it this way, meld with her this way, and—scarcely moving—make her squeak high in her throat. Brian is smiling, but not lasciviously, not in pride. He is glad. He's merely glad, but there's nothing mere in that, nothing banal. He's holding her hips still, where they want to rut at him. He is exacting. Tessa is squeaking, fighting to move, and then no longer fighting. Tessa has entered some trance. She sings in an inhuman language. Brian is nodding, reassuring: I've got you. I've got you. You're safe.

The Killer wanted Jules to fight, but she wouldn't. Justin stares, unseeing, out the sliding glass door. The penthouses both have decks with sun chairs. The regular penthouse has a hot tub on the deck. The deluxe penthouse has a hot tub in the bedroom, where Tessa's squeaking has formed the rough equivalent of Brian's name, and sweat stands out on his body, all of it, and Tessa has grabbed the fourth post of the bed, and Brian comes with a cry of surprise, and it lasts so long, it surpasses embarrassing into funny, and the minute vibrations of suppressed laughter might make the chair with wheels roll, but I don't care; this is just ridiculous.

The Thinker looks up from his game of solitaire. I hold very still. I hold my breath. The Thinker gets up, and then walks to me. Right behind me. I try to remember where my eyes were looking the last time he looked at me.

It's embarrassing to care, still, after pissing and shitting in this chair. Why live? Why wish to keep living?

Why ask these questions, when the Thinker is bending forward to check this broken body for signs of life? Hold your breath. Stare at the monitor you saw when you first fell—the one that shows the fountain in the center of the maze—while chaos took over behind you and your men bellowed from the searing, white flash. The monitor beside it (bottom row, third column) shows the employee break room. The Tupperware for Vivica's huevos rancheros is soaking in the sink. The Killer put it there and added soap. The soap is curdling. The Thinker is reaching toward my neck to check for a pulse, when his phone buzzes. He stops. His mask tilts as he considers. He's considering how unlikely it is that this broken body could be alive. Practically impossible. It's embarrassing to him that he thought such a thing, when obviously the chair must have moved, minutely, due to explainable phenomena involving weight displacement and time. He's turning away, sitting down on the floor again, and tapping his phone to read a text. Then he's looking at the monitors.

At Jules, who groans and bleeds and cries in her corner. The Killer stabbed her in areas of the torso that would not result in death. It looks like he hit her in the head with the butt of the knife—half her face is glazed in blood—but not hard enough to incapacitate her. He receives a text and reads it.

Tessa is weeping. Clinging fast to Brian and weeping. "I'm sorry. I shouldn't have—I was so mad at you for such a long time. I wasted so much time."

Brian pulls the covers over them. "Tess, don't cry." Then Brian begins confessing. Specifics about Mitch, how many conversations, how many arguments he and Mitch had about Tessa. How he, Brian, never really argued that he himself should be the one for her, though he knew Tessa loved him more. Because he, Brian, felt that was an unfair advantage, somehow. He confesses, now, how stupid that was. He laughs at how stupid, but Tessa's drying his eyes—really, this is nauseating—and he says, "It was this whole other layer of guilt. After Mitch died. Because it kind of, I can barely say it, but it cleared the way for me. With you. He even talked once about how we could share you, make up a schedule—he was high at the time, but I still busted his lip."

"Sounds like him," Tessa says, smiling.

"It was more than Mitch, though. I can't pawn it all off on him. It was me. It was—it was our parents ditching us when we were two. I've looked into it. I hired a PI and everything. Tracked 'em down. They're still alive. They've got a whole mess of kids, live in Pacoima, in this dump with a dirt lawn. They're drunks, both of them."

Tessa puts Brian's head between her breasts and plays with his hair.

The Killer is walking down the stairs of the regular penthouse, flicking blood off his knife in quick whipping motions. Spatters dot the wallpaper, the carpet. He arrives in the eighteenth-floor hallway. Crosses it. Puts his card key into the lock of Room 1802, the deluxe penthouse.

The lock flashes red.

I smile. The Thinker is boxing up his cards. There are only two keys that access Room 1802. One is on the nightstand beside Tessa. The other is in my pocket.

The Killer pushes on the door. The doors are constructed so as not to give in the slightest without card key access. They have no exterior handles, only locks. The Killer's push therefore makes no noise inside Room 1802. The Killer tries his card key again. The lock again flashes red.

I smile.

Brian says, "I saw them. I watched them. I went to talk to them, but I ended up watching, for hours and hours. Parked my bike and camped out on a bus bench across from their house. This was about a month ago. I was going to ask them—man, a trillion things. I'd planned to tell them about Mitch. The PI said they were drunks, but I still wasn't—the woman came out to get the mail, and she wasn't wearing any fucking pants. Just her underwear and this blouse it looked like she hadn't washed in forever. She watched TV all day, same chair, and about six or seven different brats—at least one set of twins—around the house, all around her. Maybe if I'd gone on a weekday. I went on a Saturday, so the kids weren't in school. I went on a Saturday so I could meet the dad, too. But the dad paints houses, and he didn't get home till almost dark, and he went inside, and in the window, the woman gets up and goes and jumps on him, right in front of the kids. He takes her up against the wall—hand to God, Tess—right in front of the kids, and the kids don't even care." Brian pushes his face into Tessa's right breast. It seems to comfort him.

Tessa also comforts him, saying, "They're missing out, not knowing you," and kissing the top of his head.

"I thought of you," Brian says. "I thought, looking at them, 'At least I can hire a PI and get a look. Tess can't do that.' And after that, I was itching for an excuse, any excuse, to come see you. So when I'm buying the paper one day and I see you on the travel magazine, I was like, 'Well, there we go.'"

Tessa says, "There we go," and then she begins confessing. About how she hired a PI, too, and he turned up five women who might have thrown a baby in a Spokane Dumpster, but one of the women was black, one Latina, so that made three, since Tessa is whitest white. How the trail led into the mountains of northern Washington State, another trail to Canada, another to Florida, and Tessa decided it didn't matter. She didn't need to know. She was fine by herself, she was okay alone. But she wasn't, she says; she isn't. She's been imagining Brian beside her in bed since he left for the motocross circuit when she was fourteen, and she's been imagining him sexually since before that, from about thirteen. She had a dream about him kissing her and touching her naked body when she was thirteen years old and he was asleep two feet away from her. Which was why she started sleeping in her own bed, down the hall.

Brian's mouth falls open. "Are you serious?"

The Killer is winding up to kick the door of Room 1802, the deluxe penthouse. He doesn't do it, because his phone lights up, in his hand, where he just finished sending a message to the Thinker about this unexpected turn of events: a scant few hours until the morning security shift arrives, two people left alive in the hotel, and he can't get to them.

Well, four people alive: there's also he, the Killer, and there's also Jules, whose cries emanate through the door to Room 1801, the regular penthouse, which the Killer left open.

Six people left alive, counting the twentieth floor.

Jules sounds—disturbingly childlike. She's still in her corner. She looks at Justin, and she cries and she cries. It never takes the form of a word, like "Help." It sounds like a siren whose batteries are dying.

The Killer reads his text and looks where Jules's cries are coming from.

"Don't," says Tessa. She hides behind a pillow. "Don't look at me like that. It's embarrassing."

"Why?" Brian says, tugging the pillow down. He's laughing. "Tess, Jesus, that's the most awesome thing I've ever heard!" He's hugging her.

"Are you sure? You're sure you're not perv'd out?"

"Baby, if you knew . . ."

"Knew what?"

Brian continues confessing. One gets the feeling he has never said the following out loud: he was twelve, for the first one. He woke up on the floor, his body cold and hot at the same time. He must not have made a noise, because Tessa was still snoring, there, in his bed. Mitch, of course, stayed asleep. Brian got clean underwear and pajama pants and changed in the bathroom, not knowing what to do. Very confused. Very, very upset. Lots of head scratching. Luckily, Troy was home that weekend, and on Sunday, when Mitch left the shed to get sodas, Brian asked Troy whether he should be worried that his peener was spitting stuff all over his jockey shorts at night.

Tessa laughs, sedately, full of endorphins and petting him. "Troy was cool about it, wasn't he?"

Brian affirms that Troy put down the five-eighths (they were rebuilding a Harley engine from scratch) and explained to Brian that no, he should not be worried. He should know, in fact, that it was a hundred percent normal. Was it a girl from his class? Yes, Brian said adamantly, yes, it was a girl from his class. Brian tells Tessa, no, it was not a girl from his class. It was Tessa. It has almost exclusively been Tessa all his life, which is weird and he knows it. He's been with other women, a pretty solid number of them, especially after Mitch died, but he has, only on maybe a half-dozen occasions, *dreamed* of other women, and he has very rarely masturbated to other women, and Tessa is now laughing and hugging Brian, and I want to vomit.

"Troy said to use tissues, hide the magazines, sponge the sheets if it happened at night. They didn't know you slept with us. I never did it with you next to me. Not once. That would've been—no."

Tessa's pensive. She feathers his hair between her fingers. Her teeth worry her lower lip, until Brian puts his thumb where her teeth are biting. She licks it. Not mischievous. Docile, like a cat.

"Tell me," says Brian.

"What?"

"What you're thinking."

She runs a finger over his eyebrow, which rises at this pause, this reluctance.

"Please?" he says.

"I stopped sleeping with him a week ago," Tessa says, and swallows. "I shouldn't have told you about him, at least that he worked here. It was only ever physical, but—"

The Killer is reentering the nondeluxe penthouse, but wild dogs couldn't pry my attention from Tessa saying,

"I tried to keep it strictly physical."

Brian looks at the bracelet on Tessa's wrist. He undoes the clasp and sets it on the bedside table; then he puts her fingertips to his mouth and kisses them. To show he is quiet. To show she should go on.

Go on, go on.

Tessa says, "He loves me way more than I deserve."

"Impossible," Brian says, and I hate him for saying it, and I hate him for getting to say it.

Tessa huffs, turns over, away from him—and Jules begins an impressive, lengthy keening scream at the sight of the Killer climbing the last few stairs; he stops at the top step, to enjoy the sound—but

Brian makes a frustrated face for all of a second before he's furled around Tessa from behind. "Tell me," he says again. "Because I need to know. This could be a problem. I'm a thousand percent sure I love you more than he does. So if you've got issues with that—"

"Have you ever felt like—like, going through what we went through, it's too much to ever explain to somebody? And the idea of even trying—you're tired before you start." She's crying again. She wipes her tears on the sheet. "What it takes to survive that when you're so small. How it never goes away, not all the way away, not ever." She shakes on a sob. Brian turns her, very carefully, so she's cradled to him. Tessa fights for a full breath and says, "If I could've told him, if I thought in a million years I could have made him understand how hard it is, even now, especially now, to feel . . ."

Alone.

I wonder if the anger is visible in my eyes. It wouldn't matter. The Thinker is composing a text message, which the Killer—listening to Jules's continuing screams like a man taking in the symphony—reads, replies to, and grudgingly obeys by walking toward her.

Whereas I, behind my death mask, roil in Tessa's self-assured, self-centered, self-fulfilling prophesy that I couldn't possibly understand her loneliness. While Brian pats and pets and shushes and squeezes, I ask Tessa, Would I be permitted to understand *now*? Now that I sit alone among the dead, death behind me, death beneath me, watching it watch you and stalk you and I'm powerless to stop it?

Just as quickly, anger is punctured by Tessa's voice in my head, asking, Are you sure I was going to say "alone"?

Brian nudges his lips to Tessa's and says, so she'll feel the shapes the words make on her own mouth, "You don't have to tell me. Or make me understand. I already know." His tongue darts out to lick a teardrop. "Don't I."

"Yes," Tessa says. "Yes."

"You wanted to love him," Brian says, "but you couldn't. You couldn't do that to him." He nips her lower lip between his teeth.

"I'm sorry," says Tessa, to Brian, to me.

They're getting turned on again. It's in their voices, but so is fatigue.

There is terrible fatigue in Jules's voice, too, as the Killer comes toward her in the bedroom of Room 1801. She moans like a toddler in a nightmare. She's wearing a brief silk nightie; it was white, and now it's red. Jules didn't help Justin fight; she sat in her corner, like this, and she moaned, like this, and when Justin could no longer fight, Jules still didn't fight, as the Killer came for her and did all this damage. There's a butter knife sticking out of Jules's right ankle. The Killer did that to hobble her. He needn't have. Terror has hobbled her.

So why does she fight now, as he reaches for her?

It's three o'clock in the morning.

It's instinct. This time it isn't more torture, more bleeding. This time it's the end. An animal knows. Jules bats at his hand with pointless, open palms. The Killer twists a fistful of her hair and pulls. Jules is dragged backward, through the bedroom. She is dragged past her dead husband, for whom she reaches, crying. It's pathetic but understandable, her display. She has regressed to a state of primal reaction. The Killer pulls her to the bedroom's stairs. Then thuds can be heard, and shrieks in time, and then they appear in the regular penthouse's entryway, and then in the eighteenth floor's hall. Blood leaves a path behind them. Jules is reaching for her ankles. Both of her ankles have butter knives through them. The Killer drops Jules against the door to Room 1802, the deluxe penthouse. He goes to the door to the stairway, opens it, and doesn't quite close it.

Brian and Tessa snuggle, speaking so low it's hard to make out under Jules's despondence, and Jules's despondence is made that much more distracting by her attempt to collect herself. She's trying to get it together. She's looking around the hallway; she's looking at the door to Room 1801 and crying anew, mumbling, "Justin, sweetie, sweetie." She is red; all of her is red. Jules licks each of her palms and tries to scrub the blood off her face. Partly she succeeds; partly she blends it. She tucks back her hair and straightens her nightgown.

"I'm not knocking on their door," Jules says. Her chin is high and proud. One might say "snobby," if one weren't, at this moment, madly in love with her. "You'll have to knock, asshole."

Jules's bravery does crumble a little when the Killer swings the stairway door wide and stands forebodingly there.

But she speaks through the crumbling. It is lovely and dreadful. "Did your mother make you those coveralls? They're nice. Very Sears."

The Killer is slow in walking to her. He is patient, standing over her.

Jules spits at him. It only hits his shin—the wounded left—but it gets the point across.

The Killer raises his right hand, which holds his blood-lathered knife. He raps his knuckles on the door, four times.

Jules screams so loudly, the Thinker, on the twentieth floor, drops a king of hearts to cover his ears. "Tessa! Don't open th—"

Even soundproof rooms have doors through which knocks must echo.

And if knocks must echo, the barest hint of a scream might do the same, no matter how efficiently the Killer was able to hack through Jules's voice box and abort the rest of the message. He avoids the arteries again. He retreats to the door to the stairs and leaves it slightly open. Jules's throat crackles like radio static.

"What's—" Tessa is bolt upright in the bed.

So is Brian. "That sounded like your friend."

Tessa's shuffling clothes, putting them on while walking. She takes Brian's undershirt by mistake. It's white, what is colloquially called a "wife-beater." Her nipples are pointed shadows underneath it.

Brian's leaping into his pants. "Wait. Wait, Tess!"

CAMERA 62, 56, 19–13, 4, 13–14, 42, X

□ □ □ □ □ □ □ □ □

Tessa's running down the spiral staircase while zipping up her skirt. She has no shoes. Brian's buckling his belt at the top of the stairs—having shoved into his boots and pulled on his shirt—when Tessa reaches the deluxe penthouse's door and wrenches it open.

It's so bright in the hall, compared to the penthouse. Jules's body tumbles backward, over the threshold, her crackling throat a slow flow of black blood, the hall light triggering a switch in the deluxe penthouse's camera feed so that it's no longer night vision, no longer green, black, and white. So that the Killer's knife, when he emerges from the stairway's door, gleams like an oblong ruby. And Tessa is bent over Jules, and Jules is whistling from the throat, and Jules's mouth mouths the word "Run" over and over again, and Brian is almost down the stairs, but the Killer moves quickly, very quickly, knife high.

It is evidently not part of the plan to leave any survivors in the hotel.

I once instructed Tessa, while she and I were boxing, "If a man attacks you and he's an amateur, yes, certainly, use a knee to the groin. But professional assault personnel wear a cup. If a man attacks you and he looks professional, then, Tessa, put everything you've got into a shin kick."

Maybe this advice plays in her head.

Maybe not.

Maybe it penetrated deep enough into her mind, when she heard it, that it became a part of her, something she'll carry as long as she lives, however long that will be.

It will be at least another few seconds, because as the Killer comes for Tessa, as Brian runs across the penthouse to save her, as Jules gurgles, Tessa crouches and curls her left leg tight to the hip, releases it with an outward snap that is like a bear trap tripped, and the arch of her foot—the powerful part—connects solidly with the Killer's wounded left shin. There is a dull *thunk*, not a *crunch* but good anyway, and the Killer makes a kind of desperate yapping noise as the pain of ripped-open cuts impedes his coordination and he windmills over the women. If the Killer were allowed to fall forward, he might impale himself on his own damn knife, but no, Brian catches him around the belly and hurls him into the kitchen. Tessa's pulling Jules up to sit against the door frame, seeing the blood, babbling, "It's okay, babe. It's okay. Don't worry," and like comments that are patently untrue. The Killer has recovered his wits, head-butts Brian, and Brian falls. The Killer raises the knife high up in both hands.

Tessa screams so loudly, the Thinker returns to the security counter. The Thinker is searching for the audio feed volume. The audio feed volume is digital. It requires a code. The Thinker presses random buttons. The foyer's chandelier goes dark, and the fountain in the maze's center lights up and jets water at the night sky. The Thinker flaps an impatient wave at the controls and goes back to his cards.

Brian rolls out of the path of the knife. The Killer uses so much force that he stabs through the carpet and into the flooring. He's trying to pull the knife free when Tessa kicks him in the face. This time, there is a crunch. There is also wonderful, awful banshee screeching that any sane person would run away from, coming from Tessa's mouth. The Killer cannot run. He tries to catch Tessa's feet as they pummel him. Blood leaks out of his mask. He catches her foot, turns it, and she falls to the floor with a thud. She hits her head, but the carpet is stupidly thick. The Killer is wrapping his hands around Tessa's throat when Brian leaps on his back. The Killer stands, reverses into the kitchen and into the refrigerator. Brian bounces off. Brian ducks a punch that dents the refrigerator, runs around the Killer and helps Tessa stand. "Stairs! Stairs!" Brian shouts as the Killer selects the biggest knife from the knife block. He pulls out a spare and rears back to throw it at Brian, but Tessa stumbles, so Brian falters, so the knife flips past where Brian's head was a half second ago and embeds into the door frame with a *thwummm*. Tessa grabs for Jules, but Jules is dead. Brian propels Tessa and himself through the door to the stairwell.

"Hurry!" Brian says. "Hurry! Hurry! Go!"

"Is he behind us?"

"No! He must be taking the elevator! Hurry, Tess! We can beat him—go, go!"

The Killer's shoulders quiver with rage. He steps over Jules. He hustles across the hall, into the regular penthouse, across the living room, into the secret elevator. He hits the "Lobby" button and turns around.

Jules, not dead, smiles at him and raises a stiff middle finger right as the secret elevator's seam sews shut. She laughs. It's a gurgling sound. She wiggles so she can fall back to the floor. She flops around as her own blood drowns her.

"Go! C'mon, Tess, hurry!"

Brian and Tessa are running past the eleventh floor.

The Killer, in the secret elevator, passes the ninth floor.

There are no lights on in the foyer. It is dark as a grave. Until headlights bathe it bright. There's a Lamborghini tracing the horseshoe of the parking lot. It's Charles Destin's Lamborghini.

"Who is he?" Tessa says, running. They are passing the eighth floor. "Who'd want to do this?"

The Killer is passing the second floor.

The Thinker is watching Charles Destin pull on Manderley's front doors. Destin curses at finding them locked. He has a woman with him. She's wearing a short, thin gold dress and big hoop earrings. Destin says something to her about "a scenario" and rolls his eyes. He takes her hand and leads her around the outer perimeter of the hotel.

The Killer is in Franklin's office. He limps past the desk and filing cabinets, out, past the check-in counter and the information desk. He goes to the stairway door and stands to the side of it, knife in both hands again, high above his head.

"Go!" Brian says. "Go, go, go!"

He and Tessa are running past the fourth floor.

The Killer is waiting.

Charles Destin is at the back door to Manderley, the one Brian and Tessa exited to visit the pool. Destin likes to bring women to Manderley for tours, though he rarely does this on Tuesdays. He is opening the back door.

The Killer's head turns to the sound of the back door. To the sound of Brian and Tessa, on the stairs ("Go! Go, Tess!") as they run past the second floor. The Killer goes toward the back door. He is most of the way there when Destin says, "Voilà!" and flips on the chandelier.

The woman screams. The Killer has the knife high. Destin manages to say, "Who—?" before the knife's length disappears into the top of the woman's head. Her eyes become all whites. The stairway door flies open. The Killer lifts the knife, and the woman rises off the ground a few inches, before sliding off and making a pile of skin and bones and thin gold fabric on the floor. The chandelier is bright, now specked with red splats from a geyser that shot from the dead woman's head, and Destin is running for the front doors. Brian and Tessa are also running for the front doors, and the Killer is limping after them. His legs are long; he is still impressively fast. As Tessa screams, "Del, oh my G—," Brian is screaming, "Go, Tess!" but Destin shoves Tessa as all three of them near the exit. Tessa slaloms to the left. Destin is a strong man, and determined. Tessa bashes into the fireplace, unsettling the mantel. Delores's head falls and rolls. Brian runs to help Tessa. Destin gets to the doors and pulls on them, taking for granted they'll open. They don't open. The Killer is directly behind him. The Killer stabs, but Destin evades, does a move from his lacrosse days, runs through the wreckage of Delores, and slips. The Killer is running for him, and slips. The both of them bobble hopelessly through the bloody lobby like a pair of children

trying to do a standing run down a Slip 'N Slide. Brian and Tessa
watch. It's too strange a sight not to watch. Tessa's perhaps thinking
how, this afternoon, Destin greeted her with a hello and a kiss to each
cheek before reading the riot act to his every other employee. Tessa
bleeds from a small cut on her right cheek, from the mantel. Her left
hand is bleeding again, through her bandage. The Killer's arm draws
back, and the knife whips forward, whirls, sticks—with a *thwap*—in
Charles Destin's neck. He falls forward.

It would appear Destin didn't bankroll this hell after all.

Brian rockets forward, pulling Tessa toward the back exit, but
the Killer moves to block them, and so Brian and Tessa of one mind
divert to the stairway door again, and climb.

"Where's fucking security?" says Tessa, her voice like a choir in
the stairwell.

"This floor, c'mon!" Brian says, stepping up to four, letting Tessa
precede him into the hallway. The carpet is white, the walls white, the
doors white with gold numbers on them, and card key locks of gold-
plated steel. Brian puts his back to the stairway door and whispers,
"We'll hear him pass us."

Tessa shakes her head, takes his hand, and leads him to a bend in
the hallway. They somehow avoided the quarts and quarts of blood
that have spilled in the lobby, so Brian's boots and Tessa's bare feet
leave no prints. Brian puts an arm around her. He lays a finger to his
lips. They listen.

The Killer is sitting on the arm of a reception sofa, pulling up his
pant leg to check his wounds. His shin is bleeding, but not badly. It
isn't that serious, but it's an annoyance.

The Thinker is pulling up a seat at the security counter. Right
beside me. He deposits a playing card facedown in front of my open

eyes. Then a card in front of him. Then another card in front of me, until both of us have five cards. The Thinker picks up the five cards he dealt this seeming-dead man and studies them. It's a hand of poker.

The Killer rolls down his pant leg and stands. He skirts the sofa, bends, and stands again with Delores's head in his right hand. In his left hand is the knife that he pulled, laboriously, from Destin's neck. The Killer places Delores's head back on the mantel and goes to Destin, who is not dead but dying. Destin has crawled so that only his feet are visible around the check-in desk, with the angle of Camera 4. There are other angles available, but they are higher in the bank of monitors, and I can't look because the Thinker is studying my poker hand. It's a good hand, one card from a full house. The Thinker makes a sound of displeasure and deals two new hands.

The Killer walks toward Charles Destin, and Destin's feet become frantic. The Killer bends to him, and his feet become still more frantic. The Killer's elbow appears periodically, in a sawing motion.

The fourth-floor hallway is high in the bank of monitors. But if one cannot look, one can at least listen.

Brian's voice (in a whisper): "What's taking him so long?"

Tessa's: "Jesus Christ, Jesus Christ, Je—"

Brian's: "Maybe he took the elevator."

Tessa's: "Christ, Jesus—"

Brian's: "How's your head?"

Tessa's: "He killed Jules. God. God, he—"

Brian's: "Stay calm. We need to stay calm."

Tessa's (hissing): "You be calm!"

Brian's: "That's the spirit."

Tessa's (laughing, sort of): "We're gonna die."

Brian's (serious): "No. No we're not."

Tessa's (crying and trying not to): "No. We're not. We're not gonna die."

Brian's: "Again."

Tessa's: "We're not gonna die."

Brian's: "One more time."

Tessa's (voice like a diamond's edge): "We're gonna live. We're gonna live."

Brian's: "We live. That's how this goes. Both of us."

Tessa's: "Right. Why's—what's—"

Brian's: "Doesn't matter. It's happening. This is what's happening now. So say it again."

Tessa's: "Both of us live."

Brian's (a kissing noise): "Where's he bleeding? I didn't notice."

Tessa's: "Left shin. And I think I broke his nose."

She did. The Killer is taking tissues from a box on the check-in desk and rolling tubes to stick up his nostrils, under his mask. He bends and rises with Destin's head in his right hand, knife in his left. He goes to the mantel and puts Destin's head beside Delores's.

Brian's: "Fire alarms?"

Tessa's (sounding regretful): "If the phone lines are—wait."

(long pause)

The Killer looks in the direction of the stairway door. He sags. He takes out his phone, taps, and types.

The Thinker's phone vibrates on the security counter. He puts down two pairs, jacks high, and taps. The Killer's message reads, "Leg hurts help with these 2."

The Thinker types, "I'll help when necessary. Division of labor." He sends, stands, and walks to the east windows.

The Killer's phone lights up; he reads. He roars and kicks the check-in counter. Then he grabs his shin and stabs the check-in counter. Then he crosses the foyer, kicking Delores's severed foot every few steps like a crabby kid with a tin can.

Tessa and Brian are hunkered low in the hallway. He's holding her with his whole body, trying to look in all directions. Tessa's telling him, "That phone. The one I took from the sous-chef earlier."

"Yes!" Brian's saying, shaking her. "Where is it?"

"By the damn dishwasher, on the fucking nineteenth floor. Jesus, shit, it takes at least ten minutes for the cops to get here."

"What do you mean? I thought your security people ran drills all the—"

"They do. That's why it takes so long. LAPD's sick of us testing their response time. After that bomb threat last week, the police chief said he was putting Manderley at the bottom of their priority list until we opened. He said to expect a ten-minute wait, and then only one car would come."

Brian knocks his head into the wall and steels himself. "What the fuck ever, it's an idea. Elevator or stairs?"

"How'd he get to the lobby so fast?"

"Good question." Brian looks at Tessa for the answer.

She shrugs. She's shaking. Brian, all around her, is shaking.

He holds a finger to his lips. Then he points to the jounce of wide steps mounting the stairs. Brian and Tessa should be panicking. Even a seasoned professional, in a situation such as this, might panic. Even a team of them. Brian and Tessa are afraid, pale with fear. Brian has wiped the blood from Tessa's cheek with his right hand, and has wiped his right hand on his jeans. Now, as they listen to the Killer—who knows exactly where they are, via text message—it might occur to Brian, as confusion sharpens his eyes, how strange it is that the Killer isn't doing a floor-by-floor search. Tessa's eyes are wide, but then they narrow, thinking the same thing. It's Tessa whose neck slowly rotates to the smoke detector in the hallway, where the hallway surveillance cameras are hidden. It's Tessa who slips from Brian's grasp and pulls him up silently. He's protesting; the steps are close. The Killer is two risers from the concrete landing on the fourth floor. Tessa pulls Brian to the opposite bend in the hallway—the right side instead of the left side. Brian looks at her like she's insane, but she motions him to be still, as the fourth-floor door clicks open and the Killer's boots sink into the plush carpet.

The Thinker texts twice, hurriedly, placing his phone on my royal flush—"Other corner!" "She's figured out the cameras!"

The Killer's pocket lights up, but he isn't expecting a text message. A ring tone would eliminate his stealth.

The Thinker springs for the secret elevator, boards, and presses and presses the button for the fourth floor.

The Killer, if he were smart, would be watching the floor for anomalous shadows, and he would see there is an irregularity to the right instead of to the left at the bend in the hallway. Tessa and Brian are flat to the wall. Tessa is closer to the bend than Brian is. He doesn't like this; it's written all over him. The two of them are watching the Killer's undaunted shadow. Then the toes of the Killer's boots. The bloodied nose of the Killer's mask, as it turns away from them, to the left of the bend. He raises his knife—and Tessa kicks, again with the bare hard arch of her foot, into the back of the Killer's left knee. At the same moment, she lets fly a fist into his right kidney, as hard as she can. Brian goes for the knife, wrenching the Killer's arm back and to an angle. The angle is unnatural for a human, but it looks oddly like a chicken wing. The Killer flails in a delightfully chickenlike way toward the floor, crashing to one knee as Tessa kicks the other knee and begins kicking him in the ribs. Brian attempts to make the angle of the Killer's arm still more dramatically wrong, but that's when a sliding noise happens inside the cleaning closet, which is right in front of them. Neither Brian nor Tessa notices; they are occupied.

The cleaning closet door crashes open, and the Thinker slashes with his standard issue Navy SEAL field knife toward Brian's heart, but the Killer's knife is flailing, and the Killer's knife clatters against the Thinker's knife with a sound like a small bell.

Brian jumps backward on reflex, and the Thinker's knife's downward trajectory catches Tessa in the right shoulder. It embeds, shallowly. She screams. The Thinker jerks it out, and Tessa screams. The Killer is struggling to get up, but Tessa's fallen onto him. The Thinker goes for Brian again, but the Killer—jostling his feet around for purchase—accidentally trips the Thinker. Brian catches the Thinker with two hard punches to the face, while Tessa sees Vivica inside the secret elevator. Her mouth falls open and snaps shut. She covers it, swallows hard, and remembers the Killer, flailing under her insubstantial weight. She walks on her knees to his right hand and kneels on it. The Killer lets go of his knife. But now his body is free. He dodders to a crouch. Tessa uses her only opening and stabs him in the side. He howls. The Thinker took Brian's punches to get a good shot at his body cavity. He plunges for Brian with the knife, but Tessa is a dervish. She turns and plunges, blindly, and catches the Thinker in the thigh. She is screaming, pulling the blade out and stabbing the Thinker in the thigh—his right—twice more, before the Killer takes a handful of her hair and grabs her neck in both hands to break it.

Brian is screaming. Brian has lost his mind. He head-butts the Killer five times in such fast succession that his movements blur on the monitor. Tessa eels out of the Killer's hold and shoves Brian into the secret elevator. She hits the button for the nineteenth floor. The Killer and the Thinker grunt in protest, but the elevator door slides shut. The cleaning closet remains open, the shelves sideways. Brian and Tessa don't have a controller. The Thinker laughs.

He points at his hip, where his controller is clipped to his coveralls. He taps his temple to indicate his own superior intelligence. The Killer nods tiredly. The Killer and the Thinker examine their wounds while they wait for the secret elevator to journey to the nineteenth floor and arrest behind the juice concentrate shelf, Brian and Tessa panicking and screaming inside about why there is a wall in front of them when the secret elevator door slides open. Their shouts and battering at it will earn them nothing, no exit. And the secret elevator will time out after ninety seconds, if the juice concentrate shelf is not signaled to move aside by a controller. Then, per programming I designed in order to reduce the risk of security team infiltration, it will return to the fourth floor, with Brian and Tessa trapped inside.

CAMERA X, 34, 33

□ □ □ □ □ □ □ □ □

What's actually happening is that Tessa is clinging to Brian, whimpering, and Brian is trying to stay between Tessa and Vivica's body. He's telling Tessa, "Don't look at her. Keep it together. Keep it together, Tess. I need you here. Little Tasmanian devil. Right? Like fourth grade all over again." Brian is checking her shoulder and shaking his head. And the secret elevator is opening into the walk-in refrigerator, where Delores boarded several hours ago, leaving the juice concentrate shelf wide-open. Brian is guiding Tessa out of the secret elevator, manually keeping her lines of sight to the front of his chest and walking sideways. He clears the disheveled barricade Delores erected and the Killer shoved past at the walk-in refrigerator door. Tessa jumps when the secret elevator hums alive and sinks out of sight.

Brian turns to her. "Tess? Are you here? Are you with me?"

She nods and makes a glugging sound.

Brian takes a rope of her hair just in time as Tessa aims sideways and vomits. She hasn't eaten much today. Bile sprinkles the red and green peppers on the walk-in refrigerator's floor. When she's done, Brian takes a corner of his shirt and cleans her mouth.

"How are you so calm?" Tessa says.

"I don't know," says Brian.

I'd hazard flying through the air with a running motor vehicle that you have to land on two wheels requires a certain stress tolerance.

The Thinker flicks blood off his thigh cantankerously. The Killer unbuttons a few buttons on his coveralls and palpates a gouge well below his right kidney. It's regrettable—but, come on, understandable—that I never taught Tessa how to inflict stab wounds for maximum damage. She asked for self-defense training, not kill tactics.

Brian and Tessa cross the kitchen. Tessa sees the cell phone and runs to it. She reaches for it, or tries to, but her right arm won't lift. She looks at it, away from it. She sways as if trying not to pass out.

"I'll do it, Tess, siddown."

"No." She's dialing with her left hand. "They'll ask for a security clearance code."

Brian checks her wound again. The knife slit her shoulder blade like an envelope. The bone is visible through a tear in her wife-beater. Brian goes to get the first aid kit, pauses by the knife block. He takes a big butcher knife and a meat cleaver.

The secret elevator is sinking past the fifth floor. The Killer and the Thinker stand ready on the fourth floor. They are angry. They are agog with anger when the secret elevator sinks into view, and in it, only the pile of Vivica. The Thinker turns to the Killer, and the Killer shrugs. The Thinker points to him, to the secret elevator, and the Thinker himself goes to the stairs. The Killer is getting on the secret elevator. Why would he check his hip for a controller that, until now, has reliably been there? He wouldn't. He doesn't. But if he did, he would see that it unclipped from his hip pocket when Tessa leaped on him and that it fell to the carpet, where it still lies.

The Thinker takes his time coming up the stairs. He believes this will be simple now, with the element of surprise and the Killer arriving ahead of him, doing most of the work.

Tessa is whisper-shrieking into the phone, "This isn't a scenario! People are dead!" while Brian puts a large bandage on her bleeding shoulder and watches the ballroom's stairway door and the walk-in refrigerator's door simultaneously.

Why would it be a problem that the Killer doesn't have his controller? If Brian and Tessa successfully gained the nineteenth floor, then the juice concentrate shelf must be opened aside—goes the logic, and the logic is correct. It wouldn't be a problem, except the controllers work like garage door openers. There have been issues with garage door openers being coded too alike and opening other garages if they're in close proximity. This has been a problem, sometimes, with the controllers in the hotel. Specifically, with the head of security's controller, which was scheduled to be fixed this week. My controller sometimes opened the door on the floor I was on, as well as the door on the floor below me (which is currently the nineteenth floor's shelf of juice concentrate). It was frustrating.

It was frustrating to feel a knife sever my spinal cord while I was in midreach for my gun, on my hip, where my controller is clipped. It is a physical fact that parts of the brachial plexus attach higher than the third vertebra.

It's impossible. But try. Move your finger. Find where it is in space—there. It is visibly moving, on the monitor for the twentieth floor. The Killer is passing the twelfth floor. He's angry; he's trembling with anger. Tessa is on the nineteenth floor, slapping the dishwasher and yelling, "He hung up! He said he's sending one unit and it'll be ten minutes and he fucking hung up. Brian, Jesus, Jesus Christ, what now?"

And Brian is taking her face in his hands. "Now? We live."

Tessa is breaking down.

"Tess? Say it to me."

My finger is wiggling an inch and a half from the button of my controller. The Killer is passing the seventeenth floor. The Thinker is climbing past the tenth floor, on the stairs, and Tessa is saying, "We live. We're gonna live," but she doesn't sound convinced.

Brian is saying, "Like you mean it."

Mean it. Reach. Remember diving underwater and swimming until you fell unconscious, brother SEALs dragging you back up to air, and seven-minute miles for ten miles, and rappelling out of choppers with a rifle already aimed, and loving her, you loved her, you still do. It's folly, but so what. She'll visit you in the hospital when all this is over, when you've rasped to the men who find you that you're alive, I'm alive, and she'll weep on your hospital sheets and you can know, then, that you did this, this inch and a half. You won't tell her, but you'll know.

Tessa is fearsome when she means to be. "We're gonna live. They're gonna die, and we're gonna live."

The Killer is passing the eighteenth floor.

The sinews in my fingers ache. It feels so good; it *feels*. The tip of the nail on my right index scrapes across the controller's button. And the wall on the twentieth floor slides shut.

And the shelf of juice concentrate, on the nineteenth floor, slides shut.

The Killer, in the secret elevator, rising to the nineteenth floor, tilts his head. He reaches for his hip. The controller isn't there. The secret elevator arrives at the level of the nineteenth floor, and the Killer pats and pats his hip as if hoping his hip will magically become a controller.

The inert skull, on the twentieth floor, on the security counter, smiles.

The Thinker is tiring. He's stomping up the stairs, passing the fourteenth floor. His thigh drips.

Brian puts the cell phone in his back pocket. He gives the knife to Tessa and keeps the meat cleaver. They leave the kitchen, unknowingly using perfect two-man SEAL team formation, back-to-back but alternating isosceles directions, to cover all ground. They're in the center of the ballroom, surrounded by tables with white tablecloths. Hundreds of white napkins have been folded into sailboats. Tessa and Brian are like scared gods in a bleached sea.

"Cops are here in ten minutes?" says Brian.

"Yeah. One car."

"That one car gets a look in the lobby, he'll call the National Guard."

"Right." Tessa's examining the disturbed areas by the bandstand, the abandoned squeegee, the table sprinkled in bits of crystal. "Won't even need to open the door. Entryway's all glass." She sees the glass behind the bandstand, noting its crackled appearance.

"You know this place," Brian says. "Do we take that hidden elevator back down?"

"I didn't know that was there. I don't know how it's controlled. Main elevator?"

"It's too damn slow. If they figure out we're on it, they'll be waiting for us."

Tessa blows hair out of her lashes, puts the knife on a dinner plate, and winds most of her hair into a bun. "I'm sorry I got you into this."

"Tess, I'd rather be with you here than with anybody else anywhere."

Her laugh sounds strange. She takes up the knife again. "That's crazy, Bri. That's Mitch-level crazy."

The Thinker has slowed. Saunters past the fifteenth floor.

The Killer, in the secret elevator, has used up his ninety seconds, and sinks. He punches the secret elevator's wall, and a hole appears.

Brian says, calm, eyes fixed and wide on the stairway door, "Do you believe in angels?"

"Nope," says Tessa.

"Mitch appeared to me the night before I did the triple. He told me I was going to over-rotate on the third turn, compensating for how he under-rotated on it. He said that's what I was going to do and it'd get me killed. He told me to shoot for even rotation, except on the third turn, because that's when inertia would start to flatten." Brian is too calm. "He said he'd help."

Tessa's silent.

"And I did it."

"You were dreaming," Tessa says.

"I was awake."

"You projected him."

"Yeah, maybe." Brian must hear the Thinker's footfalls on the stairway because his stare lasers in that direction.

On the fourth floor, the secret elevator opens and the Killer tears out of it, surging into the stairway like a rogue wave and taking the steps three at a time.

Brian tells Tessa, "Stay here," and says as he walks toward the stairway door, "It's just weird. The photo in the magazine. I knew you wouldn't sleep with a jerk like that. But I still had to see you. I thought about it every day for the past month and a half at least, but it was like somebody was telling me to wait. Then this morning, I knew this was it. Tonight, I had to be with you tonight. The whole ride up here, it was like somebody was at my back, pushing me."

"Mitch?" Tessa says. She says it not like it's a confirmation of something, but like she's talking to someone. She's looking at the cracked window behind the bandstand. Outside it, nothing is visible but night, glittering like a flawed cut of onyx.

"Yeah. Mitch," Brian says. "Quiet. He's coming."

Tessa turns from the window and grabs a dinner plate. She does it decisively, as if someone in high authority gave her a direct order. She flips the plate upside down as the stairway door pulls violently open, and Brian strikes with the cleaver, but the Thinker isn't there; the Thinker is smart, the Thinker stood to the side, knowing Brian would strike because there were no screams from the ballroom, meaning the Killer hasn't gotten there yet. And the Thinker is aiming a gun, having evidently decided these two final victims are sufficient pains in the ass that a firearm is preferable to a knife. Brian is bent forward with his assault at empty air, but Tessa throws the plate like a Frisbee, as hard as she can, and it cuts through the distance like a bad special-effects spaceship. It shouldn't smash into the Thinker's mask, but it does, it does, it hits him on the chin. The plate fairly disintegrates. There's a thunder of footsteps coming up the stairs, a primeval yell of irate pain. The Thinker shakes ceramic from his rubber face, and his dropped .45 fires a hole into the ballroom's east wall. Brian overbalances, wobbles, and chops into the backmost part of the Thinker's right shoulder.

I scream, "Why always the shoulders?" My voice comes out a croak from nearly twelve hours of silence, but it feels lovely to vent.

The Thinker shouts, drops his knife, and Brian takes two fists of coveralls and throws. The Thinker totters into a pair of tables, falls in a thoroughfare of dishes and linens and flowers, and Tessa is advancing toward him with her own knife as Brian picks up the Thinker's knife from the floor. "Brian!" Tessa screams as the Killer appears behind him, but too late—the Killer's fist still glances Brian's forehead as Brian weaves to avoid it. The Killer is exceedingly angry. He propels Brian backward, through the tables. Brian is bleeding from the forehead. The Killer picks him up and propels him past Tessa, who tries to catch him. She tries to stab the Killer, but the Killer backhands her, and she falls. Brian has dropped his knife. The Killer hits and kicks him. Directing him toward the bandstand, the stage, as if this murder will be a piece of performance art, and it will doubtlessly be exactly that. It will be what the Killer wishes he'd done to Delores, compounded by what these two have done to him, the annoyance of pain, the inconvenience. It will be pieces on every plate in every place setting, morsels left for the morning shift of the security team, who will be the first to walk through the nightmare Manderley has become. Though, somehow, the pyramid of a thousand champagne flutes still stands in the ballroom's southeast corner.

A police car traces Manderley's long driveway. It putters down the gravel at the posted speed limit of seventeen and a half miles per hour, which seems random, and it is. The randomness is what makes people look at the sign and slow. The cruiser approaches the main doors. Delores is there, or some of Delores, and most of Destin. Some of them is smeared on the windows. The police car's brakes screech like a pterodactyl, and the vehicle reverses from the main doors until its right-rear tire is twenty feet from the hedge maze. Red and blue lights begin to whirl. No one gets out of the car.

Brian's bleeding from the forehead, nose, and one ear. He's stumbling backward, and up the stairs of the bandstand, toward the glass. He trips, and the Killer kicks him, backward. Brian knocks over a music stand.

Tessa sits up. She holds her head. She roots around in her mouth and throws a tooth on the floor disinterestedly. She stands. She's walking toward the bandstand, when the Thinker grabs her ankle. She lets out a yell that curdles the blood. She takes a fork off the nearest table, basically falls with it, with all her weight behind it, and the tines bury themselves into the Thinker's left wrist. He screams. Tessa stands up, smashes her knee into his mask, and walks away from him like his unconsciousness is boring. She looks at the stage like she's watching a play she hates. The Killer is standing over Brian. Staring down at Brian. Brian is coughing. The Killer steps on Brian's chest. He begins to apply pressure. It takes a lot of pressure to crack a sternum. It'll take the Killer a few seconds.

And Tessa is moving like this is a dance. The Killer doesn't see her in the reflection of the glass, because the glass is broken. Tessa's bleeding from the mouth. She's crying silently.

"Tess," Brian's saying, gasping, the pressure on his chest increasing. He can see, as clearly as I can see—perhaps (of course) he can see more clearly—the look on Tessa's face. He's holding the Killer's foot, trying and failing to twist it, and he's twisting inside, because Tessa's decided something. She climbs the few steps to the stage, and her posture changes. All of her changes, because she's become in this instant, quintessentially, the person she's always been.

She's twenty-five feet behind the Killer.

Enough for an excellent running start.

Most would say their favorite part of the landscape here is the ocean, but a few, who want to be different—the people who most want to be different are those most likely to be like everyone else—would say they favor the mountains. I think the best part of any landscape is its highway. I didn't always. I was stationed in Hawaii when I was twenty years old. The beach near the barracks was volcanic rock, which I'd never seen. The other guys thought it was ugly or beautiful—those were the words they used—but I thought it simply was. I'd wake early and do extra PT, mostly so I could watch the sun coming up over the other islands far distant. Hardened lava made shapes against my backside where I sat. I meant to go to Kauai, and I never did. It was right there. It was so green. I thought I'd take Tessa to Kauai for our honeymoon. I thought I understood what it was to be alive, but I didn't. I never embraced my own shame, until now. I watch the far-off, winding road between the mountains and the sea, red and blue lights strung down its length, like the highway is a priceless necklace. Like it's all leading somewhere. And I am afraid. I am afraid of the pain that waits for me; I am afraid to face it alone. I am alive, and I am horrified.

Tessa moves as if this is the most natural thing in the world to do. She moves as if fear is silly, and not important, and not germane. But not not there—it is there, the fear; it always is. It simply is. The body tells the story, her body: If I am more than this body, then I give of this body, I give this whole body, for him. I am the inertia and the life. I am his life, gladly paid for. She makes no sound. No war cry as the Killer looks over his side at the subtle plud of her bare feet on marble. She needn't make a sound, for her body is saying: We are more than mere bodies. I'll prove it. I'll show you. Watch this. She catches the Killer around his waist. The Killer's mass might have stopped her if he hadn't bumbled, off-balance, at the sight of Tessa coming so fast toward him. The Killer has a knife in his hand, but his hand is thrown forward as his body's thrown backward, where smooth marble keeps traction for Tessa's hard feet, where the Killer tries to get traction with his hard boots, where he gets traction but the wrong way, heels digging, adding to the backward force, and back there, there is nothing. Music stands all moved to the front. But there's the window. The window with a bullet hole in it. The bullet hole almost like an eye in a portrait.

My eyes snap shut. I can't do anything about my ears. Or my mind, imagining:

The window blows outward. I picture it as if I'm standing at the shore at low tide, the waves remote behind me, and quiet. That dull white block blocking the mountains, most of its windows dark, the light ones so bright, so many stories—and there, where basic spatial reasoning would dictate the top is (those tinted windows at the very top must be an architectural flourish), a huge window pops like a glass balloon. The glass a bright Milky Way, shards like stars. Two people in its midst, Castor and Pollux. Or Orion, but which is Orion? Is it the Killer, knife still in his hand? Is the knife still in his hand? Or is it Tessa, calm and wordless? The Killer's scream is audible, but not hers. Not hers. Brian's yell is deafening. He chokes on her name.

I picture her descending. The wind loosens her hair. It's the color of one thirty in the morning, and so is her skirt, flying up, contrasting a downy lack of underwear and the white cotton of her shirt, breasts small but nipples hard as dark diamonds. She raises her unhurt arm. It's the sense of being in a dream and waiting to wake. A tiny distance opens between them, a function of his backward inertia or her lesser weight or both, and if he does stab—determined, still—he stabs at sheer atmosphere. He can't kill. He is nothing here. He is a joke. Tessa is thinking of Brian, and she is smiling. She's passing the fourteenth, twelfth, elev-ten-ninth—. Tessa pretends she's fly—

CAMERA 33, 34, X, 4-3-2

☐ ☐ ☐ ☐ ☐ ☐ ☐ ☐ ☐

The pool. Immense sound, glass, *crash*. My eyes open to a sudden profusion of red across the screen, dripping down. Rain of fricasseed meat into pinking water. A boot floats. Not Tessa's; she's barefoot. Where is she, where is she, a piece of her, somewhere, and then I'll know no, no.

"Tess, stop kicking." Brian is panting. He has her left arm in a death grip above the wrist. I can see only the part of her hair from this steep angle behind him, but yes, yes, yes, Brian's entire torso leans out of the enormous ruined window, his right hand braced against the frame. The veins in that bicep stand at attention. That bicep is visible because it's the sleeve he tore off to wrap Tessa's hand, long ago and far away, this afternoon in the foyer. He's not wearing his motorcycle jacket. He looks oddly naked without it.

Tessa's breathing is staccato. I imagine the dark mouth yawning wide underneath her. "Careful," she says. She's not talking about her body being suspended more than two hundred feet in the air. She's talking about Brian's body being poised above a shard of shattered window, a tip of glass inches from his taut belly, which he's sucking in to avoid being gutted.

"You have to climb," Brian says.

"How?"

"Press your feet to the wall and lean back. Then walk up."

I can't watch. I can't watch anymore. Brian's insane. Walk up? I eye the pencil, the override system. It wouldn't help them anyway. It's much too far. It's ten inches too far away. Brian grits his teeth. His shoulder is straining out of the socket. It's as painful as one would think.

An airless sob escapes Tessa. She's looking past Brian.

At the Thinker, who's rolling onto his side and sitting up.

"He's awake, fuck, he's awake," she says. The Thinker touches the cleaver buried in his arm. It's in the back of his shoulder. It missed his carotid artery. He trains the black pits of his mask on Tessa, whom Brian is ordering: "Look at me; look at me, Tess." The Thinker puts his fist under the cleaver's handle. It flips backward when he pushes. It lands with a *clang* against a soup bowl. He grabs a nearby tablecloth and begins to fashion a bandage-cum-sling.

"Tess? Tess, Tess." Brian says it like a litany.

Tessa loosens her fingers from Brian's straining elbow. "Let go, Bri," she says. "You have to run, baby." Their faces are a few feet and light-years apart. Tessa's toes must be cold in that vast nothing of space underneath her.

"No." He gasps as the knife of glass he's poised over kisses his navel. Tessa gasps with him and grabs back onto his arm.

The Thinker folds the chin of his mask to bite a knot. The sling is of phenomenal design, bracing the joint around the front while controlling blood flow in the back. His arm bleeds copiously, but lazily, splattering the marble floor. He braces himself, and stands.

Brian says, "We live or we die, Tess."

The Thinker reels, grabbing a chair for balance.

"Come on now," says Brian.

Tessa nods, and so do I. We nod. The pencil isn't that far away, not really. It's not too far for us.

The Thinker looks at Tessa and Brian, then at his gun. He's roughly equidistant between the two, but he goes for the .45, with its now-unnecessary silencer. He's tired of surprises. His footfalls are heavy, and their *plud-plud* hides the sound of Tessa's bare feet smacking Manderley's sheer, frigid face as she steps. The security counter is smooth against my left cheek, and I feel the point of the knife scraping Formica when I move, a fraction of an inch at a time, the bulk of the blade juddering minutely between those funny little bones. It tickles, but it doesn't kill me. Her feet are cold, but that's life. We're alive and we move. We're moving, goddamn it.

Brian shoves his right side against the window frame and pulls upward, using his legs. Forked tongues of glass lick the right side of his neck and nick him. Tessa leans back farther, still farther, so she can walk up that flat vertical surface like a full-sized middle finger to the universe's notions of what is possible. They're all but silent, both of them, even at the most impossible point of the whole operation, when Tessa's essentially horizontal and she takes a final step, her heel poised above the gone window, and Brian yanks backward with the full force of his weight, and she straightens and plants her foot on the stage like she did nothing less mundane than mount a sidewalk. If the ballroom were full of dinner guests, they would all stand up and applaud. If I could, I would, too. Tessa's shaking so badly, her knees fail. Brian catches her and rights her, and they speed away more quietly than any phantom. This has taken eight seconds.

The Thinker hasn't been watching. He's been purposely walking at a sedate pace toward his dropped weapon, to prolong Brian and Tessa's fear, their suffering. He arrives at the gun. He kicks a flap of napkin off its snout. He bends, picks it up, and turns with it raised. He assumes his prey are still hanging over the ledge.

Except they're gone.

I laugh out loud. A real guffaw. It hurts my throat, but I can't not, he's so pissed. He roars at the carefree, silent swing of the kitchen door. He wastes time, standing there and bellowing at the ceiling, where the cherubim look down on him, uninterested. He plods into the stairwell. The Thinker is taking it for granted that Tessa and Brian have boarded the secret elevator, and he's correct (I managed to use my controller twice more, to open the juice concentrate shelf and to close it behind them; they're passing the fourteenth floor). He's taking it for granted that the secret elevator and the hollow wall in Franklin's office will open for them when they get to the first floor, and damn it, goddamn it, he's going to be correct about that, too.

We're only three more inches from this ludicrous pencil.

We're holding each other in the secret elevator, careful not to look at Vivica.

"We're almost there," he says, I say. She holds us. She worries over our injuries and asks, "How bad?" and we tell her.

| "Well, I'm paralyzed, Tessa, so I'd say slightly worse than average, wouldn't you?" | "Not as bad as that time I landed a jump on an old seat and a spring hit my balls." |

I laugh. I turn my head with infinite caution, stick out my tongue, and taste the acrid point of sharpened graphite. Suck it to me. Sink my teeth in. It tastes like the birch bark I chew on long hikes. Brian and Tessa are passing the fourth floor.

The Thinker has mustered a jog past the sixteenth floor.

The pencil point pokes the inside of my lower lip. The taste of blood is welcome. An eraser covers a larger surface area, and more accurately simulates a fingertip. I move a last few inches, stop gratefully at the override screen, but my head is at the wrong angle to reach it. The pencil eraser clicks on the screen's Formica border. I pull a Brian, taking a deep breath and letting it out as I turn, turn. Come on now. The point of the knife in my neck sticks into the security counter like a tent stake. I feel the blade pierce new skin, but not much of it. I stop a squeal at the feeling, because then I might drop the pencil that now juts proudly over the control panel. The black screen turns blue when I tap it. The eraser floats into my pass code numbers—01311984, Tessa's birthday—like a round, pink, incandescent fantasy. The screen asks for a command. I override all systems. It asks for another code, because this is an emergency measure, so: Tessa's birthday backward.

The override system beeps, and the screen fast-motion etches a schematic of Manderley—a transparent blueprint of the hotel's bones, in pixels, building from the foyer to the twentieth floor, where we perch on the roof. Then we plunge inside, where the walls appear, even the furnishings, in a rendering as faithful to reality as current technology allows. My bloody teeth bare themselves. I look a bit mad, and I like it.

The Thinker is passing the twelfth floor. He's walking. He pulls a syringe from his coveralls pocket and jabs it into his thigh. Probably an amphetamine and painkiller cocktail. I blow through a memory of injecting one of those. Burma, I think. I had the flu but was running an op. I don't recall the op—that particular narcotic mixture effaces events nearly as well as it jacks up energy and pain tolerance—but my men called me "Ahnold" after that. *Predator* was doing big box office at the time. I snort rudely as the Thinker's pace starts to quicken. Great.

The secret elevator settles on the first floor. Brian and Tessa stand waiting. And waiting.

"No," Brian says, panic rising up in him for the first time. He can handle a fight to the death in an open space but not passive entrapment in a tiny box, and "Oh no, oh shit," and "Bri, we'll get it," and don't lose your cool now, you Tantric whippet-bodied woman-stealer. We're going as fast as we can here.

The digital override program works a lot like a first-person video game. I don't like video games, but I'm no fool: my team loves them, plays them all the time. It sets the programmer in Manderley's driveway to start. There is no police cruiser, no patrolman; my new virtual world is as empty and tranquil as paradise. I enter the front doors by tracing my path with the pencil. Through the foyer, to Franklin's office. Tap on the secret elevator.

The secret elevator opens.

Tessa and Brian bound out. The lamp on Franklin's desk glows. Tessa's limp right hand knocks it over. Brian bats Franklin's top desk drawer open. The drawer sails backward and to the floor. Adrenaline is making Brian's movements too powerful. He squats and grips a large pair of scissors; he precedes Tessa to the foyer. He turns right, but Tessa says, "Not that way," reminding Brian the front doors are locked. He tosses a look of yearning at the police car in the driveway. They go left, out the rear exit, stepping around the dead girl in the gold dress. Brian squints at the reddened windows of the pool, but Tessa's intent—pulls him by his belt loop to the left, then left again at the corner, where Manderley's glowing white edge meets the night.

The Killer's mask floats in the pool. A portion of his head floats facedown beside it.

The Thinker is passing the fifth floor. He's invigorated, running again. Holding the gun like something he treasures, holding it to his chest with the arm that's not wrapped in a perfect field dressing. He jumps at the sound of the fire alarms, the earthquake alarms, and the bomb threat alarms, all going off at once. They're of different tones but all terrible and unavoidable and un-sleep-through-able, and continuing, and continuing, like a church choir in hell, or a Brooklyn Saturday morning when one is trying to sleep in. He covers one ear with his functional hand, tries to lift his shoulder to cover the other, but it hurts his shoulder too much. He groans and I groan. Graphite is puncturing the tip of my tongue, but I don't care.

I can access wider hotel systems more easily. So easily I have to stop myself from making every faucet go full-blast, every door slam open and shut. Targeted assaults. The foyer chandelier, a stupid, expensive pinecone that dusts up every time a butterfly flaps its wings in Africa. Off.

In green, black, and white, the Thinker hurtles into the ink-dark foyer. He stays calm and commits to a direction. He runs. He remembers that the front doors are locked but not that a skinny gold-clad trophy date lies between him and the rear ex— A once-in-a-lifetime wipeout! Masked-face-first into the stain-destroyed Italian marble floor. I laugh and laugh, coughing saliva and spools of blood onto the counter. I'm a little worried, but I can't stop.

Brian and Tessa round Manderley's front. The police officer pops from his cruiser, points his revolver at them, and shouts, "Freeze!" Brian and Tessa skid to a stop. Brian puts his hands up. Tessa puts her left arm up, but her right hangs, loose and streaked red. They start shouting in tandem. Brian stops so Tessa can do the talking. I shut off the alarms so Tessa needn't shout.

"I'm the one who called," she says with admirable composure, when Manderley stops screeching. "We need help."

"Drop those," says the cop, referring to the scissors in Brian's right fist. The rookie's gun trembles so much, it could conduct "Flight of the Bumblebee." "No sudden movements."

Tessa repeats, "We need help."

Brian says, "He's got—"

A bullet strikes the police officer square in the forehead. Brian dives and takes Tessa with him. They hit the ground crawling, while the policeman folds to the driveway. Silent shots punch loud holes in "Serve" and "Protect" on the cruiser's side panel. Brian and Tessa shamble behind the right-rear tire. The whirling lights of approaching emergency vehicles are still a mile away. Brian and Tessa can surely see them. But there's only one terrible option. They nod at each other, and disappear into the hedge maze.

The Thinker is loading a new clip. He's steady; this is business. He must not lose his cool as he did in the ballroom. He's a professional, and in his profession, there must be no survivors.

This is stupid. It's the stupidest idea I've ever had. I select every light in every room. Courage is how people die. I know this; I learned this. I watched men learn it, and it was the last thing they ever learned. The Thinker is walking toward the maze. I hear a grunt come out of my throat. I look at myself in the monitor for the twentieth floor, like I'm confirming I'm really there. That poor man, his arms and legs like drop cloths on his office chair. His eyes blinking at me through salty sweat. I see you.

I tap the lights on. All Manderley's windows—hundreds and hundreds—shine bright, and darken. Brighten, darken. In varying speeds, specific rhythms—Morse code.

SOS.

The Thinker's mask stretches in a manner that suggests his jaw just fell open.

Come on, come and get me. Come on now. Leave them.

I had little hope he'd comply, and he doesn't. He turns from the hotel and enters the maze with the eerie noiselessness of a panther. I reset the override system so I'm standing in my empty driveway again. I enter the maze and walk where the Thinker walks.

Tessa and Brian went straight for the maze's center. They're a dozen feet from the fountain shooting its spray at the sky. They're cocooned in each other. I manipulate the eraser up, up, expanding my view to the maze's convoluted diagram. I'd forgotten how convoluted. It's a grid overlaid with a mess of systems: sprinklers in case of fire, arc lights in case of guests lost at night, auxiliary cameras in case of same. Tiny icons indicate where each tool of each system resides in the maze, so I'm squinting at a chessboard with hundreds of blue water drops dispersed across it, signifying each of the sprinklers. And yellow lightbulbs for arc lights, and green lenses for cameras. I coded the program to be user-friendly, but it's dizzying. It's too much.

It's tempting to think how comparatively easy it must be to take those short, quiet strides the Thinker is taking, how refreshing the smells of soil and dew he inhales in the chilly morning, how exciting the encroachment of flora all around him. The delicious challenge of picking a path. Narrow openings begetting forward motion. Switchbacks that are often the only method of progress. The rare straightaway stretching for twenty-five yards to his either side.

The Thinker does what I would do—stops at the first long stretch his turns take him to, raises his gun, and fires a volley straight across. The bullets whiz through the hedges. A rose explodes above Tessa's head. She grabs Brian's arm and takes him behind the fountain. That's our girl.

The sirens blare around the turn to Manderley's driveway, obscuring the buzz of another clip, fired lower. A rose explodes where Brian and Tessa were hiding thirty seconds ago. Chips of the fountain they crouch behind whir off as if the granite were sneezing.

The police are speeding into the final stretch of driveway. The lead car swerves and sprays gravel at the dead cop. I can hear barks of "Officer down!" even through their sealed windows. A few cops get out and try to revive him, despite his brains oozing onto their hands.

Brian's kissing Tessa behind the fountain. He indicates she should stay here. He rises. She seizes his shirtfront and yanks him down. Brian kisses her again. It's gentle, tender, profound, and complete. He's kissing her good-bye. Hypocrite. We live or we die. That doesn't work if you die for her. That's not how this ends. She loves you, and I love her, so therefore—no, forget it, I can't love you by association. I still pretty much hate you, actually. But hey, so what.

I bite down hard. I feel the pencil tip puncture my soft palate.

The Thinker looks around at a mechanical hum. It's coming

from the greenery. He peers into a hedge as the sprinkler I've set to its top level of water pressure shoots him full in his masked face. My maniacal laugh fills the twentieth floor. It's conclusively as loud as the Thinker's girlish, high-pitched cry of offense.

Which makes Brian and Tessa look up. He's here; he's right here. Stay away from right here. I select the arc light nearest to where the Thinker is standing. I'm prompted with a dropdown menu, and I drag the pencil eraser to "Switch On." The Thinker turns away—the sudden burst of light hurts his eyes—and hope hits me like excellent liquor.

I select sprinklers all around him. The second and third and fourth jets of sprinkler water make the Thinker spin in a circle. He looks up at the twentieth floor. He looks around for cameras. Good luck, dunderhead. Sid practically made sweet love to these hedges twice a week for months, and he never found one of them. The Thinker steps toward a pathway three turns from the maze's center, and I douse him repeatedly, discouraging his route, while I keep a close eye on the police's progress (there isn't much; exactly one lieutenant is behaving with capable organization—"This will be a tactical assault, so, Johnson, stop throwing up") and on Brian and Tessa.

Tessa is looking up. She swallows with effort. "He's alive," she says in a whisper. I want to close my eyes and savor the relief in her words. But I can't. The Thinker is taking another route—a bad one, one that dead-ends. I leave off the sprinklers and render live every camera in every corner of the maze—twenty-six of them, 1A through 1Z. The wall of monitors in front of me wipes clean of Manderley's bright corridors and becomes a tapestry of night vision. Only motion inside the hotel will reactivate interior surveillance. So the twentieth floor's camera remains live, showing that sad rag doll in a dark suit, flopping his neck on the counter like a dying fish.

"He's alive, Bri."

"Who?"

Tessa points. Brian stares up at the twentieth floor. I authorize a manual angle change on Camera 1, because they're looking right at it. I make the red power light blink by turning the camera off, then back on, then off, on. Sweat stings my eyes. My nose is running, and I've drooled an ochre puddle onto the counter.

"Jesus," Tessa says at the camera.

I turn it left, toward a curve in the maze. Turn the camera straight. Turn it left. Brian and Tessa stare, understandably ignorant that I have to move my neck in order to make the eraser manipulate Camera 1's mounting mechanism, and that I could at any second sever my last tenuous connections to brain function, but a grunt of frustration escapes me anyway. Seriously. *Left.*

Brian and Tessa exchange wide eyes, frightened touches, and finally, dejected shrugs that denote a resignation to having no better choice than to trust me. Which hurts my feelings, but that's nothing new. Brian puts Tessa behind him, and they mince—left—around the corner.

It's delicate work, guiding them. Brian and Tessa know to be quiet, but so does the Thinker. Luckily, the police don't. Their stampede-like preparations to enter the foyer (They rack shotguns, heft battering rams out of cases, say things like, "You're fuckin' with the LAPD this time, bitch.") amply cover the shuffle of Tessa's bare feet and Brian's thick boots on the grass in the maze. They follow the cameras' pinpoint red lights, pivoting with my aching neck. The hedges loom around them like the fuzzy green backbone of a docile monster. The cameras make a whirring sound on their stands, so I regularly pelt the Thinker with jets of cold water, to distract him. After a particularly direct hit to his nose and mouth, he has to stand and cough for several seconds.

Brian hears the coughs; he perks. Tessa focuses on Brian and ignores my next instruction, which is another right. They begin discussing an idea so awful, it's almost impressive. Tessa's communicating via hand signals that she should be the bait, and Brian is refusing this idea adamantly. Tessa is gesturing to her limp arm, and then, without further discussion and without giving me time to prepare, she runs.

The Thinker makes a last left from a long straightaway. He finds a dead end.

Tessa hangs a strategic right and left, and then runs full out. Her arm flaps like a dishrag. She appears directly in front of the Thinker for a second in the dead end's narrow entrance. The Thinker doesn't follow her—as Brian and Tessa's imbecilic plan demanded—but raises the .45, as I would, leading her progress past him.

I select a sprinkler so violently, I feel the pencil tip break off against my molar.

I fire as he fires. Tessa slides. She's freakishly graceful, except for that arm. My aim this time was to the Thinker's genitals, and between my contribution to his botched first shot and Tessa's momentary resemblance to a star pinch hitter, I'm ninety-five percent sure he didn't hit her. But she stops and lies so still and so flat on the grass, she seems to become part of it. The Thinker fires and fires, and I let him: he's leading too far. Mute bullets smack leaves over and around and past her; one travels through nine layers of hedges and puts a perfect "O" of surprise in the gravel beside a policeman, a foot and a half from his shoe. He doesn't notice. He's telling his partner about a drug raid this reminds him of.

The Thinker checks his clip. It must be his last, or he wouldn't be checking it; he'd simply load a new one. He has four rounds left. I've been counting. He approaches the blind corner in front of him with impeccable poise. He'll round it and see Tessa lying to his left, playing dead. But first he'll turn right, because he's not stupid. Brian's waiting with the scissors from Franklin's desk. He's got the blades cocked back like the Thinker is Janet Leigh showering in *Psycho*. The Thinker takes aim through the greenery, at Brian's heart.

Wouldn't it be awful if I hesitated?

CAMERA 1

☐ ☐ ☐

There is a luminescence setting on the arc lights that's so bright, it eliminates all shadows, on the off chance a small child decides to hide in the maze.

There are nine sprinklers within range of where the Thinker stands, but I have maybe a second and a half, so I can't individually select them. There are four hundred fifteen in total.

There is a speaker in each of the maze cameras, to give a panicked guest verbal directions to the exit.

There are occasions when the only route to order is through unmitigated chaos, and no verbal direction can lead the way. So the only direction I shout to Brian is "Go!" when I activate all three systems at once.

The wall of monitors suddenly blinds me, flooding the twentieth floor with white light. In the maze, every sprinkler fires at maximum pressure, every arc light blazes like an acetylene torch, and my voice explodes at top volume from twenty-seven cameras. The cameras' waterproof lenses mostly show swirls of water, like I'm looking out the portholes in a submerged submarine. My aerial view is of bright, white, frothy mayhem, lined with interlocking geometric green, the sole motion being these three figures at the bottom left.

"Brian, now now now now!" My pencil is rolling toward me. I spat it at the counter so I could shout. I have to catch it. It's moving too fast. *I'm* moving much too fast, my tongue reaching manically as if I'm Gene Simmons, live, in concert. I surge my face forward and clap my mouth shut. Got it.

The Thinker splutters and coughs and endeavors to shield his eyes, but Brian does, too. They're drenched; they're blinded; they're drowning standing up. Brian tries to grope forward. The Thinker tries to see enough to aim the .45. Tessa launches up from the grass, her hair a dense black drape from crown to waist; it shields her eyes so she can see. A she-beast, a swamp Wendigo, she plows into the Thinker. He dumps into the hedges, and the pair of them flops onto the saturated grass. Tessa has his wrist. She tackles it away from Brian and gets her finger on the trigger. The gun goes off twice; I can't hear it through the water's roar, but two teaspoons of mud hop from the ground. The gun muzzle swerves abruptly to stare Tessa in the face. She's soaked, choking, not strong enough, and I scream a stripped, cored, fundamental negative that seems to call Brian forth. He materializes in the air above Tessa and the Thinker. He lands on them like a bag of dog food. A puff from the gun takes a Tic Tac–sized piece off Brian's ear. He grabs the Thinker's wrist and twists it, fighting for a complete reversal of trajectory, a perfect point-blank into his enemy's heart. I angle a camera downward so the water sprinkles off the rim, so I can watch Brian spraining the joint patiently, his eyes crazed. The blank offense of an assassin stares back.

The gun goes off before Brian's ready. Lack of sound makes the moment somewhat anti-climactic. I can only tell it happens because Brian and the Thinker both jump. The Thinker's hands fall to the ground.

Brian pulls the trigger again. Again, again. He looks viciously into the Thinker's mask and keeps trying to empty the emptied gun.

The police lieutenant who earlier seemed capable has been having a claustrophobic's lively and convenient debate with his superiors, via radio, about how regulations dictate a Day-Glo, waterlogged hedge maze that's hissing with max-pressure sprinklers and alive with four kinds of screams, should be stormed. His superiors agree to send a SWAT team.

The Thinker shudders. Then he's still. I'd like his death to take longer. I'd like him to be a sushi platter like his partner in the pool. At the very, very least, I'd like someone to check the bastard's pulse.

Brian struggles to get his breathing under control. Tessa, only her limbs visible, bats weakly at his waist. When the sprinklers shut off and the arc lights dim to a soothing brightness level, Brian pops to standing with an obvious excess of adrenaline and hurls the gun. He barks a "Yiiiaaaah!" as he does it—guttural, primordial. The .45 crashes through a hedge an admirable distance away.

Tessa remains splayed on the Thinker, robbed of her wind. Brian asks if she's okay, okay. Okay, okay? It's evident as Tessa stands that she is not particularly okay. She's limping now. Brian puts her good arm over his shoulder. She says, "I'm okay" in concert with Brian saying, "You okay?" The overlap comforts them as they try to determine which way is out.

I activate a program I'm especially proud of: an algorithm that senses motion above three feet of height, generates the most efficient path to the maze's entrance, and illuminates footlights, guiding the lost. The footlights glow a pale, restful blue. They pulse on and off slowly, to slow a panicked heart rate. I theorized the footlights would be crucial in the event that security personnel were occupied by a hotel-wide emergency, and a guest was stranded in the maze, and no one was available to conduct a search or give verbal instructions. An earthquake, say, or a fire. Backup systems of backup systems are indispensable should fail-safes fail.

And my voice will fail me if I attempt to speak. Because of what she says as she speaks.

"We have to get to him," says Tessa. She's crying. Probably shock. Probably not outsized concern. "He's hurt—he must be. He'd have killed them both if he wasn't. We've gotta get up there."

"We will," Brian says. "Shh. Shh."

"He's unstoppable. He's amazing, Bri. He's a black belt in I don't even know how many—there's no way—if he saw me in danger, he'd—those guys would've been dead before they touched a hair on my head, so he must—he's, he's—" She's getting hysterical. It's like music to me.

Brian stops her and makes her look at him. Dripping wet and disheveled in the pulsing blue light, he cups Tessa's face, contorted by grief—grief for me, and I'm alive; I'm here. I begin activating the speakers again, to tell her what I've tried to tell her at least a hundred times in words and deeds she refused to hear or see.

Until Brian says, "He saved you. He saved both our lives. Wherever he is, however he is, he has that. So he's all right. It's all right, Tess."

My forehead isn't paralyzed. It makes ripples like a pond with a pebble thrown in when I'm at a loss for thought. Or when the thought is a terrible thing. I exhale what feels like a weight I never knew how to hold up. Not strong enough, amazingly. I'm not all right. I'm not, but he's right, I should be. Brian's right.

Brian's telling her, "He loves you, Tess. He forgives you. He understands."

In my virtual override diagram, the maze is unoccupied. Every place is unoccupied. I'm standing where they're standing, but they're not here, and I'm not there. The pencil twiddles in my mouth. The counter under my head seems softer; it seems like a pillow. Randomly, I think of the creek by the house in Indiana. Watching my brother and sister play. I had no friends of my own, but that never bothered me. I preferred to watch them, make sure they were safe as they swam. My sister wore bright orange water wings. My brother liked to splash her, but I'd tell him to knock it off. Sometimes, I'd tip my face to the sun and close my eyes. I'd think about time, and about how I didn't need to understand it. He who serves doesn't always have to understand.

I reset the override system so that I'm standing in the driveway, and I look up at Manderley, its vacuous inner light. I pass through thirty emergency vehicles. Through the police, who call for Tessa and Brian to halt when they stagger into open space.

I walk alone through digitally spotless, of-course-unlocked front doors. Through a pristinely clean white foyer with plump sofas and an inviting fireplace, a gratuitous chandelier. Past a marble check-in counter. To an empty office full of steady silence. I enter the dull, beige secret elevator. And I close it behind me.

A minute and four seconds later, Tessa's pounding on the office wall with the one arm that works. Brian's beside her, pounding with her, but looking askance at her, worried. A duo of paramedics waits by Franklin's desk with tackle boxes of stuff Tessa badly needs. She's sheet white and can hardly stand. She screams my name at the top of her lungs. I mutter, "Brian, you idiot, get her out of here," but the words come out mush, because I'm weeping.

"He must be unconscious!" Tessa says. "He might be bleeding out! Help! Help us! We have to help him!"

One of the paramedics loads a syringe, eyeing Tessa with concern. Brian gets Tessa in a bear hug from behind and sits on Franklin's desk. The paramedic administers a sedative to Tessa's neck. Brian speaks in Tessa's ear. I can't hear what he says, but I can hear Tessa's arguments to what he says: "He's alive. Help, help'm."

Several dozen patrolmen crowd the foyer, their voices a wreck of echoes, discussing how vital it is that they don't contaminate the crime scene while they tromp through blood, turn around, and request that the crime scene photographer take pictures of their shoe-prints for evidence. A beefy cop slips on Delores's liver like it's a banana peel and falls on his butt by the mantel. It shouldn't be hilarious, but I laugh. The pencil slips from my mouth, and I let it. I watch it roll down the counter and listen to its progress—it reminds me of the playing cards in my bicycle's spokes when I was a boy. It nears the counter's edge. I blink and it's gone.

Two more paramedics wheel a stretcher into Franklin's office. Brian lifts Tessa onto it. The police lieutenant tries to help, but Brian snaps at him, "I've got her." The lieutenant asks Brian a question, taking a piece of paper and a pen off Franklin's desk. Brian glances at Tessa, whose eyes still show slips of awareness. He slaps the paper on the desk, draws a crooked rectangle with twenty compartments, and slashes "Xs" here and there. When the medics begin rolling Tessa out, he hands the map to the lieutenant like he can't be bothered. He holds Tessa's hand, escorting her to the corpse-strewn foyer, through the busted-in front entrance, across the cruiser-packed driveway, into an ambulance. They load her cautiously. I have a strange, flustered reaction—the ambulance is malevolent. It's being driven by Killers; it'll crash on the way to the hospital. But as Brian climbs in after her, looking around in a similar paranoid fashion, he notices Camera 3 above the main doors. He holds there, his weight on one foot. Lithe and young. Capable.

He nods at me, once. I grin, almost hearing him say it: I've got her.

I nod in return, and he ducks inside.

A policeman shuts the ambulance's rear doors and pounds on the roof. It drives away. No siren, but its lights whirl, painting the hedge maze's tall exterior in smaller and smaller swatches, until it reaches the highway and merges. I lose track of it momentarily when it's passed by an armored van doing at least eighty. Then it's an ember glowing red to blue. Then it vanishes.

The SWAT team arrives. Twenty-two men in full gear pour out of the vehicle. Their CO looks at the maze with the affected wisdom of a wretched leader. He starts his stratagem speech by shouting, "Listen up!" and it only gets worse from there. The men nod, smack their helmets lower, and charge into the maze single file. They split at each turn so they'll cover more ground. They lead with their rifles around turns, see dark-clad figures with guns, and shout, "Freeze!" repeatedly, while the dark-clad figures with guns likewise shout, "Freeze!" repeatedly, until both parties realize they are attempting to disarm and arrest a fellow SWAT team member. It takes "Freeze!" said an average of four times for both dark-clad figures with rifles to realize this. I'm laughing so hard, my tears are streaming onto the counter and forming puddles.

I stop laughing instantly when a trio of SWAT team members successfully corners a fourth SWAT team member. Their boots are trampling a patch of muddy grass recently churned by a life-or-death brawl. But no dead man lies there.

I'm oddly relaxed, perusing monitors for him. A distant smudge of average stature skulks toward the ocean, far past the pool. He's able-bodied, still; Brian must have missed. When the Thinker gets to the shore's soft sand, he kneels. He labors at some task. The navy blue of his clothing becomes flesh. So does his face. He's taken off his mask and his coveralls. He's too far away for me to distinguish any features, but I can tell he's digging. He rolls up his clothing, deposits it in a deep hole, tips sand on top, and packs it tight. He adjusts his sling-cum-bandage into exclusively a bandage so it won't get in the way when he swims. I remember the sting of salt water in open wounds, and the memory reassures me. What a professional. He'll collect his fee and leave the country for a while. He won't kill Brian and Tessa, because he won't be paid to.

The Thinker dives into the ocean and disappears.

The police lieutenant is walking into the foyer, holding Brian's crude sketch. "Everybody shut it! We've got a diagram of where the bodies are. Where's Johnson?"

"He's puking again, sir," says a sergeant.

"Fine, Wisnewski's on point. We're going floor by floor. We've got eyewitnesses saying the perps are dead—one in a pool out back, the other in the maze out front. I've sent SWAT in there, so they might find the guy by the time we're all on our next birthdays."

"It's my birthday today, sir," says the sergeant.

"That's great, Wallace. Shut your damn face."

Charles Destin, Destin's girlfriend, and Delores are in the foyer.

Sergeant Wallace opens the dryers, finds Franklin, and has to breathe into a paper laundry convenience bag for ten minutes. The police search each floor, but not each room (they don't have card keys), so Henri remains in the dark of Room 1408 and Twombley in the dark of Room 1516. Brian knew where Jules was, so the police find her, and Wisnewski makes the intuitive leap that another body might be across the hall. He finds Justin. Brian must have described the nineteenth-floor entrance to the secret elevator, since the police knock on the shelf with the juice concentrate, with no result. Behind the wall in Franklin's first-floor office, Vivica stares at her handprint with eyes that are flattening and beginning to cave in.

The coroners drew straws for who had to retrieve the Killer from the pool. A sad old man with heavy jowls works with what looks like an insect net. He's making a pile of bite-sized pieces near Tessa's boots.

SWAT team members continue freezing one another in the maze until their CO declares, via comm link, that the area is secure. He's lying—he has no clue—but it's dawned on him how risky this is. His men try to find their way out. One attempts to crash through the foliage and gets stuck. Another shoots at the hedges until he creates a hole, steps through it, finds he spatially misjudged, and scratches his helmet inside another dead end. I almost die of laughter. I'm red faced and covered in tears by the time they're clear.

It's five twenty-eight a.m. A subtle burnish has appeared above the mountains. Police scurry across the monitors like ants. They obtain a card key and search the guest rooms floor by floor. They find Henri in Room 1408. An officer takes photos of Henri's contorted position while a coroner's assistant waits with a body bag. A detective squints at the dirty dishes in the kitchen, then at the meal laid out in the dining area. He goes back to the kitchen. When he thinks no one's looking, he steals a spoonful of cold cherry coulis from the stove and nods appreciatively.

A few patrolmen continue with the room-to-room, but they're far slower once reduced in numbers: Twombley will be waiting awhile in 1516.

Officers chatter about how they've never seen a case this grisly, this awful. They discuss the killers' probable motives—parental abandonment, socialization in the penal system or the foster system or both, cruelty to animals, bed-wetting, and a fascination with fires. They state obvious facts. They can't wait until it's a story they tell one another, in some future where it isn't a smell thick in their nostrils, where it's not people sprawled in various exotic methods of murder but victims: the victim in the dryer, the victim in the penthouse hall, the victim on the fourteenth floor, the victims in that gorgeous lobby. I hear them rehearsing what the story will become.

We become what we become by accident, a lot of us. We find a method of being and be that. Even if we think we're thinking about what we're becoming, we're often thinking around it, because there doesn't seem to be enough time.

It's five forty-nine a.m. They've arrived at the hospital by now. Brian's refusing to leave her. If Tessa were to awaken tomorrow and learn I was alive, right down the hall—or in another ward, the ward where nurses turn you to prevent bedsores—she'd become confused. She would feel she owed me something. She would come to my room, apologizing.

Or, she wouldn't come to my room, and I'd wonder why. I'd think: Last I saw her, she was screaming my name, afraid for me, and regretful, and Brian was saying there was no need for either her fear or for her regret. I might ask myself, Why didn't I end it there?

I could be a motivational speaker. I have the suits. I merely need a wheelchair I control with a mouthpiece, or—by dint of a miracle—the minuscule range of motion I'm able to regain in a few fingers. There I am, wheeling across a stage, telling weary drones with disposable income how happy I am to be alive. While somewhere, Tessa and Brian live the truth of what I'm lying about. I could remain a security expert, but only in a consultative capacity. I'll never again sit and stare at a bedlam I cannot prevent.

Or, that's all I'll do.

It's a beautiful morning. The pixels change from green and black and white to the colors of morning. You reach out and seize the future, or you become the sum total of your past, and I'm sick of it already, my future, my tenancy inside this broken body, my thoughts, my philosophies, my empty observations. I see the years spinning out before me, sure as I see the highway like an adder waiting to strike. I wish I had a star so I could wish myself brave enough to face—

Five fifty a.m. I choke on a sob that waggles the knife in my neck. A bone called the atlas holds up the head. It is named in honor of Atlas, who held up the world. It's also called C1. It will punch into my brain stem with the mildest impact, so I stop the motion, but not the sob. Motion is life. For how much of my life—even if I was running, swimming, driving, flying—for how great a portion of it was I sitting still? What I see—the cars on the highway, two of them a few miles out, a white sedan and a blue sedan, unassuming but well tended, the vehicles of men dedicated to order, to protocol, dedicated to the rule that early is on time and on time is late—what I see is not life. It's high-definition color confetti.

It's Bowles, arriving first, followed by Larson. Good men. They park in the lot, get out of their cars, and run for the main doors. Bowles is green, but he's improving all the time. Someone must have watched out for him when he was a SEAL. That's bad when you're a SEAL, but Bowles no longer is. He's a civilian. He's security, and that's nothing; there's no such thing. There never was.

A sergeant stops them at the check-in counter. They show their ID. It's a process. It takes a few minutes. They shift from foot to foot, taking in the splattered state of the foyer and glancing nervously at the ceiling, as if trying to see through it, to the twentieth floor. But they follow the rules.

The rules are: people will tell you you're brave. When you're bed-ridden, or you get a chair you control with a mouthpiece, "You're a brave, brave man," is what they have to tell you, according to the rules of etiquette when interacting with a quadriplegic. Especially one who was tall and broad, proud of it, vain. A man who exercised hard to look like Captain America. That was who he thought of, secretly, when he exercised. He was born in the late sixties in Indiana, and he thought Captain America was the best superhero. He was a strong kid, but he became so much stronger, through mental toughness, through discipline. And when someone like that has his spine sev-ered and gets to watch his strong body atrophy underneath him as he wheels through life—if he's lucky—by scraping a fingernail clumsily along a control panel, people will tell him, "You're so brave." And he will hate them. He will be wrong to hate them, but he won't be able to help it. He is not a brave man, not in that way. Not in a lot of ways.

Tessa knew that, and she waited for her knight to come for her, and he did. And I'm glad. I'm nothing but glad and grateful. They'll be here in seconds.

People will think I died after aiding Brian and Tessa. After those antics in the maze, they'll say, He must have passed out from the strain. Tessa thinks this is true already. Brian doesn't, but he'll keep his theories to himself. The medical examiner won't bother with a specific time of death. When Bowles and Larson check my pulse and find my neck warm and my body pliable, they'll take the truth with them to their graves. They'll erase the twentieth floor's camera feed. They'll say, His chair must have rolled.

No one else will guess I pushed my left cheek along the counter, back and down, away from the monitors. Thinking, not altogether flippantly, I'd better go get that pencil I dropped.

Bowles and Larson are showing the police the secret elevator. They use Larson's controller. They goggle at the sight of Vivica.

I move another half inch, hurrying.

A policeman holds Bowles and Larson back. "We need to get the body out of—"

"You don't understand. There's no other access to the twentieth floor. We have to check if our team is alive up there."

I move. Movement is life.

They move, past the second and third and fourth floor. I am nearing the edge. On the monitor, the sun winks over the mountains. It shines in my eye. The fountain is still on in the center of the maze, spraying at least ten feet high. Someone should turn that off, it's a horrible waste of wat

ACKOWLEDGMENTS

NODAK
Mom
Dad
Ya
Brock
Aubs

NOLA
Erin
Des

NODAK
Sara
Sarah

JAX
Jen

MSP
Dani
Steve
Sally

C-VILLE BN
Roy
Stewart
Tammy

UVA
Scott
Ann
Henry and Alex
Michael
the Survivor Types
Cecilia and San
Judas Tadeo

ESA
Emma
Serena

ALG
Chuck
Jane and Brunson
Brooke and Craig

OTH
Daphne du Maurier
Stephen King
Shirley Jackson
Czeslaw Milosz
Alain Robbe-Grillet
Joss Whedon
John Carpenter

SECURITY

Merrily: A Note from the Author

Questions for Discussion

MERRILY:
A Note from the Author

Anybody who knew me when I was growing up would be floored to find out I've written a horror novel. As a child, I lived in a constant state of worry and fear. I wouldn't eat spaghetti sauce because it looked like blood; I thought cats wanted to crawl down my throat thanks to *Tales from the Dark Side*; and I was sure every crime ever profiled on *Unsolved Mysteries* was going to happen to me (how unbelievably scary was Robert Stack on that show?). Every Friday the thirteenth, it was verboten at my house to even flip past the USA Network, because that's when they played the Jason movies back to back to back. The slightest glimpse of Jason and his mask was enough to make me sleepless for days.

But that was before the day I almost died.

ON JUNE 10, 1994, I jogged to an aerobics class at the YMCA. I was thirteen years old, and I lived in Bismarck, North Dakota.

Why did I jog to an aerobics class, sweat Richard Simmons–style to wicked early nineties synth, and then bop out of the Y all set to jog back home when I had the body mass index of a pile of corn husks? I don't know. I guess I have too much energy. Some of which I should have invested, that flawlessly sunny June day, in looking both ways before crossing the intersection of Washington and Divide. Because as I loped across the crosswalk in my dip-shitty innocence, I heard a car horn. I turned my head to the right. And the last thing I saw before everything changed was a white hood slamming into me.

My memory of the incident isn't fast-forward or slo-mo; it's real-time. The sky and the ground switched places. I had a second to register this and to think it remarkably strange. My thought, if narrated, would have probably read, "Huh." I had that second because I was airborne before landing ten feet from the car, which had been doing about thirty miles per hour when it whacked me. I don't remember hitting the sidewalk. I realized I was lying with my face in the gutter, my head pillowed on my right arm. I raised my head, saw my arm. And my next thought, which I voiced, was, "WaaaAAAAHHHHH!"

My right upper humerus had split clean in half, with the bone flush against the skin of my upper arm. When my hand wouldn't move, my very energetic brain went into overdrive, repeating and elaborating on my previous eloquence by causing me to scream, "WAAAAHHHH! HELP!"

I cinched my eyes shut and heard people swarming around me. Somebody covered me with a blanket. Somebody else ran to dial 911. A woman shouted, "You're in big trouble, lady!" at the girl who'd hit me; she was shaking and crying—but not nearly as impressively as I was shaking and crying. I'd switched my vocal output to a fast, whispered, "Help me, help me, help me," until I heard myself, decided I sounded pathetic, and stopped.

And *that* was the moment something truly bizarre happened. The terrified kid who had blitzed past Channel 9 every Friday the thirteenth so she wouldn't see a nanosecond of Jason's masked face—

the kid who was creeped out by marinara sauce, felines, and gaunt old Robert Stack—she went calm. A voice spoke up from deep down. From an odd, important core.

How nice that you're not in any pain.

I could hear the ambulance siren as it came closer, and that calm inner core continued to grow and observe and speak.

It's a beautiful day. You might be paralyzed or you might die, but it's a beautiful day, and there will be another, even if you are gone. Accept this as a gift, and you'll find you are far, far braver than you ever believed possible.

Keeping my eyes shut tight, I said to the woman who was crouched over me, "Tell my mom I'm okay. Okay?" I told her my home phone number, one digit at a time. "Tell her I'm okay."

I didn't mean, I'm dying, but lie to her.

I meant, Here I am in the middle of everything I've ever feared, and I'm fine. I can't believe it, but I'm fine.

The siren grew deafening. Brakes squeaked. Rattle of a stretcher. Deep male voice.

"What's your name, honey?"

"Gina."

"Gina, I need you to open your eyes."

"I can't."

"I need you to open your eyes so I know you're awake."

"I'll sing. So you know I'm awake. I can't look at my arm."

". . . Okay. What'll you sing for me?"

I sang "Row, Row, Row Your Boat" all the way to the ER, sometimes humming it, responding to questions from the nonplussed paramedic, who might or might not have noticed that I often repeated "Life is but a dream." And that it made me smile.

• • •

I'D FIND OUT later that the reason my bodacious traumatic transverse fracture didn't hurt was because it had stretched a bunch of arm nerves to the point that they snapped, immobilizing them. Basically, I'd broken my humerus in such a way that I didn't have the capacity to feel pain at the injury site for two months, after which the nerves started sending signals again. By then, the bone was well on its way to mending.

I landed, I reiterate, with my head pillowed on that arm. Meaning it could easily have been my head that sustained a bodacious traumatic transverse fracture, and if it had, you would not be reading this essay or my first published novel, *Security.*

But if I hadn't been run down that day—if the driver had braked a few seconds earlier or if I'd looked both ways before crossing—I doubt you'd be reading this, either, for two reasons.

One, after the accident, I developed an insatiable appetite for the experience of being frightened while cocooned in perfect safety. Namely, horror movies. I began to analyze them, interrogate them, and wonder how the genre, which could slip so easily into stupidity, could be so life affirming when it was great.

Two, *Security* is my first *published* novel. I wrote ten novels before it. I wrote dozens of short stories and hundreds of poems. I got rejected by more than a hundred literary journals, six MFA programs, and over two hundred agents (though for an essay collection, not for a novel). *Security* netted me an agent on the second try. And my agent is gold and I love her like PMS loves chocolate, but it took me a decade to find her. And in that decade I was poor and I was scared and I got pneumonia and cracked a rib coughing and didn't go to the doctor because I knew it would bankrupt me. I once woke up with a fever of 102.4 and decided to write in order to see how I wrote with a fever of 102.4 (the answer: go to the doctor). I clung by my fingernails to a dream that seemed completely impossible.

Because life is a dream that is completely impossible.

Security is the story of a luxury hotel just days away from its grand opening. A skeleton-crew staff is in its final preparations for the opening's big party. There's a temperamental chef, a mischievous manager, a skittish maid—and, unbeknownst to them, a killer who stalks the halls, reducing their numbers one by one. But there are also people who understand that the only security that truly matters lies in the lengths to which we're willing to go for each other.

That in this impossible dream, we make a reality out of every second.

That maybe someone or something decent is watching us. Maybe they're cheering us on. And maybe when we open our eyes, we will be just fine.

QUESTIONS FOR DISCUSSION

1. The first chapter of *Security* introduces most of the novel's characters, with Tessa getting the most attention. By the end of that chapter, which characters have elicited in you a mostly positive reaction and which a negative? What do you think makes a fictional character likable, and do you apply the same criteria when it comes to your reaction to an actual person?

2. The novel's narrator refers to himself for the first time on page 11, and then the realization of the use of multiple screens—seen in the novel, of course, as pages with split columns—first appears on page 19. Knowing what you know now, having finished the book, in what ways does the narrator's position mimic a reader's? At what point did you realize just who the narrator is?

3. The narrator's knowledge of each character's background supplies the book's exposition until we reach Brian's story about meeting Tessa. This is closely followed by Tessa telling Jules about Brian's career and Mitch's death. How does the approach of each of these

storytellers vary? Whose approach do you find most appealing? Whose is most effective?

4. The Killer takes a shower, does laundry, reads *Us Weekly*, and even goes to the bathroom as we watch. Does this humanize him and make him more relatable, or does the very ordinariness of his actions make him more menacing and more monstrous? Why?

5. As the narrator's love for Tessa and his jealousy of Brian becomes increasingly clear, how do you find yourself defining his relationship with Tessa? How does that change your impression of him in general?

6. Jules and Justin's marriage, though troubled, shows signs of genuine affection and compatibility. Had they survived the night at Manderley, do you think they could have repaired the rift between them? Would either or both of them have remained friends with Tessa and Brian? Why or why not?

7. Henri's conversation with his daughter is one he has had many times, and it strikes the narrator as surprising when he first hears it. How are Tessa and Henri similar? Why does the narrator have such difficulty understanding them, and how does he compensate?

8. When Brian sees the pool, he asks if it's dangerous. Danger and safety, mortality and luxury, surveillance and privacy, horror and humor—do these dualities undermine each other in *Security* or do they serve to heighten each element? Each scene is written with the intent of eliciting a strong reaction from the reader. What factors

within the scenes had you laughing, and which had you cringing or turning on more lights: the characters involved or the language used or the description of the scene's action?

9. Delores's heroic fight and grisly death are juxtaposed with the sex scene between Brian and Tessa. What was your reaction to experiencing graphic violence side-by-side/simultaneously with healthy, affectionate sexuality? What is the significance of Tessa and Delores screaming at the same time?

10. Why does the head of security's chapter lack a title?

11. Do you agree with Tessa that life's very meaninglessness fills it with meaning? Or do you side with the head of security, who finds her point of view admirable but misguided? If you agree with neither of them, and you had to choose which character in *Security* most represents your worldview, who is it and why?

12. The head of security claims, "Survival is about what *is*, not what might be." Do you think he is right? Could he be talking about two different types of survival? If so, what are they?

13. Tessa tells Brian the reason her relationship with the head of security didn't work out is that she didn't know how to tell him "how hard it is, even now, especially now, to feel . . ."—and then Brian interrupts her sentence. The head of security believes that Tessa would have finished the statement with the word "alone," but he soon doubts himself. What word do you think she intended to say? How does such uncertainty parallel the book's ending? How could it relate to

the head of security's thoughts on the unfairness inherent in human existence?

14. Why do you think that only Brian and Tessa survive the night at Manderley? What characteristics, strategies, or philosophies seem to guide them? Why does this inspire the head of security to act?

15. Do you believe Tessa loved the head of security? Why or why not?

16. One of the last words in the book is "horrible," but in the context of its use it describes the banal offense of wasting water. Do you view *Security* as a "horror" novel? Or do you view it as a "love story"? If the former, how would you define "horror"? If the latter, can you think of other stories in which a lover makes the ultimate sacrifice for his or her loved one? What are they?

Gina Wohlsdorf lives in Colorado. *Security* is her first novel.